LIFTED BY THE GREAT NOTHING

LIFTED BY THE GREAT NOTHING

KARIM DIMECHKIE

BLOOMSBURY PRESS

NEW YORK · LONDON · OXFORD · NEW DELHI · SYDNEY

Bloomsbury Publishing
An imprint of Bloomsbury Publishing Plc

50 Bedford Square   1385 Broadway
London   New York
WC1B 3DP   NY 10018
UK   USA

www.bloomsbury.com

BLOOMSBURY and the Diana logo are trademarks of Bloomsbury Publishing Plc

First published in Great Britain 2015

© Karim Dimechkie, 2015

Karim Dimechkie has asserted his right under the Copyright, Designs
and Patents Act, 1988, to be identified as Author of this work.

Every reasonable effort has been made to trace copyright holders of
material reproduced in this book, but if any have been inadvertently
overlooked the publishers would be glad to hear from them.

British Library Cataloguing-in-Publication Data
A catalogue record for this book is available from the British Library.

ISBN: HB: 978-1-4088-6201-8
          TPB: 978-1-4088-6202-5
          ePub: 978-1-4088-6203-2

2 4 6 8 10 9 7 5 3 1

Typeset by
Printed and bound in Great Britain by CPI Group (UK) Ltd, Croydon CR0 4YY

MIX
Paper from
responsible sources
FSC® C020471

To find out more about our authors and books visit www.bloomsbury.com.
Here you will find extracts, author interviews, details of forthcoming
events and the option to sign up for our newsletters.

Pour Mamita et Paíto,
qui me donnent envie d'être courageux.

I was sober and could have walked a chalk line,
but it was pleasanter to stagger, so I swayed from
side to side, singing in a language I had just invented.

—Isaac Babel

PROLOGUE

MAX'S FATHER, RASHEED, loved baseball, burgers, and expressions like *howdy* and *folks*, which sounded more like *Audi* and *fucks* with his eternal Lebanese accent. When his father ordered the tree house to be built in their yard, he instructed the builders with great enthusiasm, "Okay, fucks, put the tree house in there now!" He clapped his hands once and pointed at the pines that faced their home.

Max didn't know what to do in the empty tree house. Imagine it as a ship? A prison? A hiding place? It was a small particleboard box on stilts with a tiny window, a circular opening in the floor, and a ladder. His father intended it to revolutionize his boyhood, laughing about how his son wouldn't ever want to come back into the real house. So after it had arrived, Max nested up in there at least once a day out of duty. It was so well enveloped in the pines that hardly any sunlight made it through that little window. It stayed dark most of the day, like a hole suspended in the air. He invited a neighbor's grandson up once, but since it felt like an empty attic, the boy came back down after a few minutes of pacing about. The boy's lack of interest made the house more exclusively Max's, and more dreadful. Alone again, he decided to set a trap at its entrance. He emptied a tube of toothpaste around the edges of the opening and waited for an intruder. Eventually he got hungry and went home, staining his slacks with the paste on the way down.

When Rasheed came up there for the first time, he wore a khaki cap, a brown fanny pack, and his camera slung around his shoulder. He was a short man but still had to crouch to avoid hitting his head on the ceiling. "Wow," he said, once inside the barely lit space, "just, wow. This is fantastic."

"Yeah," Max said, walking back and forth in the cramped house.

"You can do many great things in here."

"Yeah, I know."

"If I had this as a boy, I would be too happy. Much too happy. Are you too happy?"

Max took a moment to transfer all the sincerity he had into his answer. "Yes."

Rasheed looked proud, comforted that he'd made the right purchase, that he understood what his boy wanted. He began shooting Max with his camera, the flash filling the box like gunfire. "Right. Now pose like a great adventurer."

Max placed his hands on his hips and put his nose up in the air.

"All right. Good. Now pose like a great thinker."

He posed like the great adventurer again, only with a variation in chin angle.

"All right. Now, maybe, like a big caveman."

Here he rounded his posture into a crescent and thrust out his jaw. Rasheed laughed and hugged Max tightly enough to take the wind out of him. He opened his fanny pack and pulled out another gift for his son: a compass.

By himself again, Max turned in a circle, watching the compass's needle insist on north, which happened to be where their real house stood.

PART ONE: SUMMER OF 1996

ONE

FIVE YEARS BEFORE Max and Rasheed would never speak again, Rocket was still alive. A gray-and-white potato-shaped dog, and blind, she was eleven years old—a year younger than Max. She got out of the bed that lay next to his and wagged the back half of her body as she followed him into the kitchen. She bumped into the back of his legs when he stopped at the counter, waving her head and turning in circles. She smiled and panted: *Hey, hey, hey, hey.* Rasheed came in and told her what a pretty girl she was.

Max had done all the cooking since he was about eight and took special pride in Sunday breakfasts. Today he prepared onion and shiitake mushroom scrambled eggs, chipotle-seasoned sweet potato fries, avocado slices, whole-grain toast, juice, coffee, and hot chocolate. He stood on a chair and leaned down on the electric orange press right as the doorbell rang. It was their neighbor, Mr. Yang.

Mr. Yang usually dropped by to bring them pears from his Asian pear tree, or to apologize about his son, Robby, though never in the same visit. Robby was his youngest child (eighteen) and had Down syndrome. Sometimes he came over naked, giggling, his chubby cheeks worm-pink, and when Rasheed or Max opened the door, he gave a long, drawn-out cry, "Hi!" and waved his hands over his head, as if celebrating his beauty from the top of a parade float. His happiness uplifted them. After admiring Robby's excitement for a moment, Rasheed typically said something like, "Okay, Robby, okay, hello, yes, hello, you are a very nice boy to come see us, yes, that's right," and walked him home.

Today, Mr. Yang hadn't come about Robby or to bring pears. He wore a fine-looking gray suit in place of his usual gardening attire. Despite his handling soil and plants all day, he was an exceptionally clean man, one whose feet, Max imagined, might have smelled of candle wax and whose silvery white hair probably felt like bunny fur. But today there was more to him than his usual spotlessness.

"Good morning, Mr. Boulos!" he said to Rasheed.

"Ah, hello, Mr. Yang. How are you?"

"I am so very well, Mr. Boulos! Today, I will have a sudden party and would like you to participate in it with us." Max abandoned the kitchen and joined them at the door. Mr. Yang nodded to him and then acknowledged Rocket with a kind squint.

Rasheed savored the phrase "a sudden party."

"Yes! For the *camukra* flower will bloom today, Mr. Boulos. It finally arrive to a bloom!" When he smiled, his cheeks lifted his huge glasses over his eyebrows.

"Oh, Mr. Yang, that is very great news," Rasheed said, and then turned to explain to Max that this *camukra* flower took fourteen years under Mr. Yang's faultless care to blossom. Today it was scheduled to open and wilt in less than five minutes.

Mr. Yang cut in to add that his great-grandfather had succeeded in this deed, though his grandfather and father had unfortunately failed. Now he, Mr. Yang, knew by some nature-defying calculation that his would come into flower today.

Max's father and Mr. Yang liked each other very much. With genuine excitement and warmth, they chatted about common-place things like the weather, traffic jams, different ways to get to the Home Depot, lawn mowing, and the deliciousness of Asian pears and other fruit. Though they knew each other's origins, they didn't speak of them. Their accents brought so much atten-tion to their foreignness in other social environments that they'd tacitly agreed to enjoy a simple, classic American neighborliness, forgetting that they ever came from somewhere else.

Once Mr. Yang had violated this understanding, causing a strain between them for a short while. He'd stopped in to ask Rasheed how to make hummus, which he'd read optimized the nourishment of a particular Chinese orchid he'd tried to cultivate before without success. Rasheed coldly told him he did not know.

Mr. Yang said, "But where you are from, I think you eat this food very much." He looked troubled by the possibility of having gotten his facts mixed up.

Rasheed stared at his feet. "Yes, it is true. But I don't eat hummus, I don't enjoy hummus, and I don't know how to make hummus." This constituted one of the rare unsmiling moments between them. Mr. Yang regarded him awhile, unsure of the meaning of this secrecy. He eventually broke away with a shallow bow and walked home. Maybe he took Rasheed's unwillingness to share his Middle Eastern know-how as a form of exclusion. Maybe Mr. Yang realized the disappointing boundaries in their friendship. Or maybe he thought Max's father had secrets involving a dishonorable past linked to hummus.

Max had no idea if his father knew how to make hummus, but he certainly never ate any with him. Rasheed had effaced his past so thoroughly that Max didn't ever think to ask about it. Other than Rasheed's generosity, accent, and a face that could pass for everything from Italian to Hispanic to Jewish to Arab, he veiled off access to Lebanon, a country Max couldn't have located on a world map. His mother had died in that place long ago, that's all he knew.

But Rasheed hadn't uprooted his ancestry entirely. Once, when quite drunk, he lapsed, confiding in Max, after a wearing day at the warehouse, that they would retire to the Country someday.

"The Country?" Max asked.

"Yes, *Lubnān*." The metallic glint in Rasheed's eye promised some kind of paradise. He told Max he would stop working and they would go—by the Mediterranean, under the sun, between mountains, in the bustling city of Beirut—when the people could be trusted again. But the idea of being surrounded by people who had only recently become trustworthy terrified Max. In fact, living anywhere but on Marion Street, in this unexceptional town of Clarence, New Jersey, seemed like a self-destructive undertaking. Why start over when you've built something so secure and knowable here?

Max never thought to ask why his father went by Reed instead of his given name, Rasheed, nor did he think to ask why they never ate Lebanese food, or why he'd never heard his father utter a word of Arabic, or anything about old Lebanese friends or family or religion or politics; nothing about his personal history at all.

When someone did ask Rasheed where he came from, he'd say, "I'm American." If they insisted, he said his ancestors came from just about everywhere. If they insisted further, he told them his relatives last resided in the Near East, and then deftly changed the subject.

When he informed Max about the retirement plan back to the Country, he stressed the importance of never telling anyone about the journey. "When we are in America we are Americans," he said. People who wore their nationalities on T-shirts and hats were idiots. He explained he would not be defined by some faraway place. We were individuals, not countries. Besides, people couldn't understand Lebanon.

Over time, and thanks to a joyful nude visit from Robby, Mr. Yang dropped the hummus tensions and came back over with pears and sincere small talk.

"Please, Mr. Boulos," he said now, "I invite you all to come see it bloom."

"Now?" Max asked, looking back at his breakfast, already beginning to mourn the eggs that were getting cold.

"Yes. It is now. I have many people in my home now. I call them early this morning after the flower move and I calculate when it will happen." He laughed, and his shoulders popped up and down.

"Yes. We will come," Rasheed said triumphantly.

"You know it will happen now, really?" Max said.

Mr. Yang looked at his wristwatch. "Normally, sometime between ten forty-five A.M. and eleven forty-five A.M. exactly."

That's incredible, Max thought.

"Wow," said Rasheed. He looked at his watch too. "That begins in under nine minutes. We're coming over shortly."

Mr. Yang rubbed his hands together. "Okay, good, see you."

"W-w-w-we'll head right over," Max echoed as the door closed. Rasheed clucked his tongue at him in disapproval. Max didn't actually have a stutter. He put it on because a handsome Doberman-faced boy named Danny Danesh had one. He associated it with Danny's success. Danny Danesh didn't technically have a speech impediment either; he stumbled over his consonants when angry or overly excited by his own jokes. He had everything going for him—class clown, most daring prankster, best drawer—and was a miraculous feat of athleticism and cool. He only had one good arm. The other was a short chicken wing with four rubbery nubs sprouting in different directions. And still he was the best basketball player in the middle school. He dribbled with large side-to-side movements with that single long trunk of an arm, crossing his opponents and dashing past them. Juking quicker and jumping higher than anyone, he consistently got to rebounds first, one-handedly tapping the ball up in the air, like a sea lion with a beach ball, until he managed to bring it down to his chest and dribble again. He had a wicked long-range shot too.

Max had been imitating Danny's trademark stutter from time to time at home, but his father remained unimpressed. The times Rasheed had seen Danny Danesh when he came to pick Max up from school, he'd guffawed at the boy. He disliked hotshots and said Danny looked like a hoodrat. But Max didn't believe his father knew what a hoodrat was; he'd also heard him use the term to describe their neighbor, Mrs. Waltzen, an ancient woman who stuffed their mailbox with pamphlets about the word of our Lord and Savior, Jesus Christ.

AT THE YANGS' it smelled of sauna wood, rosewater, and mothballs. They had a greenhouse roof that covered half of their kitchen and all of the adjoining living room, filled with hundreds of extraterrestrial-looking plants and bright flowers. Max was wearing gray sweatpants and an oversize beige T-shirt, and his father sported jean shorts and a white tank top. Vines of hair spiraled up Rasheed's neck and across his back, accumulating into a little black fire on each shoulder. He was proud of his hairiness. When they swam at the Y, he sometimes floated on his back and announced to his own submerged chest, "It is like a burned omelet!" and laughed, turning his head from side to side to see who enjoyed his very funny comment.

A wall of about twenty Asian men and women surrounded a flower sitting on a stool. They turned to briefly register Max and his father's arrival.

Rasheed called out, "Audi, fucks." Though such moments embarrassed Max, it never occurred to him to correct his father. Rasheed was a fixed entity, an unchanging, finished, permanent person, and the thought of teaching him anything was as unthinkable as training a turtle to sing. Turtles cannot sing and fathers cannot change. Neither fact demands alteration.

The men wore gray or navy suits and the women bright floral-patterned dresses and a lot of powder on their faces. Standing out two heads taller than everyone was Max's basketball coach: Coach Tim. Max went up to him and received a low five.

"Getting a little shaggy there, Maxie," Coach said, tussling Max's thick bowl of black hair. Max's eyelashes, long and womanly as a camel's, twitched his bangs when he blinked. Tim grabbed Rasheed's hand like an old war buddy, and with a lot of emotion, said, "What's ragin', Cajun?" and the two of them cantered off to whisper intensely in the corner.

They were a funny pair, Coach Tim and Rasheed—Tim, a broad-shouldered, reddish, balding man who hardly ever took off his San Antonio Spurs cap (in homage to where he'd lived most of his life); and Rasheed, a five-foot-five paunch-bellied man with twiggy arms, a scimitar of a nose, a weak chin, brown eyes that looked like little coffee beans, a hairline that started a quarter of the way down his forehead, and an easy laugh. Rasheed watched a lot of baseball with Tim at the house but never remembered the games. He didn't know the players' names or what cities teams came from or even who'd won. Max knew that baseball was like gazing at a bonfire for his father, a wonderfully tranquil and warm time to get drawn into the flickering light, and dream. Anytime this favorite American sport of his came up in conversation, he got a faraway look in his eye and said, "Yes. There is a beautiful game."

Since Tim's wife had left him four years earlier, Rasheed spent a lot of time at his house. They drank over there frequently—to lift Tim's spirits, as Rasheed put it. Max wasn't invited to these therapy sessions.

MAX NOTICED A pretty Asian girl, maybe eleven years old, peeking around a woman's shoulder. The girl was slipped inside a rich orange dress, lips painted a dazzling gloss. She took one shimmering step toward him, showing her whole body now. She stood with the composure of a magazine model, had a mod haircut and pearl earrings. A little woman. Her beauty stunned him into extreme self-consciousness. He felt spotlit, exposed, and maybe insufficient. She kept a bronze leather purse taut on her shoulder, and had tight, brilliant black eyes. Such captivating eyes made him insecure about his own. His were far too big for his face. Though adults often complimented him on how pretty they were, he'd hated them ever since a boy in his class accused him of looking like a Chihuahua. When he remembered to, he'd let his heavy lids close three-quarters of the way to make them appear smaller, peering at people through the narrow slits he left open. Teachers would often ask if he was sick or sleepy.

Tim and Rasheed laughed loudly about something, and when Max looked back to see where the little woman had gone, she was right in front of him.

"Hello," she said, flickering her mascaraed eyes.

"Hi." He swayed back and forth, sea-legged, relaxing his lids, impatiently waiting for something else to come out of his mouth.

"You look tired. You need sugar." She reached into her purse and offered him a giant wrapped cube of Chinese candy. He thanked her by bowing his head, overplaying some gentleman's role he'd just now invented. He blushed as he tried to work the wrapper off the candy. Picking it open took all his concentration. She giggled and said, "Here," bringing out another from her purse and quickly unwrapping it with her tiny polished nails. The giant cube was apricot colored. While Max put that one in his mouth and nodded to express how good it tasted, she began unpeeling the one he'd been holding. She smiled at his chewing like a mother watching her infant eat.

Mr. Yang called out, "Okay, excuse me, normally it may bloom in exactly one minute." Tim could be heard from across the room, whispering loudly, "This is so freaking awesome," to Rasheed, putting an arm around him for a rapid side-hug.

Mr. Yang turned toward the tripoded camera and gave a speedy discourse in Mandarin, probably a brief history of the flower and of what was to come. Max saw the flower through cracks made by the suits and dresses rocking side to side like buoys. It sat in a ceramic pot on the high stool between Mr. Yang and the camcorder. It was the size of a small hand, with its hairy green fingertips touching, bursting at the seams.

The little woman gave Max a third cube. He accepted it, sucking and chewing and swallowing back saliva while the two of them laughed together with their eyes, but these taffies weren't getting broken down at all. Managing the enormous wad exhausted his tongue.

Robby descended the stairs naked and waved—"Hi!"—to all the guests. Other than the little woman, most stayed faithfully glued to the flower, not allowing Robby to take priority on this big day. Max had seen Robby naked so many times, he preferred to pore over the little woman's profile, trying to ball up the taffy in his mouth and push it into his cheek so he could get a word out. He'd thought of something to say now. *Where ya from?* That's a good starter question. But she was unwrapping another taffy. Mechanically now, still staring at Robby, she handed it to Max. It didn't occur to him to decline, and he added it to the giant mass.

Mrs. Yang draped a quilt around Robby and walked him down so he could join everyone for the main event. She rubbed his back in big circles, saying something calming into his ear. His eyes shrunk, small as a mole's, his mouth hinged open, agreeing serenely with whatever poetry she used on him. Rasheed asked Max with hand signs if he could see okay, and Tim wiggled his eyebrows at him. Max said yes with his head, praying they wouldn't come over.

The room quieted. The little woman held back a different kind of smile. Max realized she was trying to conceal what she really wanted to do: laugh at his struggle with all this taffy stuffed in his mouth. A woman in the wall of people cried, "*Wasai!*" and they knew it had begun. The little woman became more girl-like, standing on her tiptoes, weaving to the left and then the right, until she found a gap to see through. She turned back, inviting Max to look between shoulders with her. His mouth spread wide at her thoughtfulness, and a long cord of apricot saliva poured to the white tiled floor. She slapped her mouth shut with two cupped hands to trap in her laughter. More people oohed at whatever the flower was doing. He inhaled violently out of mortification, and the ball of taffy got vacuumed into his windpipe.

It was too big. Not enough space around the ball to even cough, and breathing stopped for him. His chest and head got hot, and he knew some kind of explosion was under way. He couldn't make a sound, his insides throbbed in a death-panicked frenzy, but on the outside he was frozen still. The little woman's face pulsated: electric blue, violet, red, yellow. Something about his expression transformed hers into terror, her brow slanting into a roof. His lungs convulsed, pleading for relief. He contemplated her lovely face, humiliated, wanting to apologize. He tried to smile. If only he could keep still, until the flower went through its short life, and not ruin Mr. Yang's moment.

And then—*snap*. He dropped to the floor and thrashed, tearing at his throat. Everything clenched and released, then clenched and released again. His vision blurred so that he saw the heads crowded over him in unusually proportioned blobs, wavy, like he'd been sunk in a bathtub. His father elbowed through the guests so hard that he knocked a woman to the ground. He pulled Max up to a sitting position and whacked at his back.

A woman shouted, "I am a doctor!" but Rasheed wouldn't entrust his son to her.

Rasheed yelled at Max, "Come on! Come on!" He understood that the hitting didn't do any good so he slid behind him on the floor, propping Max's back up against his chest. The crowd took a uniform step back and someone stumbled over the woman on the ground and went down too, hitting the bottom of the stool, tipping the flower toward Max. He watched the pot fall over the two people on the ground, as his father taught himself the Heimlich on him. He saw it vividly. Its fresh bruise-colored stem looked too frail for that heavy head. It was about a quarter of the way blossomed to its pink insides, like tender gums or an uncovered organ. It bordered on grotesque. The flower eyed him until the pot crashed against the white tiles. Soil sprayed up to his feet. It began wilting instantaneously, turning gray and then charcoal. His eyes felt as if they were bulging out of his head.

An overwhelming calm took him, and he went limp. Nothing left to fight. Rasheed said, "Calm it down, Max, please, breathe very slowly. Please." His tears soaked Max's temple. Time for Max to shut down, fireworks crackled off in his brain.

Coach Tim's furry, red, hulking fist swung in from nowhere, punching up into Max's ribs. The ball of taffy popped out like a glistening planet, spinning away in a slow arc. It grazed a pant leg and then met with the floor, picking up a ring of dirt as it rolled past the stool and all the way to the opposite wall. At Max's first goose-honking breath—announcing *I am here. I am alive*—he kept his eye on the orange ball and couldn't believe how much smaller it was than he'd imagined.

TWO

BACK HOME, AN hour after Coach Tim had saved Max's life, Rasheed stayed glued to his son, staring with a frantic love that looked a lot like misery. He appeared drained, running off pure adrenaline, as though worry had caused his body to click over into survival mode, fighting for its life against the nightmare of losing his boy. He grabbed Max by the arm and rolled the muscles and tendons together like electrical cords, making sure his son was solid and animate. While Max poured a glass of OJ in the kitchen, Rasheed ripped him away from the counter, gripping him by the back of his neck, and plunged his nose into Max's hair, inhaling loudly. "Dad!" Max yelled, having almost knocked over his drink. Rasheed followed him around the house like a starved zombie.

Max escaped to his room and fell asleep in Rocket's bed with her. A tremendous fatigue had piled in after touching his mortality. When he woke up, Rasheed sat on Max's bed, still looking like an illness ate away at him. He presented two plates of peas and tiny burned hamburgers and a pool of ketchup. Max rubbed his eyes and breathed in the dinner, suspecting nothing had been salted or spiced. Rasheed said Coach Tim and the Yangs had stopped by. Mr. Yang brought a baby cactus for Max that looked like a green bump in a pot. He also gave Rasheed his business card to pass on to him. The card read MR. YANG: 1 (856) 567–5308.

Rasheed handed it to Max. "For emergencies."

"But I know this number." He'd had the Yangs' home line memorized since he was five.

"It is in case you forget during the emergency."

"But they still live next door, right?" He feared he'd been asleep for months.

Rasheed clucked his tongue to end the conversation.

He usually told Max wonderful stories, but tonight he narrated a joyless episode of a series he'd invented about a guy named Kip and his Man-Dog of a brother. The Man-Dog was a naked guy on a leash, behaving like a dog. Rasheed had originally introduced them as a man named Kip and this other man, Doug, but after Max fell into a fit of giggles at the misheard version, Rasheed decided to go forth with the Man-Dog character, and this probably allowed him to get a lot wilder with the stories than he would have otherwise. Kip and the Man-Dog started off by doing mundane things like going grocery shopping or to the movies, but then something fantastical would happen: they might get surrounded by incandescent lizard-men or find themselves on a meteor where the Man-Dog needed to dig and hollow out its center so that it gravitated to the earth as softly as a piece of popcorn. It turned into a joke for Rasheed to change the Man-Dog's name every time, from Sam to Brandon to Dylan to Patrick and a few others. Max pretended to be outraged by this name switching and told him it didn't match the name he'd used

the time before, and Rasheed claimed Max was the one forgetting. This evening, Kip and the Man-Dog sat in a classroom. The
Man-Dog inexplicably had magical earlobes, and flung them out
and cracked his teacher's butt while she wrote something on the
chalkboard. Rasheed mimed the whip of the earlobe by snap-
ping his fingers in an uncomfortably serious way.

After they'd finished eating, Max fake-slept. Though he never
would have said so, he felt like being alone. When his father finally
left, he counted backward from one hundred before sneaking out
to his tree house. Once up there, he thought of that final rush of
peace that blew into his body at the Yangs', like he was death's
balloon. He stuck his head out the little window and folded his
waist over the ledge, putting his weight on his abdomen. As he
tipped forward, his feet got lighter and lifted off the ground. If he
let himself go much farther, his back half would pick up speed and
fling him upside down. He'd slip out and fall on his head. He
leaned forward anyway, and it happened just as he'd anticipated.
All at once. He heard himself make a helpless karate-man sound,
hi ya, as his legs flipped up and tried to shoot over his back. His
calves caught the inside wall above the window, toes pressing
hard against the ceiling, hands squeezing the ledge, blood swelling
the brain. His black hair hung straight down. A weightlessness
cleaned out his chest as he imagined his skull cracking open and,
for some reason, envisioned only sand spilling out. He saw a flash
of his father and Coach Tim, Rocket, his bedroom, his school, the
Yangs, and again, his father, ruined. Rocket traipsed out of the
house and sat on the grass under him, yawning up at the top of his
head. He didn't want to die, oh God, he didn't want to die. Of
course, all it required was for him to push back on his calves and
lower himself. And that's what he did.

He lay on the wooden floor, his heart still thumping, and
took in the dark ceiling. He meditated on what would be worse,
dying in outer space or in the middle of the ocean at night. The

only dead person Max knew of, and who he was in any way connected to, was his mother. Rasheed had made it clear that there wasn't much he wanted to say about her, and so her ghost had been formed by abstract descriptions here and there—no photographs or letters or jewelry, just the vague sketch of a woman who seemed excruciating for Rasheed to so much as allude to. Max only knew that she had been beautiful, smart, strong, and murdered by a man trying to rob their home in that place called Beirut, Lebanon. He wondered little about her in a direct sense because he'd never had anything concrete to miss, no person to imagine or idea to hold on to.

His father climbed up a few minutes later, out of breath. "Where have you been?"

"Here."

"I've been looking." His voice sounded different in the tree house, hollowed. He lay next to Max and went quiet. Feeling the timing either perfect or awful, Max carefully broke open the silence by asking about his mother's death. That's a story he was curious about now, if only because she was a real person who had been killed by real life. Rasheed mumbled that she'd died long ago. Max knew as much, but hadn't ever gotten any specifics. Lying in the obscurity like this made it feel safe to ask. Max could barely see his father. Rasheed's features were fuzzed by the dim light coming through the window. He had a hazed shark's fin for a nose, his eyes glimmered like wet paint, and his mouth: a dry crack that parted. Rasheed shut his eyes, not answering for so long that Max started to think he'd fallen asleep.

Rasheed finally said, "You were just a baby. I was walking up the stairs of our building with you in my arms, and when we arrived to the apartment the robber had already come and killed everyone. That's it. Finished." He got up to leave. The subject had chased him out.

"Everyone?"

"Yes."

"Like who's everyone?"

His voice trembled. "Everyone is everyone. All of the family: parents, grandparents, sisters, brothers, friends, cousins, everyone. There is only you and me now. Okay?"

"No survivors?"

Rasheed started climbing down. "No one is alive."

"What did the robber want?"

"What do you mean?"

"What did he take? Jewels?"

"I don't know. I didn't care about checking for jewels."

"No one tried to fight back against the robber?"

He stopped halfway down the ladder. "Maybe they tried." He spoke like he'd just forced himself to swallow some acrid medicine. "I was not there to see. Or help."

Max wanted to tell him it wasn't his fault, but that wasn't how he and his father operated. Max didn't say whether Rasheed did right or wrong. He expressed no judgments, gave no recommendations, offered no consolations.

A teardrop hammocked the bottom of his father's eye. "Your mother cared about protecting you too much. She wore a cooking pot."

"She what?"

"She took you into the bathroom and sat in the bathtub with you, wearing a cooking pot on her head." He gave a single sad chuckle. "Really, a cooking pot on her head all day, and you in her arms. She was a sunshine, you know. She would not leave that tub."

"Why?"

"Oh. Because of war. Bombings and rockets and so on."

"I didn't have a cooking pot for the war?"

"No. You were a baby. You had a baby's head." He got stern and closed up again. His tone indicated there would be no more particulars. The cooking pot was all Max would get. And for now it felt like enough. Thanks to the darkness of the tree house, his father had said much more than he'd intended.

This brief exchange filled Max with a prideful sadness, a sort of nostalgia for family he didn't know. It added a profundity to his life that he was related to so many killed people.

HE WOKE UP the next morning thinking about the time Danny Danesh drew a giant fishbowl on the bathroom stall door. Inside the fishbowl Danesh had sketched the details of an arctic ice-fishing village: igloos, fur-hooded fishermen with spears, their children, and the chill-panting huskies that pulled their sleds. Behind the fishbowl stood a naked man, the size of the stall door, holding the bowl at the level of his genitals. His penis poked through a hole and lay in the middle of the ice-fishing village. The fishermen in the picture didn't seem to take notice of the penis. They continued gutting fish, feeding their dogs, tightening up the bags on their sleds, laughing by the fire, and so on, as though it were merely a natural element in their arctic world. Danny had boldly signed the drawing *Double D! Bitches!*

Max brought his set of fat Prismadeluxe art markers up to the tree house, planning to depict the same fishbowl scene on the back wall. During a short part of the morning a small square of light projected itself on that wall, and it would make a perfect canvas for Max to draw on. He started drawing the fishermen, but their heads kept coming out either overly circular or oblong. The fish were stick-figure-eights with eyes, the igloos looked like baseball caps, and the fishbowls turned out lopsided every time. As the frame of sunshine slid across the wall with the slow marching of day, he left a trail of more bowls, a series of lumpy penises and dog sleds that resembled a poorly rendered rock formation, and finally, a stall-door-size man with the form of a city mailbox.

Rasheed had bought Max the high-quality art markers long ago after seeing him doodle a pony on a shopping bag. In his father's mind, Max was a virtuoso at anything he thought about doing. The boy just needed the right tools or gear, and innate talent would take care of the rest. When Max started playing basketball for Coach Tim the year before, Rasheed had bought him two pairs of the most expensive basketball shoe, describing them as the "fastest sneakers on the market," presuming that now Max had all he needed to become the star player. Rasheed once got him a Stowa Airman wristwatch for looking up at a plane in the sky. He told Max all the great pilots had such watches. And when Max watched the Tour de France, Rasheed bought him fingerless lambskin biker gloves. Max liked to sit with Rocket on the front porch and drink Virgin Marys with the gloves on. Rasheed never showed a glimmer of disappointment when Max didn't become the star player, express further interest in aviation, or ride his bicycle more than before. No, Rasheed had no expectations of his son, treating him as if he'd already achieved greatness by virtue of being himself. Mostly Max appreciated Rasheed's blind faith, but occasionally it made him feel his father just didn't know him all that well.

Once the light was gone, he regretted using the permanent markers. He knew that when he saw the drawings tomorrow they would be even more disappointing, uglier.

BESIDES MAX, MARION Street was childless, save for when the neighbors looked after a niece or nephew or grandchild. He spent his time during the summer almost exclusively with Rocket, waiting for his father to come home. Rasheed had a few free hours on any given day, aside from Sunday, when not at either of his two jobs (the warehouse or the night shift at the gas station). Most evenings, they ate a new dish Max had learned from the television, and took Rocket on exceptionally short walks (to and from the Yangs', for example). She did not love walks, and when she'd had enough, she plopped to her belly. Her head, small for her neck, like that of a seal, slipped out of her collar when she stopped moving forward. They had to pick her up and carry her home in these instances. She had her own small doggie door to get in and out of the backyard as she pleased, so timing bathroom breaks wasn't imperative anyway.

The day after the incident at the Yangs', Max pretended not to notice his father staring at him while he watched *Seinfeld* reruns after lunch. Rasheed looked tired. He had an hour before he needed to head back to work. The purses under his eyes were a darker plum and fuller than usual.

"Max," he said, "please switch off the television a moment. Thank you. Do you remember the story I told you of the man who climbs up into a tree and never comes back down from that tree?"

"Yeah."

"He is an enormous man on a very small tree. He is a very lonely man and takes his shirt off up there."

"Yeah, I remember."

"The tree looks like it will break because he is too big. It cannot maintain him forever, but the man stays on top of that small tree, for years, years, and years. It rains on him, and he cries."

"Yep."

"All right, well, do you know why this man was inedibley so sad?"

He meant inevitably. "Why?" Max asked. Though he did know, he'd been told a number of times. The man was so sad because he'd lost his friends and family in a village raid orchestrated by an evil witch and her band of possessed elves. He had nothing left to live for and so climbed the tiny tree and waited for death to come. The witch left him with the ultimate sentence of never being allowed to die. Max was too afraid to ask why living forever was considered punishment.

But now the cause of the enormous man's sadness had changed: "He was so sad," Rasheed explained, "because he could not love a woman. He could not open his heart enough to love a woman."

"Really?"

"Max, I have invited a woman."

"Here?"

"We will have dinner with her before I go to my other work. I think you want this, no?"

"Want what?"

"A woman in the house."

"Yeah, no, a lot. When?"

"Tonight."

Jesus. What would Max make? He'd need to vacuum, iron his father's indigo shirt, no, his yellow one, his nicest. They must both wear ties. The counters should be rewiped. What did their home smell like? Did it smell weird in here? This might be an occasion for those citronella candles he'd bought.

MAX SENSED EVEN what he couldn't make sense of. He knew this sudden need for a woman was related to Rasheed's telling of his family's death, and more specifically of his wife's death. Their conversation, the longest they'd ever had on the topic, had relieved some of the weight Rasheed lived under, and now he was ready to move forward.

The woman with the pot on her head still hadn't inspired much curiosity in Max about her as an individual. His relationship to her was like the one he had with Kip and his Man-Dog of a brother, or the Man in the Tree. Though often moved by these characters, he didn't feel he'd missed out on knowing them personally. This woman with the pot on her head had crossed his mind a couple of times since yesterday, sure, but the story's greatest effect was on Max's interpretation of his father's sadness. That lost expression Max saw when Rasheed came home sloppy drunk from Coach Tim's, as though he'd entered the wrong house, wishing he was still at his friend's, and the desperate whimpering sounds he made in his sleep that sounded like a boy calling up from a well, they were all symptoms of Rasheed's guilt about Lebanon, about being out of the room while all the most important people in his life were massacred. This visceral understanding of his father's motives poured down on Max like a religious revelation.

His father groomed himself somewhat obsessively before the date, principally the mustache. Max offered to tidy up his ear and neck hair, one of the little jobs that made him feel necessary. He loved cooking and shopping and cleaning for the same reason: to feel like he was actually good at something—qualified. Though Rasheed said a boy Max's age shouldn't behave like a domestic wife, he looked pleased to come home to dinner, a Pine-Sol'd kitchen floor, and folded laundry, kissing Max without stating what he was thanking him for. As long as Rasheed didn't see Max doing the work, he appreciated the outcome.

While Max prepped the beef, oxtail, and veal for the pot au feu, he tried to anticipate what their guest would be like, thinking about women he'd just seen at the grocery store: a gray-haired lady in spandex who inspected her produce with a frowny face of deep concentration; another woman who spoke loudly into her cellular phone as she clomped up and down the aisles, starting her sentences with drawn-out *maybe*s, *perhaps*es, and *I feel like*s, wrapping up her thoughts with a philosophy of fatalism where everything is precisely as it should be, and happens for a reason.

He put all the meat into a pot of cold water—followed by the leeks, celery roots, and carrots he'd peeled and cubed—before turning the heat on. Then there was the checkout lady who had dry yellow hair that sat like a triangle of foam on her head, and the kind of heavy glasses that seemed responsible for her nasal voice as she commented on the items she scanned with superlative enthusiasm: "These are just the best ever . . . Isn't this the most amazing . . . Oh my God, these are my favorite in the entire universe." She leaned in close to thank Max before handing him his receipt. Her breath smelled of a mixture of white wine, rot, and babies' heads.

He pushed two cloves into each onion half and added them to the water when it started to boil. As he cut the potatoes and cored a head of cabbage, his mind made a collage of the tabloids that documented famous women's stretch marks, inner arms and thighs, creases, pigmentation scoured by whitening creams, sun-mottled skin, makeup, pregnancy, warped and bunioned feet.

He brought the pot to a slow simmer. Older women were richer, layered, bordering on mythical. They had a substance Max had studied from a distance: schoolteachers, Mrs. Yang, weatherwomen and newscasters, the female chefs on the Food Network who taught him new dishes and gave him the idea to make vodka cranberry drinks (careful not to overdo it with his father's stash), and some neighbors he'd seen around, chiefly Nadine, the attractive black woman who had recently moved into the yellow house across the street. He liked to watch her work in her yard from the living room window.

Putting the cornichons, sea salt, and hot mustard into separate ramekins and setting them on the kitchen table, he thought of women he'd seen moving about with a pleased expression, and others with a silent pain. Some exuded sexuality, some self-preservation, wisdom, courage, and others creativity and brilliance.

He slid the potatoes and cabbage into the pot of water. What were women really? He knew there was much more to them than what he'd seen. How did they stand and sit and talk at home, when away from the roles work and social expectations imposed? What did the ones whose voices he'd never heard sound like? What about when they spoke to the person they loved most? What did their faces and armpits smell like? Why did the breathtaking ones become even more stunning when distressed, when they squinted, bit their lips, brought their hands to their mouths? He wanted to know everything about them. The little he did know suggested something epic, of great importance. He intuited that they had the capacity to show him a more authentic version of himself, able to see all sides of him with a simple glance.

He removed the beef and cut it into pieces, then used a marrow spoon to dig out the inside of the veal bone.

HER NAME WAS Kelly, a secretary at the warehouse where Rasheed worked. She had a long mess of champagne-colored hair that sat bunned on top of her head, stringy and frayed. Twenty-two years old, thin-lipped, with a narrow jaw and a little waxen nose spangled with freckles, she had the physique of a prairie dog: skinny in the shoulders, belled out at the waist, small pyramids for breasts. She wore a dress the color of an old pinecone. There was a kind of weak prettiness to her. She reminded Max of a sticky-skinned girl in his class named Laura who had a bloated peach for a head.

Kelly had prevented his father from getting fired by negotiating additional unpaid days of absence for him. Rasheed had called in sick thirteen times in the past six months, and the boss wanted to let him go, but Kelly organized a petition to save his place. They didn't really know each other, and Kelly's argument was more political than personal. It had to do with how the company ought to maintain a certain number of minority workers. Though Rasheed had never asked her for such backing, and probably wasn't crazy about the premise by which she defended him, he was grateful to have kept his job. He'd missed so many days of work because he sometimes dropped into a crippling melancholy that he called the flu. These flus could keep him bedridden for a week at a time.

When Kelly arrived, Rasheed presented her to Max in a sober, businesslike manner. Then they stood in the kitchen, staring at her, as if she had something grand to reveal, as if they'd been waiting years for Kelly to stroll into their gray-and-barley kitchen and give them the answer to a question they should have been pondering their whole lives. But they didn't know the question yet, and she didn't seem to know what to say exactly.

Before it had been made evident that a woman was all that lacked in their lives, it never occurred to Max that his father thought about women at all. Rasheed didn't show signs of desire, didn't laugh at suggestive jokes on sitcoms, and behaved apologetically in the presence of women. He held doors for them and said sorry as they passed through, his hand on his heart, looking at the ground, expressing regret that his duty of holding the door imposed his body's proximity on them. Up until now, women had been authority figures best kept at a deferential distance.

Rasheed bragged about Max, telling Kelly what a nice boy he was, and how one time a custodian from his school, Irvin, wrote him a letter to note Max's extraordinary consideration for other children (always letting them cut in front of him at the water fountain, and so on and so on). Max stammered that he didn't really know what Irvin was talking about. Kelly asked about the nature of his relationship with Irvin.

"The nature?" Max said.

"Yeah, do you spend a lot of time together?"

"With Irvin?" He looked to his father for guidance, but Rasheed gave a puzzled shrug. "Not really."

She looked concerned. "I mean, how does he have your address?"

"There's a school directory with everyone's address and phone number." He felt he'd missed something, made a mistake.

Rasheed bragged about Kelly to Max now, with noticeable effort. He didn't seem to know much about her. He stated facts Max could see for himself, like her pale blonde hair, her dress, and her smile. When Rasheed ran out of physical descriptions, he began listing the organizational skills he remembered her having at work and her cordiality with even the rudest of clients on the telephone. She did not appear flattered. Then he turned and asked his son, "Max, what questions do you have for Kelly?" Max came up with very simple ones on the spot: Do you love being a secretary? Do you have pets at home? What are your favorite foods? Colors? TV shows? He learned she did not love being a secretary; her ex-boyfriend whom she still lived with had a pit bull, but she was trying to figure out some way to afford moving out of that situation; she disliked the favorite food and color questions on the basis of it depending on her mood; she watched a lot of documentaries and news, not interested in fictitious stuff.

The doorbell rang, and Rasheed went to answer.

Max and Kelly stood silently, listening. Coach Tim could be heard saying, "I need my Wahl beard trimmer, Reed."

Rasheed said something back in a hushed tone.

"Yeah," Tim shouted, making sure everyone in the house could hear, "well, guess what, Reed? I need my Wahl beard trimmer."

Another admonishing, hushed retort from Rasheed.

"Well," Tim said, "if it's not at my house, where the hell else would it be?"

Rasheed could be heard scream-whispering, "What is your problem now? You don't even have a beard. Come another time."

"I want it now, Reed. I'm not leaving without it."

Max had never heard them fight, and had certainly never heard Coach Tim whine like this. Normally, when he came over, it was to eat and watch sports. Rasheed would sit between him and Max on the couch and suddenly become more talkative. To distract himself from feeling eclipsed by Tim, Max got up to prepare snacks for them. Max also learned, and occasionally had to relearn, to be fine with never getting invited to help out with Tim's house. Tim and Rasheed were aspiring fix-it men, and usually had some home-repair project in the works: tinkering with Tim's leaky sinks, installing new tiles or a fence, painting, caulking, roofing, lighting, carpeting, etc. Max wondered why they only worked on Tim's place. And why Rasheed wasn't motivated to find the time to build the tree house himself. Anyway, Max told himself that when Rasheed and Tim were away together, it gave him more time to work on his own house stuff. Discover a new recipe, for example. He managed to see his aloneness as an opportunity more than anything.

But while they argued now, Max couldn't help but notice a light buzz of gratification move through him. He became a little hyper, maybe glad that they were clashing. No, that was wrong. That couldn't be the reason he was glad. His gladness was probably thanks to Kelly. He looked up at her as she was biting her nails and agreed with himself that she was more likely the reason for his excitement. Rasheed stepped outside and closed the door so Max and Kelly only heard muffled arguing. He bragged a little about his father to her. Maybe when Rasheed

came back, he'd understand this to mean that his son supported
his pursuit of romance with Kelly, and if she, by virtue of being
a woman, had the power to eliminate sadness from his father's
life, then Max would do whatever he could to keep her around.

"My dad saved a bird once," he blurted.

"Is that right?"

The argument outside ended with Tim tramping across the
front yard, repeating, "Fine, fine, you know what, fine."

Max continued. "The bird had a broken wing. It was on the
sidewalk. It would have gotten eaten by cats. And he just picked
it up and talked into its ear and threw it up in the air."

"And it flew off?"

Rasheed marched back into the kitchen with his brow folded
like an accordion.

"Yes," Max said to her, though that wasn't how it happened.
He now remembered that the bird actually came falling down
like a clump of filthy rags.

"The wing wasn't broken, then?" she asked, looking at
Rasheed.

"No!" Max said. "Not anymore."

"What's it?" Rasheed said, meaning *What's that?*

Then everyone looked at a different spot on the floor. After
an eternity, she asked, "Do you have any music or anything?"

Music, of course, music! Max and Rasheed rushed over to
the one CD collection they had, a boxed set called *If You Are
American* . . . Tim had given it to them a couple Christmases
ago. They'd yet to open it.

Though Rasheed didn't listen to music, when Coach came
over and they had enough vodka in them, he sometimes took
out the copper flute he'd made years before with Tim's welding
gear. Tim said, "Oh, no, oh no, here he comes, it's that time,"
and Rasheed played something distantly similar to "Frère
Jacques" as he skipped around the house, laughing into the

instrument more than playing it. Tim free-formed baseline vocals and banged on the coffee table, and Max tapped at the back of a pot or an empty bottle with the flats of his fingernails. He couldn't ever tell if the other two heard his tapping or not, if he was really part of the song. But after one of these impromptu jam sessions, Rasheed surprised Max the following day with a used violin. He handed it to Max, saying, "I think you will self-learn this one nicely." Max never figured out how to even begin doing that. He spent an hour sitting on his bed, cradling the instrument that his father could have easily rented for the day, without a clue as to how to make a melody come out of it.

Rasheed read the names off the back of the boxed set to Kelly, "We have Beatles, Rolling Stones, Bob Dylan, Elvis, Chuck Berry, Michael Jackson, Simon and Garfunkel, Linda Ronstadt, Frank Sinatra, Al Jolson, Duke Ellington, Louis Armstrong, Tony Bennett, and Kate Smith. What's your preference?"

"What do you usually listen to?"

"Oh, everything here is very good," he said.

"Yeah, everything here is good," agreed Max.

"How about some Stones?" Kelly suggested.

Rasheed stared at the names a while. "Ah. The *Rolling Stones.*"

She smiled in a sweet way for the first time. "Yeah, that's great."

Rasheed played the music too loudly. Max served up a salad and then the pot-au-feu that he'd been working on since three o'clock. They slurped and chewed to the blastings of "Brown Sugar." Max studied Kelly to gauge whether she liked the food or not. He couldn't tell if she was mildly disgusted or if her scrunched face was one of appreciation. She didn't look anything like his mother, or at least not the bleary image of her that fluttered in his mind as he ate. He pictured her as having an inviting roundness, short black hair, amber skin, and relaxed caramel ponds for eyes. As much as he batted that image away, it kept flying back at him.

Kelly asked Rasheed what it was like being an Arab man in the most racist country in the world. It took him a while to hear the question clearly over the Stones.

"What do you mean?" he said. "It's a very good country. Our neighbors, the Yangs, for example. They are very successful, the Yangs."

"Oh, come on," Kelly said, spearing a sliced carrot, "that's not what I'm talking about. You must pick up on the way the media depicts Arabs, right?" He said no, and she wrinkled her forehead. "You're not conscious of how vilified Arabs are?"

"Excuse me," Max said, "what's vilified Arabs exactly?"

She didn't answer and sat through "Paint It Black" and "Wild Horses" looking depressed. She thanked them for the nice food and excused herself before dessert, claiming she had a capoeira class.

"Capoeira?" asked Rasheed, looking into his bowl. "What is this capoeira? You didn't say you had capoeira before. Max made a *tarte aux fruits*."

"Sorry. I really have to run." She patted Rasheed on the shoulder and Max on the head.

Rasheed came down with the flu later that evening, collapsing on his bed like a groaning, felled tree. He stayed down for two days, missing work.

DURING THESE FLUS, Rasheed's bedroom transformed into a muggy, dim box. The bitter air in there felt like a giant dog panting in Max's face when he came in to bring his father's meals. The ceiling fan stirred the soupiness. Below the fan lay Rasheed's bed with souring sheets, a bedside table, and a lamp. His window, the size of a big photography book, hardly let in any sun during the day. Rasheed insisted on keeping it shut and the blinds drawn. He refused the ceiling light too. Max lit a candle in there, and shadows flowed over his father's cheeks like black water.

Rasheed's breathing sounded sandy. It rattled and stunk. Max had nightmares of finding him dead, a dusty green corpse, unrecognizable except for his black hair. It reminded him of the skeleton in his school's science lab they'd dressed up in a mustache, wig, and goggles. But he never let on that he detected anything out of the ordinary about his father's health. Showing concern made Rasheed feel like less of a father, like he'd failed his son. So Max charged into that murky room, inconsiderate of the grave quiet, and demonstrated how little concern he had for his father's well-being, far too engrossed in the joys of his own childhood to notice that he lay in bed all day.

Max blabbed about what hilarious things he'd seen on TV or what an awesome seventh inning the Astros had against New York, imitating Tim's enthusiasm for sports as best as he could. He tossed Rasheed's meals on his nightstand carelessly. Rasheed only ate a couple of bites a day, and Max gave the rest to Rocket. She came in there with him, following the food. He tried to get her to stay, dragging her bed in so Rasheed had company, but she wouldn't stick around that airless space for anything.

During another flu, Max had tried the strategy of lying liberally. He recopied paragraphs from various adventure novels, combining pieces from *Swiss Family Robinson*, *The Beasts of Tarzan*, *Tom Sawyer Abroad*, and *The Hobbit*, and presented them as stories he wrote, reading them with his best funny voices. Another time he invented a neighbor named Wesley, and said how Wesley and he wrestled in the park together for hours. Rasheed grumbled that he shouldn't wrestle black boys. They're too strong. Max didn't know why his father assumed Wesley was black and told him that he was neither black nor strong, and after a while of nothing else passing between them, he excused himself, saying Wesley waited for him now. He tiptoed out the back, and sneaked up into his tree house.

Rasheed disappeared sometimes too. He'd be bedridden for a couple of days, and when Max went in there on a given evening, the bed would be empty, the car gone, and he'd see his father again a day or two later. Max would never get the story on where he'd been. Once, after having not seen him for three days, he placed a chair atop Rasheed's bed, wobbled himself stable on top of it, reached up to the fan, and taped strips of legal-pad paper on each blade. Though they couldn't be read in motion, on them was written, *I Am Much Too Happy*. He believed this could help prevent his father from leaving again. When it spun, the five imperfectly aligned pieces of paper formed a yellow oval that looked like half of an infinity symbol. When Rasheed returned home that night, looking awfully tan, and saw what Max had done, he admired it a long time before announcing, "It will never come down!"

"Where did you go?" Max said.

"I had to play catch-up, missing so much work, and so on and so on."

Max did not demand a better explanation. He had long believed it preferable not to try solving all mysteries. When you only have one person in your life, you must live with their ambiguities.

But still, Max worried. He'd begun to feel uneasy about Rasheed's income after learning of hourly and minimum wage jobs in a social studies class a month earlier. He thought about how many hours his father put in. Was this a sign that they were short on money? Why did he need to work so much? Max's anxiety got bad enough for him to eventually open Rasheed's bank mail. He discovered two statements. The first was for an account with a little under $4,000, with deposits from the two jobs Rasheed held at the time. The second account contained

$620,000. It showed three previous deposits, each for $5,000 on the first of the month from something named Ziad Jabbir through the Banque du Liban. Max decided it didn't matter who or what Ziad Jabbir was. He simply felt great relief that his father had some money. Rasheed must just love working those extra hours.

Ordinarily, Rasheed recovered from his flus in time to keep his job, but when he didn't, he got hired elsewhere with amazing ease thanks to his affability. He'd worked as a bus driver, a custodian, a gas station attendant a half-dozen times, a baker, a car washer, a Sports Authority clerk, a barista, a bank clerk, and a used moped/scooter and ATV dealer, and he'd had a number of different jobs involving painting, landscaping, shelf stocking, construction, delivery, and moving.

AFTER RASHEED HAD recovered from the Kelly episode, Max asked him, "What's going on with Coach Tim?"

"I don't know. What's going on with Tim?"

"He seems mad or something."

"He's fine."

"Oh. I thought there was something about a beard trimmer."

He caterpillared his eyebrows. "If you have to know, he is jealous about Kelly coming over here."

"He knows Kelly?"

"He knows she is a woman."

"And he doesn't like women?"

Rasheed actually shouted the word "Ha!" before walking away.

Max liked it when he accidentally said something funny.

COACH HAD ALWAYS been a rock. Such a strong man feeling jealous about Rasheed empowered Max's image of his father.

But also, Tim's sudden flakiness affirmed that Max and his father were special, inseparable. Their duo was unconditional. No woman or beard trimmer could ever pull them apart.

MAX DIDN'T KNOW much about friendships yet. That summer he mostly cooked and cleaned at home, did the laundry and the ironing, sipped on vodka cranberries, sat nervously in the tree house, walked or stood or lay with Rocket, and watched loads of TV with and without his father.

At school Max had mastered discretion. He'd created the ideal distance between other kids and himself so that he didn't stand out as anything at all. Gracefully forgettable. A lot of kids wanting to be left alone committed the error of sitting slumped in the farthest corner of the cafeteria, trying to isolate themselves, a fatal mistake that made them prime choices for abuse.

At first glance, it seemed these kids got stigmatized because of the way they looked: Jimmy Williams, who was rumored to bathe with his little brother, did happen to be gaunt and buck-toothed, and he wore cheap plastic tennis shoes that were three sizes too big for him; Tina Marques, who supposedly sniffed her own shit, was indeed a lamentably awkward runner in gym class, smelled of onions, and had an irrational overdevotion to piano; and, sure, Jonathan Givard, with his weasely grimace and peanut butter perpetually smeared across his chin, was said to fuck yogurt.

But the origin of such reputations could not be blamed on careless presentation—after all, even among the popular boys and girls, few were blessed with physical elegance at that age. It was that these kids presumed they were screwed from the beginning and thus stood too far from the center of attention. They were the crows that hopped about the outskirts of the playing field. Their distance and quiet, born out of a lack of confidence,

made the others forget their humanity. They became degener-
ates without feelings. And for the most part it was the years of
being treated like this that prompted them to stop caring about
fashion and hygiene and acceptable behavior. Their torment
had started as far back as pre-K, when they chose wrongly by
keeping from the core. And now they were the result of social
exclusion.

The solution, too late to share with these young crows, was
to maintain a middle distance. Physically standing or sitting
close enough to someone like Danny Danesh to hear him
clearly, laugh at his jokes, and learn to see his moods coming,
taking that extra step back or forward when necessary. True
invisibility.

Max dressed more or less like one of Danesh's sidekicks, who
dressed more or less like Danesh, which came out to navy blue
cross-trainers, baggy jeans, and earth-toned T-shirts with
modest zigzags. No one would have ever guessed the depths of
Max's admiration for Danny Danesh, how he considered
Danesh's alteration of the bake sale sign posted in the halls—
from BROWNIES AND BEVERAGE FOR A BUCK to BROWNIES AND
BEVERAGE FOR A SUCK, with a red Sharpie marker—to be one of
the bravest things he'd seen anyone ever do. Danesh did it in the
middle of passing time, at the height of foot traffic. Max had no
idea what it felt like to be without fear, to risk being singled out
as the wrongdoer.

Max had gained total control of his face. He never allowed
himself to look upset or lonely, jealous or bored, only problem-
free and easy to please. He stayed hidden in this way because he
didn't believe he had interesting thoughts to contribute,
convinced that the images and words scrolling in his head were
private and valueless. Living the middle distance so effectively
and for so long caused him to know himself as an indistinguish-
able person. As part of the blend. He didn't dream of it being

any other way, and considered himself lucky to have found such safety. It was no longer a strategy or role but who he perceived himself to be: nobody—a boy with none of his own opinions, and no real sense of humor. Laughing when others laugh just means you pick up on social cues.

Max didn't realize Danny Danesh wasn't necessarily funnier than him, it was just that his humoristic strong suit simply wasn't the same as Danesh's: deciding who was the most gay among his group of friends at any given moment. Max laughed sincerely at situational comedies on television, some books, and the adventures of Kip and his Man-Dog of a brother. But he didn't know those different types of humor were transferable to real life. He couldn't see that his classmates exploited such a thin slice of all the comedic styles available. The gay thing was the pinnacle of funniness at his school, and if you couldn't wield this material competently, then you weren't one of the funny ones. Humor, like everything else, was defined by the confident, who didn't have to be any different from the delusional. If you were unflinchingly convinced of yourself, then you were equipped to be a leader.

THREE

KELLY RETURNED ON the evening of the longest day of the summer. She'd gotten laid off from the warehouse, and after they asked her to pack up her desk, Rasheed took her out for lunch. After finishing his shift, he picked her up at her place and brought her to the house. The two took multiple trips from the car to the house to bring in her suitcases and then a rucksack and then three other bags. Max worried it would be interpreted as resistance if he asked for more clarification on why she appeared to be moving in with them right now. For reasons no one explained to Max, going back to wherever she lived yesterday wasn't an option.

She wore a military-green beret, and hesitated over where to put down her luggage. Rasheed showed her to his bedroom. Setting her baggage down in there, she kicked off her shoes and came out to officially greet Max. She had a bubbling warmth that gave her the appearance of a completely different person from the other night. She brought her face so close to Max's that the heat of her nose touched the tip of his, and she spoke as if overwhelmed with gratitude, "I hope you know you're a beautiful boy."

He was confused but also proud. He had the feeling they were doing her a great service by taking her in, maybe keeping her safe from someone or something that caused her harm. There was no prearrival shock or excitement this time, no more bragging or interviewing; she was already in, and here to stay. Maybe their dinner the other night had gone much better than Max remembered. Maybe all of that clumsy conversation had just been shy courting. Rasheed looked thankful that it had all been determined for them. They didn't have to think about whether she'd be a good addition to the house or not. Some unclear set of circumstances made it so she simply became the addition: the first woman Max would ever share a home with. Rasheed gave his son a silent isn't-this-great! expression with two thumbs up in the air.

The phone rang while Kelly unpacked. Max picked up in the kitchen, where he had started making pasta, a moment after Rasheed had already gotten on the line and talked to Coach Tim from his bedroom. Max caught the second half of Tim's sentence, ". . . shit, it's because I care too much about you, Reed."

Max liked the sound of that—his father deserved such appreciation—but as he was hanging up, he heard Rasheed whisper menacingly into the phone, "Just-leave-us-alone-goddammit-do-you-fucking-understand-shit-man!" Max couldn't imagine why Tim's jealousy should warrant such a reaction. Tim must have done something else, something indefensible.

At dinner, Kelly talked about what a blessing it was that she'd been fired. "A clean slate," she proclaimed. She could finally focus on her real dream of starting a nonprofit organization. She hadn't yet decided what kind of nonprofit but knew she was finished working crummy jobs just to pay the bills, and it was time to apply her skills toward something that aided those most under the oppressive control of Big Brother.

"Whose big brother?" Max asked.

"Oh, Maxie"—she turned to him—"I'm not surprised you don't see the oppression all around. You're so adorable, no one would ever do anything but admire you." Max had never been looked at like this, like he was appetizing, and it sparked an unprecedented discomfort in him. His father radiated with joy, thrilled by Kelly's new babying tone.

She struck Max as the near opposite of the little woman at the Yangs'. Where the little woman was a girl acting as a full-grown woman, Kelly was a woman speaking like a little girl. But having seen her behave so differently before, Max couldn't be sure which version of her was the more natural one.

She continued, "You see, Maxie, some people are treated worse than others in this world. You're one of the lucky ones, so you're not forced to be aware of that ugliness."

"Okay, yes, good." Rasheed chuckled nervously. "Please, have more noodles." He pushed the bowl of pesto and goat cheese pasta Kelly's way.

"Oh, thank you." But she didn't take any. "What I'm saying, Maxie, is that the world is still an unfair place with a lot of unlucky people who didn't do anything to deserve their unluckiness."

"That's right," Rasheed said, "and we are very happy and lucky people—so." After receiving a look of unyielding patience from Kelly, he added, "But in many ways Kelly is right. It's very important to be nice to the unlucky ones."

Kelly nodded. "Exactly. I guess that's all I'm saying. And the way to help the unlucky ones can be complicated by the government because of how it is controlled by private interests that profit off of keeping the unlucky people down."

Rasheed said, "Could be, okay, yes, could be. And we have a happy life here and will always be nice to other people." He nodded at her emphatically. "Any people, lucky or not lucky."

"Yes—," said Kelly, "and, well, I'm excited to start helping the not-lucky ones. That's the main idea I was driving at. I'm going to take full advantage of this wonderful new living situation"—she reached over and shook Max's and Rasheed's arms simultaneously—"to start really planning how to help more. Does that sound good to you, Maxie?"

"Yeah," he said, assuming it was his fault that he still didn't understand whose big brother was involved in this tangle of luck and help and new living situations.

She said, "It's been my dream since I was a little girl to help the unfortunate."

"That's just—wow," Rasheed said, enormously pleased now. "We support this very much." He stuffed his cheeks with pasta. "Everything is starting to feel even more fortunate than before, huh, Maxie?"

Max gave a big, persuasive smile. "Yeah."

For the following couple of days, Max mostly avoided Kelly, staying in his room with Rocket, or in the tree house, only coming out to the kitchen when he heard her going into her and his father's bedroom. She spent most of her time doing research by borrowing documentaries from the library to hone in on what cause she wanted her nonprofit to center around.

When she and Max did cross paths, she hugged or patted him with the detachment of someone handling one of those life-size apes they have at toy stores. He finally braved up enough, partially out of boredom, to join her on the couch to watch the documentaries. She'd scoot closer, rest her head on his shoulder, throw a calf over his thigh, wrap her arms around him. He wanted to like it and couldn't understand why she made him so rigid. Why couldn't he relax and take pleasure in the human contact? His father supported it, trusted her—this was exactly what they'd wanted, right?—so why the blockage?

He also noticed she systematically put her hands on him the moment his father came back from work. Rasheed walked in, and she found and held Max, sometimes even going into his room and lying in bed with him. And he had the strong impression that only when he entered the room his father and Kelly shared did Rasheed suddenly pet her head or cuddle up to her. So Max too, in an effort to adapt to this new style of life, rushed to touch Kelly when Rasheed came in on them, commanding himself to sit close enough to her for their knees or shoulders to touch, eventually putting his arm around her. A bizarre competitiveness developed where Max simulated increasing affection for Kelly, trying to be as physical with her as his father was (or maybe even a little more), and Rasheed, in turn, seemed to grow incrementally more touchy-feely with her too.

Kelly gradually dropped her kindergarten-teacher affectations when alone with Max, addressing him in a casual way: "Hey, pass me the remote . . . Want a glass of OJ? . . . Hit those lights for me, thanks," like a roommate, but as soon as his father showed up, she reverted to speaking to him like he was a puppy. It felt like a show to Max, but since the other two were so delighted by the dynamic, he adjusted to it. This was what having a woman in the house felt like.

She smoked exactly two cigarettes a day, talked to herself about the documentary she'd most recently watched, and cleaned.

The cleaning was more like her daily exercise, scrubbing counters and mopping as though someone was timing her. She raced Max to be the first to disinfect the toilet or reorganize the fridge or to get to work on Rasheed's pants and shirts. He knew he should welcome her help, but couldn't she find some other way to contribute besides stealing his tasks? And her idea to cook as a team the night before had proven more of a nuisance than anything, slowing Max's whole process down. He silently disagreed with the way she chopped veggies, and the order in which she pan-fried them.

He played Simon & Garfunkel while he vacuumed the living room now, and turned it down when he saw her put on her headphones, listening to what sounded like fast Latin music in her Walkman as she dusted the television. Aside from Gloria Estefan's *Mi Tierra*, her three other cassettes were *Various West-African Rhythms*, Salt-N-Pepa's *A Salt with a Deadly Pepa*, and *1940–1980 Songs of Revolution*.

He got hooked on her documentaries. They covered themes of poverty, sometimes war and genocide, dictatorships, and uprisings. Subject matter ranged from the Khmer Rouge killing squads to the Bay of Pigs, Franco, Baader Meinhof, Steve Biko, Nelson Mandela, Simon Bolivar, the Rwanda massacres, the Holocaust, racism in the United States, Frederick Douglass's biography, the Black Panther movement, and the evils of the CIA. Max learned more about the horrors of humankind that summer than in all the history classes he'd taken.

None of Kelly's documentaries conveyed good news. The films were narrated by the voices of men you'd think had been living underground for fifty years, smoking, drinking whiskey, and dissecting maps. Max watched cop batons come down on bloody-faced black men, still shots of gun executions and hangings, emaciated children sleeping in the mud, the ghostly newspaper-print smiles of victims or villains, prisoners crammed like chickens, orphans clawing at a roll of bread, the bloated and the diseased, lesions that looked like shreds of tongues, piles of twisted bodies, and court cases that decided the ends of lives. Most disturbing were the people on the screen who remained calm and reasonable in interviews, with humor and a warm gaze, but had perpetrated some of history's most inhumane acts of violence. It was this two-facedness that challenged Max's sense of safety worst of all.

The evils flickering on the screen mixed with his proximity to Kelly's body forced him to shed a layer of skin. His life had been so simple before Kelly and her documentaries, so undisturbed and regular. And while he missed how uncomplicated things were before the world outside of Clarence began creeping in, this darker form of learning absorbed him absolutely, and he spent more and more time with Kelly and her films.

He surprised himself when he asked her to get a documentary about the civil war in Lebanon. She was proud of him for making the request and from that point on asked for his opinion on what they watched. She started cursing around him too, and he liked that. It excited him when she verbalized her moral and political stances with intensity. Though she usually wasn't speaking directly to him but more to herself, her views challenged him in ways that had never crossed his mind and that no other adult had ever brought up: health care is a human right and the government should treat it as such; of course gay marriage should be legal; it's unethical for anyone to make over a few hundred thousand dollars a year when others suffer dire poverty, and there should be a nationwide salary cap enforced; if redistribution of wealth creates a just society, then inheritance should be illegal; if you really believe in fairness, then do away with national borders and establish a world democracy; guns ought to be banned, period. He and his father didn't discuss the rights and wrongs of the world, and school had never insisted much either, let alone introduce the stimulating philosophies Kelly asserted.

The images of the Lebanese civil war documentary gave some visual context to the country and its conflicts, but the story itself remained a confused mess. There was no government or police in the Lebanon of this movie, only militarized clans, missile-striped skies, cadavers that took time to decipher as such, wailing mothers, slow zoom-ins on bullet wounds that looked like squashed cherries, and groups of children hiding behind dilapidated walls from masked men with machine guns. Max could not have imagined a greater hell.

It was around this time that he became truly afraid of death. An opening cleared inside him, and the terror that enlaces everything rushed in like bleaching light. All things seemed qualified to kill him now. All planes were capable of dropping bombs, all men of pulling out revolvers, all coughs and sneezes and meats and fruit of being the start of lethal viral epidemics, and the roof of his tree house was always on the verge of collapsing on his face, either disfiguring or ending him.

He told his father that they'd borrowed the documentary on his home country, and Rasheed demanded he stop watching such depressing things. In fact, he ordered Max to stop watching documentaries with Kelly altogether. Max acquiesced immediately, feeling he'd been saved from his own wretched curiosity. He knew he couldn't have given it up alone.

Kelly said, "But why? These films tell the truth. What's the harm in that?"

Max clamped up. He'd yet to hear them disagree since she moved in. They'd exchanged nothing but cuddles and smiles. Rasheed said, in a weirdly polite tone, "This disturbs everyone, honey; it's not important to know about all the bad truth in the world."

"Let's ask Max what he thinks," Kelly said. "Do you find these documentaries disturbing or educational?"

He hated the responsibility of making decisions for himself. He shrugged and said, "I don't know. They're okay, I guess."

"Not okay," Rasheed said.

"Okay," Max said.

Kelly snorted and shook her head. "Okay."

Max tried to respect his father's wishes, but every time she put in another documentary, he felt judged as a coward for walking away. After a day of depriving himself of the films, obsessively wondering what he was missing out on, he came back to the couch. She seemed to respect his defiance.

She asked what he thought of the Lebanese documentary, and he said it was hard to follow.

"You ever talk to your dad about this stuff?" she asked.

"I don't think he likes talking about that."

"Yeah, I noticed. Why do you think that is?"

He said, "When we are in America we are Americans."

"Yeah? And being an American in America means you can't talk about the Middle East?"

He wanted her to leave it alone. Her questioning felt like a violation of something that had been vaulted away for good reason. He trusted his father's avoidance of this topic. Couldn't she be satisfied that Max was already disobeying him about the documentaries? "I don't know."

"What about your grandparents? What do they have to say about the war?"

"I don't have grandparents."

She looked confused. "I mean on your mom's side. I know your dad lost his folks, but your maternal grandparents are alive, right?"

He didn't know how to disagree about such a black-or-white fact. Should they go back and forth, *No they're not, Yes they are, No they're not, Yes they are,* until one of them tired out? The suggestion that any of his relatives were still alive gave him slight vertigo. His heart tipped forward in his chest and he stared up at the ceiling for the rest of the conversation. *No one is alive. There is only you and me now.* His father's voice enabled him to be blunt. "They all died. Killed by a robber."

"A *robber*?" She intently watched the credits of the documentary, as if she were carefully reading the individual Arabic names, looking for someone in particular. "So, did that happen pretty recently then?"

"Not really." He hesitated before choosing not to tell her where they'd all been murdered and that his mother wore a cooking pot on her head. He had been trained to accept his mother's story as a closed case and feared Kelly would question this in ways he couldn't account for.

HE STAYED IN the tree house a lot when Kelly didn't have a documentary playing. He'd already spent at least fifty hours sitting up there that summer, sweating in the dark raised sauna, confronting the infinite ceiling, and letting his mind go to sauce. When the light permitted, he drew on the walls some more. For the first time in his life, he found it simpler, more gratifying, to invent than to replicate things—like Danesh's fishbowl—that had already happened.

He filled the space around the fishbowl sketches with his imagination: a quilt of water spiders bobbing in unison to the sound of dancing helicopters overhead; gargantuan, sand-colored tongues wrestling in snow, their saliva melting everything, connecting the world with the seas, where they dominated as sea monsters, Kip and his Man-Dog of a brother floating by their side in a tree house–submarine. A couple of woolly mammoths trudging through the desert en route to that oversize golden peanut that awaited them on the horizon. A pack of smiling wolves lounging by the fire, playing marbles and chatting with overweight ninjas who wore mittens (hands were hard to draw).

The process was cathartic, but once he stepped back, he immediately disliked what he'd made. So much so that he took on the project of erasing it all by coloring the back wall black. He exhausted a dozen markers, getting pleasantly woozy off the chemicals. In the small rectangle of light from the window, the black turned an oil-spill blue. He gazed into that oil spill, replaying the stories of Kip and his Man-Dog of a brother, or the enormous man in the tiny tree, or even the mother sitting in the bathtub. He joined all the characters up, having them plod across the oil together (Kip had uprooted the tree and carried it around with the enormous man swaying up top) as they searched for something in a vaguely urgent way.

Other times the tree house was a coffin. The dimness, mildew, and his echoed breathing created an escalating panic in him. He withstood the feeling of being buried alive for as long as possible. At the edge of hyperventilation, when his hands and feet tingled and his heart raged against his chest, he climbed down and pulled himself across the yard to go back home, rest, and learn more about the world's atrocities.

THAT EVENING RASHEED brought home a bag of empty cans from the soda that he and coworkers at the depot had drunk all day. He decided Max would love stomping on them in the kitchen, and took photos of him grinding his teeth, his heel about to come down on the can. He clapped when Max squashed one in line with its butt.

Kelly stepped into the bathroom. When Max heard her turn on the shower, he crushed a Fanta and then casually asked, "How come we don't know any other Lebanese people?"

"Bravo!" He clicked the camera. "Why should we?"

"I don't know. Just seems like maybe we'd know at least one."

Rasheed set up another can. "You know, Maxie, these Lebanese, they don't know about being adaptable. They are stuck in the past always. They think they are part of the modern world because they wear shiny watches and perfumes, but they are a strange mixing of corrupt show-offs and very traditional and religious." He looked away from Max. "Also, I don't find interest in talking about who hates who in that country anymore."

"That's all they want to talk about?"

"No. Sometimes. Anyway, I don't like when they talk about this. It's not good to remember how they are crazy over there. And if I'm with Lebanese, it's like I have to think and talk like them, like a crazy person."

Max stood among a population of twenty-plus cans, some flattened and others bent in half, all shining their different aluminum colors. Thanks to the documentary he'd seen with Kelly, it was easy for him to imagine a country of crazy people. He remembered an old man, coated in soot and concrete dust, screaming Arabic into the camera as he dashed by. But how did those crazy people behave when not fighting? Or were they constantly fighting?

He asked, "The civil war is over, right?"

"The big one is over, sure, but there are always more wars going on, or about to go on. There is still so much hate. So much baggage and so many outside countries wanting to make a mess of everything all over again." He set up two cans for Max and told him to stomp down on them at the same time. Before Max leaped up in the air, Rasheed leaned in closer and whispered, "This is why culture is stupid, Maxie." He let his camera hang from his neck. "People think it unites people, but the truth is, it separates even more. We have a good life.

We don't need culture or religion or things like this. We don't need to swear to some kind of group or talk about past things so much. We are individuals, so why come together under a flag or something and say that because we like the same food or soccer team or politics or time of prayer that we are all the same?"

Surely Rasheed had the right to have social and cultural preferences; to distance himself from traditions and mores and a history he felt didn't correspond with him anymore. "People still hate each other over there?" Max asked.

"They love too much also. When you love too much, it's worse than hate. You do horrible things to make sure your love will not be harmed. Loving too much makes life very difficult. Makes you afraid. Makes you behave badly."

"Did my mom hate people?"

"No, your mother had no hate inside her. That is not true. She hated artichokes very much. She said they tasted like seawater." He smiled at one of the flattened cans.

"Was she funny like you?" said Max.

Kelly turned off the shower. Rasheed stared at the bathroom door and then back at Max. "I nearly forgot! I brought you something else. Something better than cans." He left to get a book from his bedroom: *Robin Hood*. "Long ago you read me that fantastic story you pretended to write while I was under the weather, and I knew you needed to be reading more fantastic stories like this one." Max swallowed, incredulous that his father had known he'd lied. Rasheed knocked on the cover. "This is a great one, but you know, always before reading a book you must count the pages."

Max laughed and accepted the book.

"No, seriously. Make sure none of the pages have fallen out. There is nothing worse than when you are in the middle of a great story and you find there are pages gone. This makes the story a kind of bad mystery. A very frustrating one." Rasheed kissed the top of Max's head and went to his room to change into his work clothes. Kelly followed in after him, wearing a towel. Max waited for his father to come back out before bringing his heels down on the two uncrushed cans at the same time.

FOUR

Probably the most peculiar Kip and Man-Dog episode was the time they were killed. They'd found themselves hanging on to an enormous rope in a dark void. The Man-Dog couldn't hold on any longer, his grip weakened, and he plummeted. He caught the very end of the rope with his teeth, pulling down on it in such a way that it clicked on a light—they had, in fact, been left to hang on the lightbulb string of an evil giant's closet—but the Man-Dog's sudden tug of the rope bucked Kip off and now caused him to fall. The Man-Dog instinctively jumped after Kip, and they both free-fell to their dooms. It was the first time they had ever died. Max was certain this meant an end to Kip and Man-Dog stories forever but, the following night, they were alive again.

FIVE

NADINE AND RODNEY lived in the yellow house across the street. They were a good-looking young black couple. Max had watched them through the living room window as they moved in at the beginning of the summer. Nadine got out of the car first, and possessed his attention utterly. She walked with a slow and uncommon confidence, her gait wider than a woman her height normally had, cutting the air with her thick thighs and pulling everything she passed in her wake. Facing her new home, she put her palms on the top of her butt, which bowed out enough to make a little shelf. She had her tightly wound dreadlocks tied back, and wore dark jeans and a peach-cream tank top. Rodney got out next, dwarfing their car. He had a celery-green linen suit on that day, his rack of muscle sitting underneath his clothes like a bulletproof vest. He stood with the self-important posture of someone who had a military career, chewed enormous wads of gum, and coached Little League too aggressively.

Sometimes, when Max saw Rodney and Nadine outside, doing yard work, he made himself a vodka cranberry and settled into the living room to observe them. Rodney's voice was loud and intrusive, and his immense body seemed capable of withstanding anything. Nadine's breasts didn't look cumbersome at all—full and big, but light for her. A layer of strong fat covered her body; she wore it sensually, and seriously. It shivered when she moved, making a queasy feeling in Max's belly that reminded him of lying in a hot bath, where his eyelids weakened and he breathed from his mouth. His line of sight stayed tied to Nadine's waist, waiting for the moments she bent over and her shirt rose so he could see a sliver of her cinnamon-brown stomach.

On weekends she dressed casually (T-shirts, jeans, sandals), and for work she had a funky-professional style: chocolate pants, a lion-colored sash, and a cream silk blouse; a thick turquoise beaded necklace draped over her all black skirt suit and a wide rhinestone belt; a vintage orange dress made of wool with a baby blue head wrap. When he learned from the Yangs that she was a doctor, he imagined she put on a white coat over all her cool clothes as soon as she got to work.

She had other admirers too. Mr. Jenkins, a light-skinned, mustachioed old man with a fedora, sat on his porch and watched her as if he beheld an angel in the natural world. When he saw her, he took off the fedora, pressing it to his heart, and showed off the pomade brilliance of his parted hair. And Mr. Jenkins's granddaughter, whom he looked after some weekends, with her fuchsia beads adorning the tips of her dancing braids, regarded Nadine with the awe of having spotted a real-life princess. Nadine had been over to the Yangs' a few times, and they were charmed by her knowledge of flowers and of Chinese literature.

Rasheed had never introduced himself to Nadine or Rodney, or any of the black neighbors. The only other houses on

Marion Street that Max had been inside of were Coach Tim's and the Yangs'. He didn't know what it looked like in any of the black homes, and they didn't know what it looked like in his.

While Max watched Nadine working in her yard one day, a bee rammed up against the living room window from the inside. The bee wouldn't accept not going through the glass; doing so would have acknowledged a wall at the end of the universe, where space froze into an impenetrable block, posing as a continuation; a moving picture. Refusing this discovery, the bee bashed its head against it, over and over.

Max got a cup and a piece of paper from the kitchen to catch the bee and throw it outside. He trapped it, opened the front door, murmured a couple of words to the cup about liberty that resembled a Coach Tim pregame speech, removed the piece of paper, and drove the cup forward like a dagger. The bee flew about five feet away, and then, as if connected to a string tied to Max's front tooth, turned around and blitzed his face. Max actually shouted the word *No!* as it bombed down on him, its stinger curled under itself. When it plugged him right between the nose and lip, he barked in pain. The bee imbedded in his skin, its legs wriggling, fizzed like an electric charge. Max started head-banging and slapping at his mouth, his fight instincts convinced this was his demise. Nadine dropped her hose and ran over. Once he saw her approaching, he calmed down and looked at her in embarrassment, the dead bee now in his palm.

"I'm so sorry, I'm okay," he told Nadine. "It's okay, I'm sorry, I'm fine."

Leaning her round face down into his, she said, "You sure?"

"Yes."

She scrutinized the dead bee. "So weird how he's willing to die just to hurt you a little, huh?" Her breath was hot and clean.

They both examined its coiled body. Max looked up at her. There's something surreal about seeing someone up close you've only watched from afar. Everything about it is surprising, somehow less realistic. She was one of those people who, the closer you got to, the more sublime her face became. Her brown skin seemed to emit light. She had high cheekbones and large canoe-shaped lips.

His eyes were open too wide, and he closed them halfway. "Maybe this one wasn't right in the head," he said, then immediately regretted it, realizing it didn't fit with what she'd said. The sting puffed up under his nostril.

She smiled her bright teeth at him, one of the front ones slightly overlapping another. Max thought of a pair of crossed legs. "We haven't met yet. I'm Nadine."

"I—Max," said Max.

"I-Max?"

"I mean, I am Max."

She laughed, and he felt himself levitating.

Kelly appeared at his side and introduced herself. Then she leaned stiffly against the doorframe, like a tipped vase. Looking nervous, she straightened out and put her arm around Max. How different these two women were. Nadine had a health and assuredness emanating from her that made Kelly seem anemic somehow, damaged. A gray lung sitting next to a pink one.

He'd noticed a few times before in the grocery store that Kelly treated black people like walking miracles. They were the ultimate minority in her hierarchy of subjugated peoples. She seemed to be simultaneously praising and pitying them. Speaking to Nadine quickly and with random gigglings, Kelly told her that she'd just moved here and also just got fired and also just escaped an abusive relationship and also just doesn't get along with any of her family members and is also fresh out of friends she can trust, ha-ha. When Nadine glanced down at Max, Kelly clasped his shoulder more tightly.

"Well, listen," Nadine said, "you guys should come over for dinner sometime. I think it's long overdue that we get to know each other."

"Absolutely," Kelly said, a little stridently, "we will definitely take you up on that. And you too, don't you hesitate to come over anytime!"

"That's great. It was nice meeting you two," Nadine said. "I hope your lip feels better, I-Max."

She turned to walk home, and when Rodney came out of the house, Kelly nearly bolted toward him, passing Nadine and extending her handshake well before she'd left the driveway, as though it towed her to him. Max returned to his observation point behind the living room window. Rodney changed his default bored and moderately offended expression into a broad, youthful smile. He stood straighter, chuckled a lot, and ended up inviting Kelly into their home. Nadine followed in after them. To distract himself from wondering what it was like in their house, Max took a shot of vodka, chased it with cranberry juice, and watched the Lebanese civil war documentary again.

Over dinner, Kelly told Rasheed she'd met the neighbors and how nice they were. She couldn't stop talking about them: Nadine's doing her residency at Bell Children's Medical Center to become an internal doctor, she's a Democrat, an avid reader of literature, a music lover, and so pretty. And she's only twenty-six! Can you believe it? And besides becoming a doctor, she's done everything you can think of. She lived in Nepal for five months, volunteering at a leper colony, and lived in this Buddhist monastery in Thailand after that, but didn't really identify as Buddhist anymore, and before all that she went to high school in Paris because her dad was a diplomat from Cameroon. She can't understand where Nadine found the time to do all she has in so few years. And the boyfriend, Rodney, he's ex-military, writes some kind of political column now, and wants to start a business that sells—she forgets, some kind of workout machine through a mail-order catalog or something.

While putting a forkful of spinach, arugula, tomato, and honey walnut salad in his mouth, Rasheed said, "And her father was a political person who committed suicide. A very corrupt man."

Kelly and Max exchanged a look.

"What?" she said. "How do you know that?"

"Mr. Yang reads the international newspapers."

After dinner, Max got Mr. Yang's business card out and dialed the number he'd known by heart for seven years. He liked holding on to the card while he dialed. Mr. Yang explained that when he met Nadine and heard her last name, he asked if she was related to a diplomat he'd read an article about years ago. She said that diplomat was her father. A man caught up in all kinds of illegal activities. He came home one day, walked past his wife and children, stepped out onto the balcony of their Paris apartment, and dove into the street. Mr. Yang remembered a strange detail in the article: that before killing himself, he had gotten a haircut. Mr. Yang stopped on the word *haircut* like it was a small garden potato he was trying to swallow. Max had never heard Mr. Yang being so emotional and didn't dare ask why the part about the haircut choked him up.

MAX HAD JUST fallen asleep when Kelly came into his room, waking him up to say good night. She climbed into bed and spooned him. A new line was being crossed here—hugging in the dark. He had an erection, and loathed his body for it. Lying there with his eyes split wide open, he felt numb and invaded, as if awake during surgery.

She said, "Lucky boy, there's so much pain in the world and you are so lucky to have a roof over your head and plenty to eat and people who love you so much."

"Thank you," he whispered, though he didn't understand her regression. Hadn't they exceeded this baby talk? Hadn't she been discoursing on world politics and ethics just this morning, convincing him of a more socialized world where we take care of those born with a lesser lot in life? It was perplexing to admire her ideas but despise her physical company.

"He's seen dead people before, you know? Women, children, you name it. He's been there."

"What?"

"Your dad. He knows about death. The things we see in those movies, he knows them firsthand. That's why he doesn't want to be reminded."

"Oh." He rubbed his eyes. "Yeah." He wondered what his father could have told her thus far. It took Rasheed twelve years to impart any specifics to his own son, and Kelly hadn't even been here a month.

"He knows about losing people. Close people."

"Yeah."

"His wife. And lots of others."

"His wife." The ceiling felt like it was slowly lowering. "My mom." It wasn't Max and his father's private story anymore.

"I think so, honey. I think so. He told me about the time she invited a peasant into their home to teach him how to read and write. Sounds like a remarkable lady. Her dad was so pissed off when he came home to a street man sitting with his daughter." She laughed.

Max didn't know anything about that. His mind conjured up an image of a bathtub running over with blood and dirty dishes. "Did he say anything else about my mom?"

She wormed her body closer, clearly in the mood to feel needed. "Honey, I really don't know much about the story. You know he doesn't talk about that stuff. But I'll ask him for you, okay, sweetie? I'll tell you everything. I promise. I love you. I love you just for being you. You don't have to do anything but be yourself to be completely loved by us. Isn't that lucky? Wouldn't it be beautiful if everyone could have that?"

"Thank you. Yes." Conscious of his erection again, he felt her presence become intolerable. Even her body heat felt invasive and dirty to him now. He lay unmoving, as if he hid between a whale's jaws; the smallest movement would cause her to snap down on him. He suppressed an urge to scream. She perceived his discomfort enough to release him, but didn't leave.

"I don't think I can sleep," he said, meaning, *Because you're here*.

"Just try, honey. Just close your eyes. I know it's hard." She brought her arm over to hug him again and accidentally grazed his penis through the blanket. She pulled away as if burned by it.

"Sorry!" he said.

"No, no, that's okay, honey. There's nothing to be embarrassed about. That's really normal. It's fine." The honor in her voice repulsed him. *It was like this when I woke up! It has nothing to do with you!* he wanted to yell. He just wished she'd leave. Instead, she said, "You know, when I was your age, my mother made me feel ashamed of that kind of stuff. She told me those urges were evil. And that was wrong. She made me feel so—unclean and alone." She brought her face closer to his. Her breath was sharp and everywhere. "There's nothing shameful about your urges, Max. You're allowed to feel that way, and you're allowed to relieve yourself too. You know that, right?"

He couldn't possibly respond. Why was she talking like she was being helpful?

"Wait. Do you know how to relieve yourself?" She said. "Have you let yourself do it before?"

This he couldn't answer intelligently either. Of course he knew how to relieve himself. But out loud he resorted to the quick shirking response he always gave when supremely uncomfortable. "I don't know."

She lay in silence for a while before eventually sighing. "Okay. That's okay. What you can do is rub it against the bed, up and down. You'll sleep like a baby right after, I promise. It's all right. I'm going to walk you through this. I'm not going to leave you, honey. Don't worry. Now turn over onto your stomach." Indignantly, he did. He turned away from her, facing the wall. "Good. Now go ahead," she said, "move up and down so it rubs against the bed." Unsure as to why, when she told him what to do, rooting him on in eerily soothing tones, he obeyed. He rubbed slowly at first, then with a certain determination. Kelly patted his back, like she was burping an infant. Rocket exhaled loudly, and Max felt pathetic but couldn't stop. He rubbed harder and harder, and gradually brought himself closer to her, turning to face her with his eyes sealed shut. Her hair touched his face. She didn't move away; she lay still, repeating, "It's all right, you're doing fine, you're almost there," until he found himself actually rubbing it against her thigh. Their skin never made direct contact, and she showed no sign of there being anything remotely sexual about it on her end. This made it so much worse, as though she were making a brave sacrifice for him. When he came, she said, "Goooood," like when a dog fetches a stick.

She swept his bangs off his sweaty brow and kissed the tip of his nose. He heard her lips part into a smile. "There. Now you know how to do it. Anytime you have those urges, you can just do that by yourself and feel good about it, okay? No shame." Before leaving, she imposed a final meaningful pause that seemed to say, *We've just shared something so special.*

DANNY DANESH ONCE drew a naked woman on his stomach, her legs spreading open from his bellybutton. Fascinated by this image, Max went home and did the same to himself, staring at the disproportionately large vagina in the bathroom mirror. He put his pinkie inside it like Danny had done for his friends. The physical discomfort of touching the knot of scar tissue back there was something Max kept going back for well after he'd scrubbed the woman away. Whenever he needed to be uncomfortably invigorated, he jammed his pinkie into his navel. It had the same allure for him as licking a nine-volt battery over and over, or continuing to sniff the air when something foul lingered in it.

He was lying in his tree house now, cramming both pinkies into his belly button, when he heard his father's voice. "What are you doing in here?"

Max, who'd been grunting from the discomfort he caused himself, sat up. "Nothing." It took a while to make out the outline of his father's head, poking up into the tree house.

Rasheed said, "We are going to play board games with Kelly. I bought the Game of Life today. Come inside."

"All right. Dad?" he asked his father's shadow of a head. "Did my mom teach a peasant how to read in her father's living room?"

"What are you talking about?"

"Kelly told me."

Max stared at him long enough for Rasheed to feel the need to say something more. In a single breath he said, "She got into fights with her father when he came home and saw bunches of peasants sitting around the coffee table. That's all."

"Bunches of peasants? I thought it was just one peasant."

He sighed. "Listen, there may have been one or there may have been bunches. I don't remember. The point is she wanted to help the world, like Kelly. She was incredibly tough cookies, just like Kelly. So tough that she didn't tolerate people very well who asked too many questions about her or who didn't care about the Game of Life." He slapped the tree house floor twice to get Max moving. "Okay, come down now."

Max avoided Kelly's eyes as they played the board game that didn't resemble anyone's life he knew of. Rasheed and Kelly drank and laughed a lot as they played. They looked happy. Max felt sad but did an excellent job of hiding it. He went to bed before they finished, claiming he was just sleepy.

The next morning, Sunday, his father's day off, Max shuffled into the kitchen and poured himself a bowl of Bran Flakes at the round table. He disliked the gaps that the round table made up against the corner. There existed a profound unfairness in those two being forced together.

Instead of eating, he squirted yellow dish soap into the bowl and watched the dense globules refuse to mix with the water and cereal. He wanted an egg to crack into the bowl now. What would happen? Would the yolk join the soap? Rupture and smoke around the bran flakes? Float at the top, like a sun? Would everything blend together into a brownish wet cement guck, a thick substance he could sculpt with, or throw at someone's stupid unwelcome face?

He opened the fridge in search of the egg but got sidetracked by a brilliant red apple sitting on the bottom shelf. A puddle of milk gleamed a few centimeters from the apple, yellowed and motionless. The apple was lighter than it should have been. Probably meant a cushion of air separated the skin and flesh. He took an angry bite, and smacked up and down on the floury consistency and that web of cold skin. He spat the patch of apple into his palm and squeezed it into a kidney-shaped lump, then pressed it back into the apple where he'd taken the bite. Placing it in the milk puddle, he rotated the bitten and replastered part away from him so that it faced the back of the fridge.

Kelly came out wearing a brown T-shirt and dirty-white terrycloth shorts. "Ready for a big breakfast?" she said. "I'll need some ingredients from the store." Her thighs were diagramed with veins and olive-green bruises.

Max wondered what she was playing at here. He stammered, "I just, it usually just takes me a second to plan out what I'm going to cook and everything, so—"

"I know. But I'm going to take care of it this morning."

He should have expected this day to come. On previous Sundays she had managed to simultaneously compliment the meal Max had prepared while slipping in stories of her own breakfast achievements from her past life. Now, finally, she would be the head chef.

"Max," Rasheed called from his bedroom, "go to the store and get her the ingredients for breakfast, please."

"Okay," he said.

She handed him a list and twenty dollars. "Hey," she said, "I'm not trying to take over or anything, but I'd be lying if I told you I didn't make a mean frittata." She blew him a kiss before going back into the room with his father and shutting the door.

Outside, he saw Rodney raking leaves into a trash bag. The rake looked brittle in his hands. He boomed at Max, "Hey there!"

It took Max off guard. They'd never exchanged a word before. "Hello."

"Shouldn't you be in school?"

His eyes beaded about. "It's summer." *And on top of that it's Sunday*, he wanted to say.

Rodney squinted a little harder than the sun had previously made him. "I'm Rodney."

"Hi, I'm Max."

"Good to meet you, *Jack*." The way he said it, Max wasn't sure if Rodney had misheard him or if Jack was some kind of nickname. "Too bad it's only now you say hello. After how many months of living across the street from me?"

You've never said hello either, Max thought.

Rodney winked. "I'm just messing with you, man. Hey, make sure that bike seat isn't too high. Don't want to injure the goods, know what I mean?"

Max looked down at where his goods met the seat and mumbled, "You got it." He started riding off but stopped when Rodney continued talking.

"I met your mommy the other day."

"My mo— Oh, that's not my mom."

Rodney said, "That's not very nice. You think she'd appreciate you saying that?"

Max inspected his front tire awhile, unsure of why the truth wasn't nice. He had a quick fantasy of dropping the bike, diving across the lawn, and spearing Rodney in the chest with the top of his head. Of course, Max would bounce right off him.

Rodney gave another wink. "Well, all right, Jack-O. A pleasure meeting you anyway. Remember what I told you about the goods."

Max gave a downward nod, and Rodney returned it with an upward nod. Max favored the downward nod because it resembled a bow of respect. The upward nod was aggressive. It seemed to be saying *What?* with the chin, *Yeah, what?*

KELLY'S BREAKFAST WAS quick and uneventful. Her frittata didn't taste right. The next day he was home alone and felt a queer stillness in the house. The creaks took odd priority; the clicking of Rocket's nails on the kitchen floor sounded loud as a slow typewriter. He followed her to the front door, where she stood staring at it. She sat down, looked back at Max, and then again at the door. He peeked through the living room window and saw Coach Tim standing out there. Max waited another minute, but Tim didn't ring or knock. Eventually Max opened up anyway.

"Oh, whoa— Hey, Maxie." He was wearing mirror sunglasses. Max could see two funhouse reflections of himself and Rocket in Coach's eyes.

"Hi, Coach. What's up? My dad's at work, but—"

"Yeah, I know." He looked terrible, fatter. His apple cheeks and massive bull-like shoulders had always given him a hunched aspect, but now he was especially stooped. "I came to check up on you, actually. How have you been?"

"Really good."

"I hear you all have a new roommate."

Kelly had left early that morning, maybe to the library. Something had happened between her and Rasheed the night before. There was a lot of angry whispering. At one point he heard Rasheed hissing, "I don't care! Don't ever talk about those things with him, do you understand? Keep what I say to yourself." It ended in Kelly storming out of the house at four in the morning, saying, "I didn't sign up for this shit, Reed." Max went to the living room and saw her walking laps around the block, talking to herself. She came back in at around five. She didn't so much as look at Max, ate a bowl of cereal, and then headed out again. He worried that it had something to do with how he had rubbed up on her, but his father's gentleness toward him that morning reassured him that their fight was about something else.

"Oh, yeah. Kelly," Max said.

"How's that going?"

"It's really good." Things weren't really good with Kelly, Max knew that, but he was complicit in the ways they were least good. He couldn't complain because it might lead to her telling Rasheed what would cause irreparable harm. Max also wanted Tim to believe they were doing well without him, that Max and Rasheed were enough and that no new person in their home could threaten the indissoluble pair. Men and women could come and go in Rasheed and Max's life and the two of them would be left standing close and tall, no matter what these unpredictable people did or didn't do.

"Yeah?" He took off the sunglasses. Puffy half-moons cradled his eyes.

"Yeah."

"Your dad seem all happy and everything?" He laughed.

"Yeah."

"Huh." Coach stared at Max's feet. He tottered back and forth and then took off his cap to scratch his scalp with his crab-colored pinkie. With the hat off he looked like a big baby. "And what about you? You really like having her around? I mean, like, things are better?"

He felt his face getting red now. "I mean, it's been pretty good."

"Good. That's great."

"Yeah," Max said. "Great."

"Great."

"Yeah."

Tim had disappeared from their lives. They used to see each other nearly every day, and though Max usually got pushed aside when Tim came over, he suddenly missed him, more than he'd previously known. Max looked at Tim's expansive chest and then up at his clean-shaven chin and then down at one of his furry red fists before saying, "So, I'll tell my dad you came over."

"No, no, don't. Do me a favor, and please don't."

"Okay."

"*Psh*, yeah right, like all I need now is for him to think I came over. Anyway. I wanted to make sure you were all right." His voice cracked a bit. "So, you playing any ball this summer?"

"Nah. Haven't been playing much."

"Well, you should keep that J in good form for next season. We'll need you to drain those midrange jump shots."

"All right." It embarrassed Max to talk about basketball with Coach Tim. Max had no J. He drained no midrange jump shots. Coach gave him way too much playing time during games, which was not fine by Max and not fine by Danny Danesh, who couldn't trust Max to catch the ball when he passed it to him from behind his mothafuckin' back. Max was the third worst player on the team, but the absolute worst when under the pressure of a real game and the paralyzing resentment of his teammates for being the starting small forward. At the huddle before games, when Tim announced the lineup, Max fantasized about saying, *No, Coach, you know goddamn well I'm not the man for the job. Put Ben in. Ben's been working so hard in practice. He's earned it.* And then Ben, Danny Danesh, and the rest would take a moment to admire Max for putting the team first. But Max didn't do that. Max did only what he was told.

Tim smiled and gave him a soft slap on the cheek. "Maxie, I want you to take good care of yourself," he said, and walked away.

Max badly wanted to say something lively and natural before closing the door. He eventually called out, "I will, Coach. I'll make tandoori chicken."

"What?"

"You should come over for dinner tonight. I'll make tandoori."

"That'd be real nice." Then, for some reason, he spoke like they do in old Westerns. "Maybe some other time, kid." He walked on. "Maybe some other time."

KELLY WAS OUT of the house all day. In the evening, Rasheed had insisted on taking her and Max out to the Olive Garden, saying he had very big news to share. At the restaurant, Max only glanced up at Kelly when he was sure it wouldn't lead to eye contact. He couldn't stop thinking about their transgression. She looked like she hadn't slept in a week, her eyes cupped by slate and violet bags. It didn't take long before she unleashed her new and mysterious animosity on Rasheed, calling him an asshole under her breath when he bought a round of drinks for another table after they'd chuckled at one of his jokes: something about the Mafia eating spaghetti and meatballs. Rasheed either didn't hear her insult or pretended not to and ignored it when she scoffed at him for ordering more food, which in truth was more than they could possibly eat.

"Flashing money around like a kingpin. It's disgusting," she said.

Max held his breath, letting his head get hot, something that had begun happening when he was extremely nervous. It confounded him to see his father treated this way. He didn't believe Rasheed could have done anything reproachable enough to deserve this drastic change in attitude. This was because of some stubborn allegiance he had to his father but also because he understood that Kelly was wise and sensitive only when it came to large groups of people or subjects—like wars, class and race, governments, nations—but proved handicapped when it came to assessing the nature of individuals, and how best to interact with them.

Rasheed dipped a breadstick in his smoked mozzarella fonduta. "Darling. I am not a kingpin. A kingpin never eats at the Olive Garden."

"Forty-five million people are hungry in this country," she muttered, "not to mention those starving all over the world. Makes me kind of sick, is all." Goose bumps breezed up Max's thighs. An image of a famished Laotian girl, lying in street garbage, from the documentary *My Laos's Infamy* hijacked his thoughts. Then he remembered the shrapneled face of a Palestinian boy from the Lebanese civil war film. The boy's little brother had to dig the pieces out of his cheek with a needle and then sew him up. The stitches were black and thorny and wet as a sea urchin. The thought spoiled the strips of eggplant on Max's pizza, and he picked them off.

His father had brought them here tonight to announce that the warehouse he worked at had filed for bankruptcy. They'd given their employees two options: to get laid off with no bene-fits, or to work for six months without pay in a cost-saving drive until the warehouse could afford to compensate them again, hopefully with a raise. Rasheed stayed optimistic. He saw this as a big opportunity to make advancements. With all the people leaving, if he stuck around, he'd be sure to get the promotion.

"They can't do that," she said.

"Yes, they can. They did."

"I don't even think it's legal."

"It is legal, yes, as long as we agree to it. We become like volunteers. And I think it will be hard for the six months, but afterward it will be better. I really think so."

"I worked there too, Reed, remember? There's no way Don is converting it into a volunteers-only workforce."

"He is."

"Fine," she challenged him. "I'll come in and talk to Don myself."

"Not a very good plan for me. He fired you."

Kelly's shoulders shuddered with disparaging laughter. "Reed. This cannot be for real."

He looked at Max and then back at her. "It is real."

"So this was the big news. This is why you took us out to dinner. To tell us you're not getting paychecks anymore." She snorted. "Bottom line. How does this affect that thing we were talking about?"

"What thing?" Max wanted to know, trembling at the thought of them having discussed what he and Kelly had done.

"Well," she continued staring at Rasheed, "your father and I were talking about starting a nonprofit. You know, contribute some good to this world?"

"Yes. This is still a very nice idea," said Rasheed, looking for the waiter to ask for another soda.

"It's not just a very nice idea, Reed. It's what we talked about. Remember?" Dread overcast Rasheed's face. "When are you going to give back? Don't you think you've taken enough?"

Why didn't his father stick up for himself? He'd lost his cool for much less in the past. He flipped out when he'd learned that Max's school requested, on Flag Day, that Max stand by the flag of his country of origin. At the time, Max didn't know he was Lebanese and couldn't decipher what Mr. Jobson meant when he slowly repeated, "No, Max, your country of OR-igin. Do you understand OR-I-GIN?" When Max came home asking what his country of origin was, explaining why he wanted to know, Rasheed called the school and shouted into the phone that it was none of their goddamn business. Rasheed also had no qualms about shushing intimidating people in movie theaters, yelling at other drivers on the road, or calling people out for cutting in line, and he gave far too honest feedback to waiters when they asked him how he was enjoying his food. But here, nothing. Total surrender.

And Kelly, who had sided with the underpaid laborers in the documentary *Unionize or Starve*, remained untouched by Rasheed's struggle. But again, the film surveyed a mass of people and an ideology she strongly supported. Rasheed was only one person.

The table was poorly centered, and a lamp hung directly over Rasheed's seat, casting a cone of blond light around him alone. A man under interrogation. His skin looked ashy. "You are right," he said. "There are so many causes for the human race, but money is a little bit tight at the moment, and perhaps it is not the best time."

"How about refugee camps in Beirut, Reed?" she baited. "Maybe we can help out over there? What do you think about that?"

Rasheed's face crumpled, and he shook his head from side to side, *Please, let's not do this here*. What was Max missing exactly? His father had lost his job and said he couldn't afford to start a nonprofit organization yet. This made him a bad guy? Prioritizing himself and his family over an undefined cause in the interest of an undefined population?

Then Rasheed told them the second reason for this occasion at the Olive Garden. He hadn't been able to make rent payments, his bank accounts were in the red, and his credit cards all but maxed out. They'd received their first eviction notice the day before. The bank had rejected his application for another extension on a loan, and though Mr. Yang said they could probably ride out the legal process for up to two years, Rasheed didn't want to live somewhere he wasn't welcome.

Max remembered the account with the Ziad Jabbir deposits. He had no real sense of how long $620,000 lasted and didn't know if Ziad Jabbir still made monthly payments, but it crushed him to think of his father working so much and still failing to afford the lifestyle he'd set out to provide. Max's fretfulness had nothing to do with the idea of getting evicted or being poor. The immediate anxiety was the thought of his father considering himself a loser. Max did not ask about the Ziad Jabbir deposits now. It was none of Kelly's business. It wasn't any of Max's business either, really. He didn't even want it to be. He just wanted Rasheed to go back to commanding the ship like he always had. Max trusted him completely. Rasheed had never been one of those cryptic dads that children in movies think of as either heroes or monsters, vague and impressive, impossible to read, and living some kind of double life. He knew about those fathers, but his, Reed Boulos, was anything but inexplicable. Max knew him well, knew his habits and preferences, could virtually read his mind, and knew that he wasn't even capable of lying for the wrong reasons.

Kelly's laughter changed pitches as Rasheed explained the new conditions. It was the helpless laughter of a person submitting to the absurdity of not having any control or semblance of purpose. She caught her breath. "So your story is this: You get told you won't make any money, that you're going to lose your house, and you decide, Let's go to the Olive Garden!" Her laugh broke into a hoarseness that seemed to tear at her lungs. She slapped at the table with startling power.

Max had been holding his breath again. A pressure formed in his skull, and he could hear little pops, like soda water. "Hey!" he heard himself blurt.

It seemed as if all the people in the restaurant whipped their heads around to look at Max. He made eye contact with Kelly for the first time. Anger flowed over her face. This woman could destroy him in a single sentence, at the mere allusion of the orgasm he'd had against her body. His gaze fell to her fettuccine plate, and her stare burned the top of his head.

Finally Rasheed said to her, "Darling, tell us more about your nonprofit idea." He smiled sadly. His reasonableness incensed

Max. Max couldn't say anything, but why wouldn't *he*? Max put his hand up his shirt and jammed his pinkie into the back of his belly button, giving himself a surge of dull pain.

"Oh, the nonprofit I've wanted to start my whole life? That I keep getting sidetracked from by men like you? Then what? I tell you about my dreams, and you tell me about yours, and then what? You get your end of the deal, and what do I get?"

"What deal?" asked Max without lifting his eyes back up to her.

"What do I get?" she repeated louder.

His father looked scared. "I don't know, darling, I must think a little bit about these things, okay? Please, maybe we can enjoy the meal now, and talk about this later." He reached for her shoulder, but she yanked it away.

She finished her drink. "I don't want to talk about this later. I'm done talking."

WHILE RASHEED WAS at work the next day, Kelly stayed in the bedroom and wept. Max had never heard a woman cry in real life before. She sounded like an ensnared animal. Every whimper made the bones in his arms and shoulders shake like a tuning fork. He knocked lightly on the door. "Kelly?"

She went silent. He heard her sniffle and then get off the bed. She took a deep breath, locked the door, and spoke more gently to him than she ever had. "Go away, Max."

By nightfall, the coldness of her silent treatment blew through the house, dividing Max and Rasheed. Everyone stood apart. Max couldn't imagine how to address whatever was going on with either of them. Kelly was too unapproachable and powerful, and his father had become too sheepish.

Their home turned into a quiet, suffocating space, and when Max and his father did talk—never about the mysterious scorn breathing through the house—it felt playacted and awkward. Rocket became even lazier, looking dispirited. The cactus Mr. Yang gave Max wasted away, the tree house stunk of yeast and raccoon urine, and Max no longer took pleasure in cooking, for no one looked forward to eating together.

His father, for the first time in their relationship, started complaining to him about money problems, but the strangest part about it was that he only did this when Kelly was in earshot. Everything he said seemed to be a reminder that he worked like a brute and didn't have the cash to invest in any kind of new business, which was, as far as Max understood, precisely what had upset her at the restaurant. For example, as Rasheed was zipping up his bag in the kitchen, preparing to go to the second job he'd gotten at an all-night diner where they actually paid him, it was only when Kelly came in to pour herself a glass of water that Rasheed told Max that the diner was not the great change he'd hoped for, but he would do it until his other job started remunerating him again. Max could actually see Rasheed's words aggravating Kelly's pale skin. Plus, Rasheed continued, if he did his job well enough they might promote him from dishwasher to busboy, and that was a step in the right direction. Kelly compressed her lips so that rays of wrinkles fenced in her pink mouth, marched out of the kitchen, and locked herself in the bathroom until Rasheed left. Why did she hate him so much? And what was she still doing here if she hated him?

She began spending time with the neighbors, not the Yangs or Coach Tim, but virtually all the other families on Marion Street, especially Nadine and Rodney. She didn't watch documentaries anymore. Max overheard her saying to Nadine on the phone that she needed to get more involved with the community to understand the system and its workings on the actual people. She sought to study the local underprivileged population, to better sculpt her nonprofit vision and decide what form her help would take. She volunteered at the homeless shelter, taught GED prep courses at the county jail, and involved herself with the neighborhood watch, which consisted of her and Mr. Jenkins. They put together neighborhood safety tracts, reminding people to call the police if they witnessed anything criminal going on. She also joined a gospel choir at the church a few blocks from Marion Street, along with an awareness group downtown that combated racism.

In an unexpected moment of enthusiasm, Kelly gave Max a short speech like in the documentary days, maybe rehearsing for an upcoming meeting with her antiracism group. "The results of the Mamie and Kenneth Clark doll experiments haven't changed since they first did them in 'fifty-four. It's still the same percentage of black kids who call the white dolls pretty and the black dolls ugly. How horrendous is that?" She then talked about racist remarks made by politicians today, and what institutionalized racism had done to black people, listing statistics for unemployment rates, alcohol and drug and spousal abuse, prison rates, schizophrenia in young black men, and neglected school systems in predominantly black neighborhoods.

Rasheed walked into the kitchen just as Kelly was describing the racist hurdles their very own neighbors faced. He was visibly pleased by her chattiness and asked lightheartedly, "Racism from what people? We and Tim are the only white ones on the street!"

Without looking at Rasheed, Kelly placed her palm on her forehead and took a deep breath of lost patience.

"What? I love African Americans!" Rasheed proclaimed.

"You are not white. Arabs are not white. No matter how light-skinned you are, you will never be considered white." She excused herself to go to her gospel church.

Rasheed turned to Max and forced a smile. "It is very good she is wanting to help others. I am pleased about this."

Kelly spent more and more time with Rodney during the day. At first she mumbled excuses around Max for why she went over there—"Out of eggs. I'll go see if the neighbors will lend us some"—and then came back hours later, eggless. She eventually stopped giving pretexts and just hung out with Rodney for hours on end. Max gathered from his living room observation point that she tended to leave a few minutes before Nadine got home from work: sometimes at five, sometimes at eight, and other times early the next morning, presumably when Nadine worked night shifts at the hospital.

Rasheed never asked how Kelly passed her days. He never complained about anything but his finances, and otherwise he tiptoed around her, in admission of guilt for having done something awful. Irredeemable. Even though it was Max and Kelly who had done something irredeemable.

MAX WAS IN the tree house even more now, alone in that clammy obscurity, with the labored breathing and light-headedness that his fear of death brought on. Now more than ever did he feel he deserved the punishment of lying in that box.

Sometimes Mr. Yang called up to the tree house window, inviting him over for tea and saving him from himself. Max watched videos with Mrs. Yang and Robby. They put on the subtitles for him when they played reruns of Ricky Wu, the bounty hunter the police contacted when they stumbled upon an unprecedentedly complex case at the start of each episode. Mrs. Yang sat openmouthed, half-smiling at the TV, scrubbing blue and green mold off soy-paste patties with a brush. She fermented them for two weeks in an electric blanket, making an aroma that Max visualized as a yellow-gray cloud of sweaty butt and dirty socks. Amazingly, the cloud stayed contained around the blanket, its smell never extending farther than a couple feet from its origin. At the Yangs', everything seemed superhumanly under control.

After she finished cleaning one patty off, she placed it in a large bowl of warm water between Robby and herself. The patties broke down into paste, creating a dense, batter-textured liquid. She placed a whole egg, shell and all, in the bowl and salted the paste until the egg rose back up from the bottom. This meant it was done. Max never thought to ask how she used the paste.

He never thought to ask why the Yangs did a lot of things: why they woke up at five every morning when they had nothing in particular to do that they couldn't accomplish later in the day (trimming bonsais, cleaning windows, drinking tea, plucking pears, watering the lawn, and carefully opening mail); or why Mr. Yang took such pleasure in crouching to the floor and removing Mrs. Yang's shoes for her while she watched TV, and how she hardly noticed him doing this; or why she cut his nose hairs, when, given the angle, Max knew it was easier for him to do it himself in the mirror; or why Mrs. Yang stroked her chin like she had a pointy goatee; or why she held purple grapes between her fingers as if they were exceptionally rare and fragile, placing one in front of her O-shaped mouth and sucking it in with a sudden inhalation. Her eyes brightened as she bit down and burst the grape open. And Max didn't get why the Yangs forced an hour of arts and crafts on Robby every day, when Robby clearly didn't give a shit about arts and crafts. For Robby, the name of the game was chaos: squirting glue, mangling construction paper, throwing glitter in the air and watching it snow down on the Yangs' black and silver hair.

Max and Mrs. Yang sat cross-legged, backs against the couch. Robby was asleep on the cream carpet, snoring. It sounded like a snowy television set being turned up and down. He wore a fuzzy strawberry pajama suit, and his shoulders twitched every once in a while from the fabulous adventures or terrors that seizured his dreams.

As the Ricky Wu credits rolled, Max surprised himself by exclaiming, "I don't understand why my dad and Kelly live together."

"Oh?" Mrs. Yang said.

"Just seems like if you don't really like someone, you shouldn't live with them, right?"

"A person will accept many bad thing in order to not be a lonely one."

"But he was less of a lonely one before. We were fine."

"You must know that this is not the same," she said. "Maybe you do not know the good thing she provide your father."

"I've heard of sex, Mrs. Yang."

He didn't know he was making a joke until she erupted into her sirening laughter and Mr. Yang's boyish giggle bounced in from the greenhouse. Robby woke up in a state of alarm, and Mrs. Yang pressed her hand on his forehead. Tranquilized by her touch, he plunked limply to the carpet again.

"Okay!" Mr. Yang said, coming into the living room, pointing at Max with his pocket pruner. "But also it is very hard to know what a couple is really like behind the closed door. Not only with the sex, Max, but in all way. People have so many different need. You cannot understand a couple when you are not inside the couple. Only the couple can really know the couple. And even they do not always really know."

Max said, "I thought he needed a girlfriend to feel better, but I've never seen him look worse. And he doesn't do anything about it. Just lets it happen."

"Then you must let it happen too," Mrs. Yang said.

SIX

Y EARS BEFORE THE tree house, Max believed anything he
planted in the backyard had a good chance of growing
into a tree. So he buried things like chewing gum, dried spaghetti,
hard-boiled eggs, a mug, some of Rocket's hair, hamburger
buns, a bottle of San Pellegrino. Today, long after he'd understood that none of those things would sprout into magnificent
trees, he crawled around the yard with Rocket, trying to dig
them all back up to throw in the garbage. His desire to clean
had spanned underground. He didn't find most of the stuff, but
he did unearth a petrified lemon that had been painted gold.
Yes, he remembered it now. It was the most gorgeous lemon
he'd ever bought, and thinking himself clever, he decided to
invest it into a tree where more lemons like it would grow,
rather than just indulge in it straight away. He got the idea to
paint it gold many times over—because it was too difficult to
leave such a perfect thing alone—and after five or six coats, he

planted it. When nothing happened for long enough, he forgot about it.

He contemplated the hardened little fruit a while, holding it up to let the sunlight shatter against it. Cracks in the gold paint showed threads of the lemon's black and red skin. He felt a baffling hatred toward the lemon. He pitched it at his tree house as hard as he could. It flew through the window and knocked around loudly before lying still.

SEVEN

O N THE AFTERNOON of Max's thirteenth birthday, a week before his summer break ended, Rasheed took him shopping. During car rides Max imagined his eyes shot lasers that cut down trees. His rule was that he had to retract his lasers for non-trees. Any homes, metal poles, stores, people, etc., would in fact deflect the laser back at Max and destroy him and his father.

They'd driven to the store in the '77 Toyota Celica. None of the doors opened from the inside anymore. Rasheed had to roll down the window, reach out, and find the handle on the exterior to pop it open. When parked, Rasheed asked for the window crank in the voice of a doctor demanding a scalpel. Max got the tool from the glove box and slapped it into his father's hand. The screw thread on the inside of the crank was mostly stripped, and it took a delicate touch to catch it on the door and get the window to come down. With only one crank, Rasheed was strict about keeping it in the glove compartment, as if someone might steal it. When Max had once teased him about this, Rasheed asked, "If you think this is so funny, you may tell me where the three other window cranks went, huh?"

After Rasheed got his window down and opened his door, he jogged around the front, making a funny blowfish face through the windshield, and opened Max's.

In the department store Rasheed insisted on buying Max any shirts or pants he glanced at. Watching his father spend money on things he didn't need was a guilt-ridden experience. When Max told him he didn't want so much clothing, Rasheed said, "It's a big pleasure for me to buy you gifts. Do you want me to stop having this pleasure?"

At one of the T-shirt racks, Rasheed gazed at a fluorescent ceiling light as he worked his thumb and pointer into his nostril, extracting a hair. He held the white-rooted hair to the light and examined it as though he'd found a bone that might be the missing link to a prehistoric mystery. Max mustered the courage to say, "Kelly seems a little upset these days."

"What? What are you saying, Max? What happened?" Rasheed dropped the nose hair.

"I mean, are you two happy behind closed doors?"

"What is this question?"

"Why is she always acting like you did something horrible?"

"Oh, come on. She is having the rough patch in her life, Maxie. Be bigger hearted, please. We don't have very good work situations, and she feels maybe unstable." He put a hand on Max's shoulder. "When a woman is feeling like this, we must be even more patient and loving and tell her everything is all right. Never forget this. When she is upset, you must wait nicely for it to be over, like bad weather. There is nothing to do about it. It will pass. Like weather. Right?"

"Right." Though with bad weather you take cover, or put on more layers. In any case, you defend yourself.

BACK FROM SHOPPING, they pulled onto their street to drop off their things and get dressed up before going out to dinner. There were cars lined up along both curbs. "Wow," Rasheed said, seeing a party through Nadine and Rodney's living room window, "a lot of African Americans, huh?" They parked in their driveway and Rasheed asked for the crank.

For at least ten minutes, Rasheed tried catching the screw to get the window down. The crank had finally been stripped clean and would not work again. They were trapped.

"Why is it like this?" Rasheed said. His breath was harsh because he never drank water. He said he already ate food with water inside it—"like apples, hamburgers, pieces of pie, all of these things have water inside. I don't like to be chugging liquids directly, this makes me feel like I'm drowning, and I want to vomit."

It was dusk. The tendons in Rasheed's forearms twitched, shaking his canopy of arm hair as he tried the crank again and again. He tried all the windows, but none of them worked. The lights in the house were off; Kelly wasn't home.

"Okay," Rasheed said, "I must break this window."

"Dad." Max thought they should back out of the driveway and honk at the neighbors' party. Someone would surely come out to help them.

Rasheed ignored him and stabbed at the window twice with the crank, like in a horror movie.

"Dad?"

The crank sliced his hand open, and he yelped, "Shitman!" Blood flowered out of his palm. Rasheed took off his shirt and wrapped his hand in it, the red soaking through. Flustered, Max took off his shirt too and handed it to him. Rasheed contemplated it for a second before tossing it on the dashboard.

He ordered Max to the back of the car so he could lie on the passenger seat and kick at the driver's window. The musky smell of his father's body odor and blood stung Max's nose as he climbed to the back and got on his knees, looking out the rear at the party across the street. Kelly was over there, in their living room, drinking a cocktail, talking to some lady. Rasheed kicked once. "It's a very strong car." He unwrapped his hand; the bleeding had stopped.

An enormous black woman came out of the party and into the street. She wore a royal blue ruffled blouse and long skirt combination with glossy white shoes. A gold cross the size of a big starfish rested on her cleavage, glinting in the sundown. Max slapped at the window to get her attention, shouting, "Excuse me! Help! Help!"

"What are you doing, Max?" his father asked, his bare legs bicycling the air, jean shorts riding up to his crotch.

She peered at the car for a beat before her eyes exploded into panic. She saw a shirtless boy begging to be freed, and Rasheed's woolly legs kicking in the background.

"Oh my God!" she shouted. "Help! Help!" Her voice was astounding. No distress signal or gong or horn had ever resounded so loudly. Max motioned for her to open the door, and she hustled over. As soon as he put a foot on the driveway, she snagged his wrist and yanked him behind her.

"Okay. Good," Rasheed said, writhing his way back into the driver's seat. She saw the totality of this hairy, shirtless man with a bloody hand and threw the back door shut. She leaned her back on the front door, not knowing he was imprisoned in there anyway. "Oh no you don't!" she screamed. Her volume had attracted a swarm of guests from the party; at least twenty people flowed out and headed over.

"What's it?" Rasheed said, leaning his ear against the window.

With little space between the driver's door and the shrubs that separated the Yangs' property from theirs, the people had to pack tightly to see what was happening. The sun had set, and everyone turned into agitated silhouettes. Rocket howled inside the house. Robby sang, "Oh! Oh! Oh! Oh!" jumping up and down, unsure if he was overjoyed or frightened. Many still had their drinks, holding them above heads or over people's shoulders like at a crammed concert.

Max said, "It's okay, that's my dad," but somehow his voice didn't work. It came from his throat, not his belly, and didn't carry over all the other noise.

The woman kept wringing Max's skinny wrists, looking over his head at the others, saying, "We got to get him to the police station. Where his parents at? Where they at?" Max thought he repeated the words *No* and *Wait,* but he was so overpowered by her jerking his wrists around that he couldn't be sure if he spoke the words or just mouthed them. The Yangs protested with their thin voices but were smothered between taller people who chattered excitedly. Max spotted the top of Coach Tim's San Antonio Spurs cap. He just loomed there, watching. Kelly was far behind Tim, still in Nadine and Rodney's yard. Was this really happening? Were the Yangs the only people willing to help Max and his father? And couldn't Max do anything other than get handled by this hysterical woman?

His father was tapping on the window, saying, "Hello? Excuse me, wait a minute— What's it— Hello?"

Nadine pushed through and said to the woman holding Max, "Let go, Leslie, can't you see you're scaring the hell out of him? What's going on here?"

Leslie did let go of his wrists but then took him by the shoulders. She slowly shouted into his face, "Yeah! What's going on here! Son?"

Rodney's deep chuckle came from behind the crowd.

"Whoa, Leslie," Nadine said, "these people are our neighbors. That man in there is his father. Calm down." She looked to Max for backup. He nodded urgently. "Some way to make a first impression. I have yet to even meet the man. Les, move out of the way so he can get out." She glanced over her shoulder. "Where's Kelly?" Everyone quieted down. Rocket continued whining in the house. When Leslie lifted herself off the car door, Nadine apologized to Rasheed through the window, looking at him as though he were a terrariumed creature she was inviting into freedom, telling him it was okay, it was all right, he could step out now, it was safe. No one understood he was trapped in there and only they, on the outside, could release him. Nadine must have thought he stayed inside out of fear of Leslie. Not hard to believe. Harder to believe was Max's delayed action, how he too was trapped, inside his own body.

He finally spoke loudly enough. "We got locked in the car. He can't open it from the inside."

That's when Rodney intervened, putting himself in the middle of Nadine and Leslie and Max. He let his gigantic body fall onto the car door, blocking Rasheed's view. He put a hand in the air, calling for a moment of silence. "Now wait a minute," he said, speaking with the slow irony of a stand-up comic building up to his punch line. "Before we open this door, we should at least be sure that it is not what it seems." His mixture of too much cologne and alcohol and sweat made him smell like an overly ripe banana.

"No, Rodney," Nadine said, reaching for the door handle.

"Hold on, baby." He winked at her and pressed himself harder against the car.

Mr. Yang's faint voice could be heard again from the cluster of guests. "Stop this. It is not right. You must open his door immediately!"

Someone else in the crowd said, "Yeah, give it a rest, Rodney. Let the man out."

"Now let's not beat around the bush here," Rodney said. "Shouldn't there at least be an investigation? Just to be sure?" Nadine shouted for Rodney to stop, but he ignored her. A grin curled his lips. He was having a good time.

Another man in the crowd said, "Rod, get out the way."

"No, no. We can't take the risk of covering up for some nasty-ass pervert. I mean, what if this man did molest this boy?" Rodney laughed.

Max shrieked, "He didn't!"

Rasheed understood it clearly now and started punching the window, shouting, his voice muffled by Rodney's mass blocking the door. "What! Pervert? Are you crazy? This is my son! This is my son! Get me out of here! Max, open this door!"

Max looked for Tim's help and saw that he had stepped back into the street, watching from farther away. He was the only other person with a big voice and body who could stand up to Rodney. Why wouldn't he help? Max hugged himself as though he'd suddenly gotten very cold.

Rodney looked at Max. "Oh, come on. I'm just messing around. Everyone knows that."

Shaking his head in disappointment, Rodney moved out of the way. In the dark, Rasheed was a faceless, tortured beast. They gaped at him, observing his fury. Leslie said, "I think he Russian or something."

This was too much for Rodney. "He Russian! He Russian!" he said as he bent over, slapping at his thighs like a person simulating laughter, repeating, "He Russian! Whoooeeeeee! He Russian!"

"What the hell's the matter with you, Rodney?" Nadine said as she let Rasheed out. Rasheed pounced out of the car, shoved past her, and went right for Rodney. The guests leaped forward to stand in the way, a martini glass breaking on the ground, and formed an impassable barricade. Rodney stayed barely out of reach, smirking at Rasheed's hopeless aggression.

Rasheed kept yelling, "How dare you! How dare you!" as he tried in vain to grab at Rodney between the others.

Rodney laughed some more, telling him he needed to chill out, it was just a joke. Everyone was squished together into one swaying organism. Bodies pressed against Max in all directions, someone's drink spilling on him. His chin dented the roll at the top of Leslie's back, his nose in her weave, and his pelvis grinding against her. Nadine kept ordering Rodney back home, but he wouldn't move, he was enjoying himself far too much. A head taller than everyone, he looked like a spoon standing in the middle of a thick milkshake. Rasheed brandished his teeth, trying to thrash through the net of people. Max had never seen him so infuriated. Nadine pushed Rodney back through the others as hard as she could, aiming to get him off the driveway and across the street. One of the guests holding Rasheed back said, "It's okay, no harm done. It was just a stupid joke," but when Rasheed started screaming, "You dirty animal," at Rodney, "you stupid stinking animal!" the energy shifted. People stopped wanting to reassure Rasheed and did less of a job at restraining him. Nadine looked back at him with revulsion for the use of that word: *animal*. Gasps traveled all around, along with clicking noises and loud exhalations.

"You're just a sad little bigot," Leslie said.

Max had forgotten to breathe for nearly a minute and let out a wheeze of air, trying to wrap his mind around why *animal* was inherently racist when pointed at a black person. Suddenly, by uttering that word, Rasheed had deserved it all. He deserved getting locked in and accused of molesting his son. Deserved being disrespected and neglected by his girlfriend and best friend. *Animal* was the word that did it—that made him bad.

The guests gave up on him. They wanted to go home now. The barricade loosened up even more. Rasheed charged forward. He jabbed his fist at Rodney but came up short, clipping Nadine in the ear. She hollered and grabbed the side of her head.

The universe froze. Rodney took in a big gust of air, barreling his chest out even more. He walked through Nadine, not checking on her as she held her ear. "Now you've done it, butt fuck," he said. "You Russian faggot piece of shit. You faggot pervert, racist MOTHER FUCKER!"

"Stop it!" Nadine said, getting in front of Rodney again to drive him back, but to him she was only a strong wind.

A couple of the other men in the crowd tried to stop Rodney but had little more success than Nadine. Max's eyes swept for Coach Tim one more time, even crying his name, "Tim!" But Coach was farther away than before. He responded to Max's plea by averting his gaze and walking home, cap in hand, scratching at the top of his head.

More guests tried to help Nadine hold Rodney back, telling him it was okay, no harm done, it was a simple mistake, Nadine will be fine. But Rodney strode through them like they were stalks of corn. He reached over a small man to grab Max's father by the bloodied wrist with his right hand, took another step, and flattened him against the car with his left. He spread his fingers wide, spanning most of Rasheed's naked chest, pinning him. Rasheed tried to squirm out of Rodney's grasp but quickly understood that he was in the grip of a man three times his strength. People pulled back on Rodney but couldn't move him. He lifted his great flag of a hand and swung down on Rasheed's cheek. He slapped him back and forth, unhurriedly and carefully, like he was performing a public lashing. Rasheed squalled with each hit. The longer Rodney battered him, the less anyone tried to stop it, as if it were too late now.

"Oh my God," a woman said.

Max clasped the bottom corner of Rodney's shirt and stared up at his father's head twisting one way and then the other: forehand, backhand, forehand, backhand. He pictured grabbing Rodney's trunk of a neck and breaking his knuckles on that anviled face, but he was stuck; the scene had stupefied him. He tightened his fist around the piece of Rodney's shirt. Rodney smacked Rasheed five or six times in all, and the whole thing probably lasted only seven or eight seconds, but when he'd finished, Rasheed's face was raw and his nose oozed a slow, thick blood. Shirtless, his neck too weak to hold up his head, and his hand threaded with congealed blood, he looked like a giant newborn monkey. Rodney tossed him against the car and brushed Max's hand away.

Rasheed threw his arms on the roof to steady himself, heaving for breath. The guests shuffled apart and made a narrow corridor for Rodney's exit. Shame had infected everyone. People mumbled and scattered, got into cars, most of them leaving, some riveted into place. Nadine and a few others tried to help Rasheed into his house, but he flinched away from them and would only use Max as his crutch.

Max looked back to see Coach Tim standing on his porch, having watched it all without doing a damn thing.

Kelly had her arms crossed, still at the edge of Nadine's yard. She glowered into the road, her shoulders bouncing up and down. It took Max a moment to realize she was crying. He'd never seen her cry, only heard it from behind a door. She went back into Nadine and Rodney's. Who knew what kinds of things she told them. That Max's father beat her? That he beat Max? That the Bouloses were hateful and racist? Russian? Perverts?

THE YANGS CALLED the police, but since Rasheed had attacked first, not much could be done, and besides, Rasheed didn't want to continue the fight. Over the next few days, he and Max shared a quiet disgrace. They had difficulty looking each other in the eye. Max stayed inside with Rocket, sipping vodka cranberries that were headier than usual and watching Nadine and Rodney's house. The idea of running into Nadine terrified him much more than running into Rodney. It made him short of breath to think of her seeing him and his father as prejudiced. He would have to excuse Rasheed somehow. He could claim his father had a sort of Tourette's syndrome, or that the word *animal* in his language meant "dickhead" and nothing else.

It was Coach Tim who had hurt Max most of all. Tim was no coward. He had not been too stupefied to act. No, of course not. Max's anger funneled itself almost entirely into him. Rodney was so clearly evil, Rasheed so clearly the victim, and Nadine so clearly the heroine. Kelly's opportunism and untrustworthiness felt inevitable somehow. His feelings toward these people, though strong, weren't particularly confusing, but Tim's inaction gnawed at him to the point of wrath. Max felt swindled. This man who had once been so loving toward them suddenly became the enemy, which felt no different from him having been the enemy all along, making their shared past instantly disingenuous, part of some larger deceit and fickleness. It only took jealousy about Kelly for Tim to drop them. Or was it even pettier than that? Was it the beard trimmer after all?

Pacing back and forth in the living room, Max fantasized about the putdowns and guilt trips he wanted to break Tim with. He'd swear to never, ever play basketball for him again, and tell him the reason he had done it in the first place was out of pity, because Tim was such a jealous, lonely man. Tim was beneath Max and Rasheed, and they spent time with him out of charity and goodness, but now it was evident that he deserved every ounce of the dejection that led him to drink like a fish. It was no wonder his wife had abandoned him in the middle of the night, or that Danny Danesh called him a bald cup-a-fag behind his back. Coach Tim was a bald cup-a-fag. Fuck Coach Tim. Fuck him and everything he stood for.

There was a terrible disparity between the man Max now felt he needed to become and the kind of man he actually enjoyed being around. He admired Danny Danesh, for example—to have had his boldness and power in the moment his father was getting slapped around, to have had the courage to fight back, would have been a godsend—but Max didn't care for Danesh. At the end of the day, Danesh was callous and mean. The trouble was, the men Max did care for were the gutless ones he feared becoming someday. Like his father, for instance, who let himself get trampled on by Kelly, or like Mr. Virgine, the art teacher who spent most of the class imploring students to sit back down or stop throwing paintbrushes. He was one of those permanently embarrassed people, incapable of toughness, and with a deep phobia of being offensive, especially regarding political correctness. If he said "African American," it sounded like a new word he was timidly testing, or a question. And he referred to any female above the age of eight as a woman.

Max had stood near him once on the playground and overheard him speaking to Mrs. Marcus, saying, "Oh my goodness! What is that woman doing to him?" It took a while for Max and Mrs. Marcus to understand he was talking about a fourth-grade girl, Tiffany Stangl, straddling a little boy and giving him the typewriter, slapping at his face and drilling his chest with her fingers.

The other kids saw Mr. Virgine as a big joke. Once, in the middle of class, Danny Danesh had walked up to another kid and handed him a cigarette, less than a foot in front of Mr. Virgine.

Mr. Virgine said, "Excuse me, Danny, excuse me—what was that?"

Danny contorted his face violently, confidently. "What! I can't even borrow him a pencil, yo?" as though Mr. Virgine had challenged his basic human rights. The classroom turned gruesomely silent, and Max could tell Mr. Virgine feared his students might riot against him if he insisted. It was in this moment, when he backed down and the classroom chatter resumed, that Max really fell for him. He fell for Mr. Virgine's timidity and gentleness that went unhonored in a world run by the Danny Daneshes and Rodneys and Coach Tims. It perplexed Max that the good guys were the puny ones, the duds. They were what Danny Danesh called dick bags, and what a difficult life a dick bag seemed to have. Max had no idea how to avoid such a fate. He wanted to be courageous like Danesh, but did that mean he was required to become an asshole?

EIGHT

MAX PUT ON his fingerless biker gloves and went to his tree house with a bundle of blue nylon rope. He sat Rocket on the ground underneath the window so he could lower the slipknot he'd made down to her. Trying to get her to step into it, he wiggled the lasso around, but she only smiled up at him. He climbed back down and placed her paw in the lasso, tightened it, and went back up. The object of the game was to rescue her from some outside threat by lifting her into the tree house. She started whining the moment her body weight resisted the pull of the rope, her front paw raised above her head. He ignored the clear message that he was hurting her and kept pulling. He pulled for much longer than he should have—until she was standing on quivering hind legs—stubbornly committed to the fantasy of saving her. Finally registering her cries for what they were, he dropped the rope and inhaled the same chilling breath as when he jumped off a swing and soared for that one death-promising beat. He ran down to her, unfastened the knot, and saw how raw her wrist had gotten. She licked his face, having either forgotten or forgiven that he had caused her pain. He put his ear to the top of her head and wept. His tears rolled off her forehead, and she batted her lashes to keep them from going into her eyes.

NINE

KEYING INTO THE house, having come back from the grocery store with some quinoa, greens, and duck meat, Max heard Kelly laughing. It was a happy laugh without a trace of sarcasm. It liberated something deep inside him; a tiny well was uncovered and a soft lightness got in. An agreement had been reached. Or maybe Rasheed had at long last stood up for himself, and she respected him for it.

He stepped in and saw she wasn't laughing with his father. Of course not. His father was at work. She laughed with Rodney, sitting at the round kitchen table pushed into the corner. She got up and wiped at her smile with the back of her hand, pinching her faded sea-green bathrobe closed with the other, so drunk she had difficulty keeping her body straight. How long had Max been gone? It couldn't have been much more than an hour. Rodney stood up too, his cheeks shining under the fluorescent ceiling light that he was a few inches away from. Max noticed for the first time that his features were offset, giving a boxer's crookedness to him. As Max placed his groceries on the living room couch, avoiding getting any closer, the first person his protective instincts jumped to—before his father or himself or Kelly—was Nadine. He thought of Rodney sweating on top of her and then on top of Kelly, one after the other, and it sickened him. He despised this man's cheating and winning body. Maybe there existed an unconscious fragment of envy.

"Hey, little man," Rodney said, rattling Max's chest with his baritone voice. The same bottle of vodka Max had been drinking from sat on the table next to a bag of corn chips. Rodney strutted over and palmed Max's head, giving it a slight squeeze as if he held a water balloon he could burst with little effort, and then smirked, apparently finding something funny in the feel of Max's head. He winked at Kelly, then picked up the bag of groceries and brought it to the table. "Anyway, Kel, we can talk about all that stuff later. I've got a phone meeting in a few minutes." He walked into Rasheed's bedroom to get his coat and shoes. He then sat at the kitchen table, slowly laced up, and left without another word.

Now it was Kelly and Max in this small gray-and-barley kitchen. "You're home early," she said with a guilty, flirtatious smile, her eyes blunted by the alcohol.

"Early from what?"

"I don't know. When does school start?"

"Next week. His coat and shoes were in my dad's bedroom?"

"Come here, Max," she said. "Please sit down."

He didn't. "You're having him over in the bedroom?" He tried to swallow down the razors climbing up his throat, unsure whether this feeling was weakness or rage.

She swayed back and forth, searching his face. Her mouth warped, the muscles slacker on one side. Her gaze vacillated between blankness and a look of amusement and then profound despair. She steadied herself by putting a hand on the back of the chair. Her stringy hair was greasy and tangled like horseradish roots, her skin blotchy. "Hey, don't you think it's a little weird your name's Max?" she slurred, and gave a silly, tired laugh. "Kind of funny for a Lebanese kid, isn't it?

He suggested she go lie down.

"You do know that you're Lebanese, right? You were born there and everything."

"So what?" He regretted giving her an opportunity to expound. He held his breath, his face immediately getting hot.

Before answering, she secured a second hand on the chair to steady herself. Her face clenched, and it looked like she was about to break down, but she managed to shake it off before going blank again. Her robe split open and stopped at the tips of her nipples, the inside halves exposed. They were a tender blood-orange color. The green bathrobe, her pasty creased stomach, and her burlap-colored hedge of pubic hair made him think of a corpse. It was too much of a body, too well lit under the kitchen's white light, so much so that he saw her in parts and layers: tissue, fat, muscle, organs, veins, tendons, bone. The way she looked at him—this half-naked drunk woman who'd helped him masturbate, who fucked the man that beat his father—caused a pulse of indignation that thundered up to his eyes. He became light as death.

"Has your father ever told you what a shitty husband he was to your mom?" She waited a while. "God. How do I put this gently? There isn't any way to, really."

"Then just be quiet," he begged. "Please."

"Be quiet?" She put a hand in the air, as if it dammed her temper, and then sighed. "Okay. No, you're right. I'm sorry. You don't deserve this." She continued with the artificial sternness of a drunk: "But believe it or not, I'm actually trying to help you."

"Why are you still here, Kelly?"

"Excuse you?"

"Why don't you just leave us alone?"

"Whoa, whoa, whoa! Talk about built-up bullshit in that head of yours! Ha! Let me make something perfectly clear. Your dad is not the victim, my friend. In fact, I'll tell you what." She leaned forward over the back of the chair and sputtered, "Don't trust another word that comes out of his sick mouth." She picked up her empty cup and squinted at its bottom, as though something hid down there. "You're actually lucky I came into your life, because I'm going to give you the chance to learn about the lie you live."

"This is so fucked," he said.

"Oh, you have no idea how fucked it is." Even with her two hands on the chair, her hips lilted back and forth as her head rolled around in little circles. She moaned and sat down in the chair. Vicious again, she said, "What—my sweet, warm, soft, handsome, lovable Max—would you say if I told you he's lied about all of it? He lied about me and what I'm doing here. That's right. Time to take responsibility for my part in this. I confess, I shouldn't have ever come here. He lied about his money. He's got plenty of it. Yep. Not to worry. And worst of all, he lied all about your mom." She paused dramatically, seeming to think silence would allow her words to sink in as truth. "Oh, and my personal favorite is that he even lied about what your real name is."

A hateful buzz whirred in his ears as he held his breath again. "You should go lie down."

Matter-of-factly, she said, "You're both too scared to live an honest life. Let me break it down for you."

"I really don't have any idea what you're talking about."

"Oh, right, okay, I see. You don't believe me, right?" She stood back up in an attempt to be intimidating.

He took a step closer, preparing to catch her if she fell. "You haven't said anything."

"Exactly wrong!" she pointed a shaky finger at him. "I'm saying everything! You're just not listening! It's important to listen, Maxie. Are you ready to listen?" She planted both hands on the table and slowly sat herself back down. "Jesus, you have no idea. So fucking sad." She slapped at the table like an infant demanding food. "So fucking sad so fucking sad so fucking sad so fucking sad!" He'd seen his father smashed a hundred times, but never like this. She eventually spoke coherently again. "You're a teenager, for Christ's sake, and he treats you like a baby, like an actual baby that can't understand anything. And you let him. You're such a special kid. You're such a good boy—but it's time to grow up and see what kind of person he really is. You deserve the best, Max; you deserve to know about your mom and what he's done to give you this precious fake life you have. That's what I'm really trying to tell you about here." She gagged a couple of times. "Don't look at me like that, you little fucker. Is it all really so hard to believe? Are you really that goddamn blind?"

He breathed somewhat normally again, relieved that she didn't have anything substantial to say. "It's like three in the afternoon. You should go lie down. Sleep it off."

Tenderly, she said, "You know what else?"

"You still haven't said anything." He went over and put her arm over his shoulder to get her up and take her to the bed. He was sorry for her, and that felt incredibly good.

"You don't think it's screwy he pretends to not be from where he's from?" She smelled like old flip-flops. "Level with me. In all honesty, you never once thought about that as being a little off?" Letting her feet drag, she said, "Oh, and he's not just a self-hating Arab. To your father, the only things lower than conniving terrorist Arabs are black people." Max laid her down on her side of the bed and closed her bathrobe. "Have you seen the way he looks at black people? How he talks about them?" Max went to get a bucket to put next to the bed. She shouted to make sure he could hear her from the bathroom. "For some reason, Asians are immune to his pecking order! Good for the fucking Yangs, right?" Her laugh was interrupted by more gagging. This time it came all the way up. She puked corn chips and vodka and bile into the bucket Max had brought just in time.

These words, *racist, lying, self-hating*, were too absurd and unspecific to worry about, like the baseless, generic insults kids used at school all the time: *fag ass, mother fucker, punk bitch*. Kelly lifted her head and with gravelly overtiredness said, "He's a fucking racist, please tell me you at least see that part? Just as a starting point. It's going to kill me if you don't at least see that. Think, Max. Learn to think. I know you see it."

New bubbles swelled his throat. "That's all very interesting, Kelly," he said. "Maybe you can tell me what you're doing here with this racist then?"

She let her head fall heavily to the pillow and shut her eyes. "Your daddy's right to treat you like a baby. You're too young to get any of this." He started to close the door. "But Max, when you do grow up, just ask him. You never ask him a fucking thing. You must have questions. I know you do, it's written all over your naive face." He closed the door and heard her say, "Ask him about your mom, Max!"

With this, she'd stomped and cracked a sealed casket deep inside of him.

WHILE KELLY SLEPT, Max came across Mr. Yang's business card and decided to give him a ring. Mr. Yang asked if he'd gone out of town, and Max said, "No, I'm still next door."

"Oh," Mr. Yang said. Max asked how his flowers were doing. "They are very well, thank you."

"And what about Mrs. Yang?"

"Oh, she is doing very well too."

"How about Robby?"

"Oh, Robby is a very happy young man."

"Good, Mr. Yang, that's good." Max said. "But let me ask you something,"

"Ready."

"If a person did something bad a long time ago, but they're generally good now, do you think that means they're still pretty good, and so it doesn't really matter what they did in the past?"

"Hm." Mr. Yang didn't answer for so long that if it hadn't been for Robby singing in the background, Max would have thought they'd gotten disconnected. "It depend on how bad maybe," he finally said. Max heard him snipping away at a small tree or plant.

"Well, I don't really know how bad exactly. Let's say it could be anything."

"Impossible to judge anything."

"Okay, let's say this person killed like twenty people, but like twenty years ago or something. And ever since then he's been good, and really wishes he hadn't killed all those people. And wants to just forget about it all."

"Twenty people a lot of people. A lot of people with a lot of family."

"I guess even killing one person is kind of a lot, in a way. Okay, what about if someone is hiding secrets from his own family?"

"That depend. Why is he hiding them?"

"I don't know."

"Is it to protect them or to protect himself?"

"Them."

"That might be all right."

"And if it's to protect himself?"

"This is less honorable."

"Yeah. Okay. Thanks, Mr. Yang, I've got to go feed Rocket now."

"Max?"

"Yes?"

"I think all that matter is that he a good man now."

"Who is?" Max asked, suspicious of Mr. Yang knowing something he didn't. "Who's a good man now?"

"Does not matter. Anyone."

"Huh. Okay. What about wife-beaters?"

"Sorry?"

"A man who hits his wife. Or is like really mean to her. That's seriously bad."

"Yes, it is a terrible thing. Max, is something wrong at home?"

He briefly inspected the kitchen, checking that the table was in its usual place in the corner, the fridge looked stable enough, the window intact, nothing overtly broken. "No, why?"

"Come over to visit soon."

"I will."

After hanging up, he went to lie down on the floor next to his bed. Rocket waddled over and clambered on top of him, clumsily setting her front paws on his thighs and her hind paws on his chest. Once she'd found her footing, he patted her side as she panted proudly at the closed bedroom door, like an explorer on a raft, nearing the mainland. Her tail brushed back and forth across his face.

HE NEEDED TO tell his father Rodney had been in the house. He knew that. But when he saw Rasheed in the kitchen that night, his cheeks still discolored from Rodney's hand, Max was incapable of giving him bad news. Instead he walked out the back door and climbed up into his masochistic space.

Ten minutes later, Rasheed came up into the tree house and lay down next to him. It was the first time they'd been up there together at night. A little moonlight glowed through the tiny window. Just as Max had decided to tell his father about Rodney— here and now, under cover of this dark box, no excuses—he heard himself ask about his mother: "Did you and my mom get along?"

"Sure. Like two of the best peas."

"So you were nice to each other? Even up until the end?"

"That's right. We were always very nice to each other."

"Until the robber came?" Max felt younger than his age. He spoke with a babyish register, wanting to be coddled with reassurances.

"Yes."

"Why did the robber kill everyone? Why would he do that? Why didn't he just rob them and leave?"

"I already told you about this," Rasheed said.

"Kelly says I should ask you again."

"She did? What else did she say?" He sounded livid.

"Just that."

"What else did she say, Max?"

"Nothing."

"You're sure?"

"Yes."

Rasheed took a lot of deep breaths. "You know, Max, you have been thirteen years old for some days."

"Yeah."

"You will be fourteen someday."

"Yes."

"Okay. I will tell you about something. There are parts you don't know about." Of course, Max didn't know most of the parts.

"Yes." Max sat up and rested his back against the wall under the tiny window, anxious for the story to seize him. He felt it could develop his life into something clear and important.

"Okay. But do you know why I am telling you this?"

"Because—"

"No. Because I don't ever want to have to speak it again."

"Okay."

"All right. Your mother and I lived in Ras Beirut," he started. "We were best friends. We grew up together. She was a sunshine, you know. She studied political science at AUB and was very smart, very radiant, very brave. Everyone in West Beirut loved her. We made a baby, this was you, and she loved it very much." He said the word *loved* as if it choked him.

"Where did you two meet, in a class?" Max asked.

"This is not the story I am telling now."

"Okay."

"In the beginning of the war," he continued, "we lived in my parents' home. My father was a dentist, you see. I helped him when I wasn't at school, and then assisted him full time when I graduated."

"I thought you studied economics."

"I did. My father," he said with a declarative finger pointing at the ceiling, "Muhammad Imad el din Boulos, was the most famous dentist in Ras Beirut. Everyone knew him. We lived in a very nice building—al-Nada building—very near to AUB. In less than five years, the people of this building—the rich people, the journalist people, the Saudis and Gulfies—fled away because of the war.

"My father would not leave the country. He said, Why should we be chased by the idiots running around with guns, and so on and so on. The apartment was also my father's dentist office, and he continued to receive patients in our home on the sixth floor. He thought the war was about to end, always sure that in a week or two it would be ending.

"Refugees, homeless people, and snipers took over the empty apartments." Rasheed's eyes scanned the black ceiling. They shone and swept like flashlights whenever he got immersed in a story, as if seeing it play out in front of him. "We heard the shooting and the bombing often. The top apartment of the building had a swimming pool on the roof. When the rich family left that apartment, it transformed into a bordello."

"A what?"

"Where prostitutes work. We heard the parties they had with different militia until the early morning. One day a rocket went through our window, over the dentist chair—with a patient there—and out the other window. This is when my mother and your mother took you in the bathtub and put cooking pots on their heads.

"There was one pistol in the house, and your mother kept it in the tub in case she needed to protect you from any bad people." He looked at Max. "Nothing mattered to her but you."

"And you too, right?"

"Yes, all right, me too," Rasheed said. "You never cried. We worried you might be a deaf child. Even when that missile flew through the living room and over the chair you did not cry.

"Sometimes I left the apartment and walked up and down the stairs of the building with you in my arms, to let your mother and my mother rest, and so on and so on. Eleven floors, up and down, maybe two or three times per day. You loved these walks too much."

He raised his hands in front of him and studied them with the horrified gaze of someone who'd strangled an innocent person. Why did he look so guilty? He smelled like an intensified version of himself: musk and sawdust. "We lived with maybe fifteen others in the apartment at a time. Grandparents, parents, brothers, sisters, cousins, and friends that had no more home. We had many friends. Even friends of friends we didn't know very well. Different militia would also come and get their teeth checked. In the middle of the war. Imagine. They respected these appointments. Not always, but yes, mostly always."

"They paid your father?"

"No. My poor father, not so many paid him for his services. And sometimes the militiamen did surprise us, men with guns who wanted their teeth cleaned early because they were moving to another part of the city or something. Some of them kept on masks that they lifted past their mouths. But because we lived in Ras Beirut, these were all leftist Muslim groups that fought for the same side. The city was divided in this way. It did not feel very risky to have different militiamen coming and going. We knew them from before. These were the same boys I went to grade school with. They were taxi drivers or fruit vendors or concierges in the neighborhood. They came in to check for the cavities or maybe to make the gums stop hurting.

"Your mother and I decided we had to leave this place. She wanted to take you away and join with her parents in Paris. They had left years before. All she cared for was getting you to safety. You were the center of her life, you see? And now she said, Enough is enough, we must leave this bathtub, we must leave Beirut. We must leave this crazy country." He swallowed at the height of a big breath. Max recognized this as a technique to overcome a lump in the throat. "During a pause in the fighting—there was a pause for two hours every day so people could do their food shopping, and so on and so on—I walked to an MEA travel agency."

"The fighting stopped? Like, for lunch?"

"Yes. Why not? There were usually no mortars during these pauses, and I was lucky because the phone lines were working, so the MEA agent sent a telex to the airline, and like this we had a flight to Paris the next day. I was very excited to tell your mother. We had to pray that there would be no big problems before leaving. But on the walk back, two boys with guns took me into the parking garage underneath our building."

Max sat up straighter. "What did they want?" he asked, guessing one of these two was the robber who would kill his mother and the others later in the story.

Rasheed didn't answer for a while. He turned and a bit more moonlight hit his face. The grooves at the corner of his eye looked like a fan of spears. "They were very confused boys. It was strange that two rightist Christians would dare be in the middle of Ras Beirut like this. They wore big crucifixes. Maybe it was some kind of suicide mission, or maybe they wanted to prove something to their leaders. I don't know. Anyway, they were disguised as poor civilians, and frightened and very nervous, and so young. Maybe fifteen or sixteen years old only. They said to me, 'We know Abdul al-Masri has made an appointment to get his teeth cleaned. Tell us when he is coming.' They were talking about some leader in the local Mourabitoun militia. I said I did not know when Abdul al-Masri had an appointment—I did not even know who that man was—but if he is an important man, he will not come to our office, he will send for my father. They said they still wanted to know when was his appointment. I told them, 'Okay, let me go upstairs and check and I will come back to tell you.' They said, 'No, we must come up with you and stay until Abdul al-Masri comes.' I said, 'Do not do this. Everyone will know you are not my friends.' But they told me this was not my choice."

"How did they know that this guy had an appointment?" Max said.

"Someone who stayed with us must have sold the information, or told another person who told another person. So I took them upstairs and introduced these boys as friends and said they will stay with us for some days before moving on and trying to make it to Syria. Everyone knew this was not true, and became very afraid that these rude boys now lived with us. One of them never left my side, and the other stood always with my father. They studied the appointment book and saw that the man they were looking for was scheduled to get a root canal in two weeks. The boys became very loud and angry with my father because they wanted him to explain how he knew Abdul al-Masri needed a root canal. It was true, it is unbelievable that Abdul al-Masri knew by himself that he needed this operation and made an appointment for two weeks later."

"So how—"

"It means my father had looked inside Abdul al-Masri's mouth before. Maybe he had come in dressed as a layperson or maybe my father went and visited him one day during a truce, we can never always learn the true story.

"The rude boys didn't trust my father and decided to stay two weeks until the appointment. We had the flight the next day and I could not even go into the bathroom and be alone to tell your mother about this. I didn't want to tell these boys we were leaving. I couldn't know what this would make them do, if they would become angry, or want to take the tickets or money or what. They became more and more paranoid.

"I went into the bathroom and your mother asked the boy that followed me to leave, and when he said no, she stood up in the tub with you in her arms, and the cooking pot on her head, and looked him in the eye. She said he should be ashamed of himself, not even allowing a family to have a few moments to be alone. The boy pointed his gun at her. I was so afraid your mother would take out her pistol she had in the back of her pajamas."

"Where was your mother?"

"My mother? She was with my father then. I don't know. But, thank God, your mother had such a power in her look that she didn't need any pistol and the boy lowered his gun back down and left the bathroom to give us the moment alone. I told her about the tickets and she said we would go. We would sneak out in the night and go. No problem. Nothing can stop us."

A long pause. "After, I took you on a walk up and down the stairs, with the boy always walking behind us. It is then that we heard the gunfire. We ran back up to the sixth floor.

"In the hall I hid behind a corner and saw men, maybe Abdul al-Masri's men, shooting into our apartment. Probably someone told them that the boys were staying with us. The boy behind us ran toward the men and was shot down immediately. We stayed behind the corner and I heard your mother scream and shoot all the bullets from that pistol. She had no fear in her scream. Only strength. She hit two of the men. They shot back. I held your ears against me and I prayed for I don't know what: that your mother survived, my sisters, my father, my brothers, my cousins, my grandparents, my friends, and so on and so on. And then there was no more scream, or any noises from inside the apartment. We waited until the men left. When we went inside there was nothing."

He stopped there.

"Nothing?"

His voice knotted up again. "What do you want me to describe here, huh?"

Max superimposed images from the Lebanese civil war documentary onto this story, imagining a dead boy from the Sabra and Shatila massacre as the boy who ran up to the sixth floor with Rasheed. That boy who launched himself into death as Max's mother emptied her pistol out, screaming. The wounds in the boy's stomach and neck grew more vividly in the playback of Max's memory, gaining more color, puckering and moving like an aquatic plant, and threatening to stink.

Max wondered why his father had once called her murderer—
or, now, murderers—a robber. None of these characters seemed
like robbers. Rasheed knew the difference between the words
robber and *militiaman*. It couldn't have been carelessness. No,
Max rationalized that he'd used the word *robber* at the beginning of the summer because he wasn't ready to share the real
story with his son. And now he trusted Max with the true
version. There was always a reason behind the pace at which
Rasheed revealed information. If this is what Kelly had meant
about his father lying about his mother, than she was even more
ridiculous than he'd thought.

"I brought you up to the bordello, and we stayed with the
ladies there. It was then that you started crying. They let us
sleep in the pool shed. It was small, almost like this." He
knocked the floor of the tree house with the butt of his palm.
"And you screamed, always a horrible scream, until it was time
to take the plane. You screamed for two days. Then we went to
Paris."

"When did we come here?"

"Short time after. I told your mother's parents the story, and
they said we could not stay with them. They were too angry
with me. They bought us plane tickets for America and gave me
some money to start this life here."

"But they don't still live there," Max said.

"No, they don't live anywhere. They died of old age very
young."

Max's trust renewed itself fully. And now more than ever did
he believe his father deserved to know the truth about Rodney,
and all the awful things Kelly had said. It was the perfect time
to say it. Rasheed had just opened up to him in an unprecedented way. He should confess the terrible thing he had done with
her that night too. But he didn't. He just let the pitch silence of
the tree house hold it all in. He wasn't yet strong enough to

break his father's heart, or maybe he was starting to understand that Rasheed wasn't strong enough to have his heart broken.

HE LAY IN bed the next morning, his father already at work, when he heard the front door crash shut. Kelly had left a note on the kitchen table: *Too bad it worked out this way. Rodney and I left for good.* —K

When Rasheed came home he stayed seated at the table. His skin and eyes looked dehydrated. His cheeks were a deflated, craggy, dried-up mess, like a turtle's.

He said, "I'm sorry, Max. She's gone now."

"I know, Dad." Max had the urge to say, *And thank God, it's about time.* The astonishing thing about it all was how Rasheed didn't understand that she had never cared about them. How could he have been so blind? So stupid? Maybe he'd seen Kelly as a symbol of something, her actual personality being irrelevant. Maybe she represented hope, simply by being a woman willing to live in their house, of distracting him from the guilt of surviving that day in Beirut so many years ago. But how could a man three times Max's age believe that any woman would do? That one was as good as another? When his father put his head in the crook of his arm and his shoulders shuddered, Max felt his own knees about to buckle. He scolded himself. Rasheed should be as blind as he needed. Lying to one's self is a basic right. A necessary tool for survival.

The following day, Rasheed didn't get out of bed for work. Max peeked into his room and saw him lying on top of his covers wearing last night's clothes. He took off his father's shoes and put a blanket on him, hearing him mumble that he must have caught some flu virus and needed a little rest. He didn't get up for three days except to go to the bathroom. This flu cost him his night shifts at the diner. Max answered the phone calls from his boss, first passing on the warnings and then that they were letting him go. Rasheed didn't respond to any of the news.

During one of his father's bedridden days, Max met Nadine up close again. She knocked on their door. Her face was stoically set, taut and smooth.

She wanted to speak to Rasheed. Max told her he was in bed. She considered this awhile before asking where Kelly and Rodney had gone.

"I don't know exactly," he said.

"You don't know exactly, huh? When did it start? The affair."

"I—don't know."

"Well, it must have happened over here a heck of a lot of the time, right?" She spoke with the cold detachment of a detective assembling information.

"I'm sorry. I really don't know much about it."

"You sure?"

"I believe so. Yes." He stepped out of the way to invite her in. She walked into the kitchen like she'd been there a million times before, her fantastic hips rising up and down like a teeter-totter with every step. Their home would never be the same. It belonged to her now; she could do with it as she pleased. She'd gotten his father out of the car that day, and she could get him out of bed if she wanted. Max was eager for them to meet again. For her to save him.

She sat at the table, and Max joined her. She said, "How are you doing with all this?"

"I'm fine, but my dad's not."

"That probably means you're not fine either." Her stoicism lifted some, and she put her hand on his thigh. Her touch and light smell of perspiration proved that he'd never been filled with real physical longing until now. It differed from the sensation he got from admiring pretty girls in school, women on TV, thoughts he masturbated to (even if they were often of Nadine), or when he'd rubbed up against Kelly. Here he felt a pull to disintegrate inside her.

"So, were you and Kelly friends?" he said. "I mean, did you think you were friends, before?"

She raised an eyebrow, unsure of whether to take it at face value or as underhandedness. "No. I guess you could say we weren't really a match."

"Oh. What about Rodney?" he said.

"Did he ever come in here? Inside your house?"

"Yeah." It hurt her, and he wished to take it back. "You are a sunshine," he said.

"Excuse me?" The right side of her mouth stretched out a confused smile. He leaned in and whispered, "I didn't like Kelly much."

"Why's that?"

"It just felt all wrong from the beginning. She just kind of showed up one day. I never really knew why."

"Is that right?"

"Yeah, it was always weird, even when I told myself it wasn't. And then suddenly she was the boss." It amazed him how gushingly he spoke to her, like he desperately wanted to tell her everything. "I mean, really, I can tell you're worth like a thousand Kellys. Rodney's loss, I guess, right?"

She looked both sad and appreciative of his efforts, then held the bridge of her nose and laughed down at her lap. It opened up Max's breathing, and he sat up straighter.

"You don't have to say those kinds of things. I'm not fragile as all that. Rodney and I weren't much of a match either."

"Okay."

"How long has your dad been sick?" she asked.

"I don't know. Three days."

She looked around the kitchen awhile, maybe searching for clues about Max and Rasheed, about their unhappiness. Were they unhappy? Did they seem unhappy? He hadn't swept or dusted or mopped in a few days. She probably thought this kitchen was an unhappy place.

"How are you getting food and everything?" she asked. "Does he eat?"

"I get the groceries and do the cooking anyway. But when he's like this he hardly touches anything. It's the flu."

"The flu. You do the cooking? Really? By yourself?"

"Yep." Max got up and made some tea. For a few minutes the only sounds were of boiling water, the opening of drawers and cupboards, setting of mugs, tearing of tea bag wrappers, and the pouring of the water. He brought it all to the table.

She shifted her blank, remembering gaze from the ceiling to the refrigerator. He wondered about her father's suicide, about his getting a haircut before jumping off that balcony. He pictured a man in a blue suit with tiny black hairs sprinkled on his shoulders, lying on the street, blood draining from his head; her as a young girl, leaning over the balcony and seeing her dad down there. Then he thought of his mother, dead in the tub. Who'd gone into that apartment and cleaned up? Who'd buried her? Who lived there now? Or was her skeleton still lying in that bath today with a pot on its head? He wanted to tell Nadine his mother had been killed. But she'd actually known her father, knew what she'd lost.

"The two of them disappeared like smoke or something," she said.

"Who?" For a second he thought she'd read his mind. "Oh, yeah, Kelly and Rodney. I know what you mean."

"It's not like they did us any good, but damn, was it sudden."

"Yeah. Would you like some more tea?" he offered, though neither of them had touched their cups. He half stood up to look into hers and then said, "Oop, sorry, okay." When he sat back down, his knees were between her open legs.

She stared vacantly over Max's shoulder at something in the living room. "This writer I like once wrote in a story, 'Absurdity is punishing me for not believing in it.' You go on living like you've understood the pattern of your days, like everything makes sense, and that's when you get hacked down and reminded you don't really control any of this trip."

He was embarrassed he didn't know how to respond. He glanced up at her, then down at the table.

She looked at him intensely enough to make him blush. "I'm sorry. I'm not sure why I'm bringing any of this to you. Like you haven't been through enough." She laughed in a self-denigrating way. "I'm tired. Not thinking straight."

Her face swirled into itself, like water going down a drain. She repeated, "Sorry, I'm just tired," and that triggered the waterfall in him too. He didn't know why or from where, but he had an endless stream of blubbering. Both of their faces soaked in it now. She brought her arms around his shoulders and pulled him near. Her sobs dampened the top of his head. After a moment, he readjusted and buried his face in her breasts, breathing in the wonderful humidity they made together.

He cried harder and harder, at one point actually squealing into her bosom. Nadine laughed and bawled at the same time. When he lifted his face, he saw wet marks in her shirt that looked like one of those drama masks, not quite the comedy or tragedy one, but something in between.

His father's health came to mind. "You're a nurse, right?"

Her voice was sweet and static. "No. I'm a doctor."

And then Rasheed hovered over them. Seeing him on his feet was a miracle brought on by their holding and lamenting. Unshaven, dry-lipped—his skin as gritty and gray as the margins of a newspaper—he smelled of a damp cave. Max was about to introduce Nadine properly for the first time. He would have tried to communicate, *Here she is, after all this, we've found her. This is the one who will know how to love us.*

But before Max said anything, Rasheed looked down at her and spoke very evenly, "Get the hell out of my house." The stillness those words created was like driving in the pounding rain, and abruptly passing under the quiet of a bridge. So ominously calm that they may as well have been floating in space.

She stood up, putting her face two inches from his. Someone who didn't know any better would've thought they were about to kiss. They faced off for a long five seconds, and then Nadine moved her head up and down, as if registering all she needed to about this man. As if all the pieces had fallen into place now. Max wanted to know what pieces she saw.

He started to miss her the instant the front door clicked shut. He had no idea he feared his father until this moment alone in the kitchen with him. A new emotion arose that he'd never experienced, at least never so strongly. A heavy disappointment, maybe even a form of dislike. His father had cast out an obviously sacred woman. Rasheed sat in her seat and proceeded to look ugly.

"Why did you do that?" Max said.

"I don't want those kinds of people in my home."

"Those kinds of people?"

That was not his father sitting there. Max was not looking at his father right now. No. Rasheed had been fully taken over by the flu. It had consumed him, and now he was a host for its malevolence.

MAX LAY IN Rocket's bed, feeling inadequate, his fantasies bouncing back and forth between demanding that his father apologize to Nadine (then remembering there was no sense in that, because he'd only be talking to the flu), and the looping sexual fantasies he'd succumbed to since her visit. He dreamed of going over there, and of her opening the door, covered in beads of sweat, wearing only her underwear. He concentrated on the way her bra hugged her heavy breasts. She unclipped it and let them fall. That fall happened in slow motion, like the greatest conceivable deliverance. One heavy breast and then the other. It replayed over and over again. He was shirtless too, and pressed up against her. He set his hands on top of the big curve at the small of her back, and she clinched and clawed at him, breathing hard, just a couple exhalations from breaking down.

The following morning, Rasheed showered, shaved, and got a job at a Polish pastry shop. The day after that, he got hired again at a gas station he'd worked at three or four jobs ago, presumably calling it quits with the volunteer position at the warehouse.

TEN

IN THE NIGHT, Max stalked across the yard. The lawn was moist and bristly at once. It sounded like he was walking on a field of fish skeletons. His adrenaline thudding, the grass grew louder. Light trails slithered past. He climbed up into the tree house and let claustrophobia envelope him, practicing his idea of absolute aloneness.

ELEVEN

THE EVENING BEFORE his first day of the eighth grade, Max slopped down an unusually strong vodka cranberry. Fortified, he crossed the street and knocked on Nadine's door with two Tupperware containers in hand: one filled with Maryland crab cakes and the other with two cold pepper-crusted skirt steaks in a bordelaise sauce. When she opened the door, he hugged her as if she was all that'd ever been absent from his life. The Tupperware containers overlapped and rested on top of her bottom. She tensed up initially, surprised at this contact. He didn't expect it either, and flushed a little.

She gently pushed him away by the shoulders. "Well, hey. How you been?" She smiled, her teeth burgundied with wine. He could smell such sweet and warm things coming out of her home—like her and like tomatoes and salted pork and caramelized onions—and it felt ten degrees hotter than Max's house. She kept him standing there, her eyes sprung wide, waiting to see what had brought him over, like he might have news to announce. Stopped up in the same way as with the little woman at the Yangs', he was silenced. What was it about beauty that cleaned out his head, paused his lungs, froze him in a state of idiotic panic? He was like one of those movie characters who stare dumbly at an oncoming train that is five whole seconds away from pummeling through him, its horn blaring for him to get off the tracks: *You have plenty of time! What are you doing? Move out of the way!*

He had no good reason to be here. Maybe he'd hoped they would cry on each other again, the heat of her mouth and tears on his head, but she wasn't anywhere near tears. She appeared fresh, young, even prettier than the day before.

Seeing he had nothing in particular to report, she invited him in, poured him some juice, and refilled the wineglass sitting on the countertop next to the stove. One bottle had already been emptied, and the other still had three-quarters left. There was a brightness to her house, and when he opened the Tupperware on the red-oilclothed kitchen table, his food looked grim and flaccid. The vodka in his system allowed him to find this a little funny, and they laughed at it without stating why exactly.

"No really, it looks lovely," she said.

"Just some dinner I thought we could have."

"Well, let's join forces."

He jumped when she plopped both pepper-crusted skirt steaks into the pot on the stove, bubbling with sauce and meat and greens, but then he found this funny too.

She wore sweatpants and a baggy white V-necked T-shirt. While humming a tune, she put the crab cakes on two yellow plates. She took a big swig of wine and asked him to go turn on the record player. Her visible tipsiness put him at ease. He went into the adjoining living room and dropped the needle on a Joe Cocker album already on the turntable.

So much of her home was plastic. Nothing like he'd have imagined. The couches and chairs all had clear plastic coverings. When Nadine and Rodney had moved in, he assumed these coverings were temporary protection for inside the truck. And then there were the plastic figurines on plastic surfaces, either nativity scenes or unfamiliar little mythical creatures or medieval soldiers. She had blue plastic lawn chairs, and plastic cups and plates too. The kitchen floor was a honeydew-and-brown speckled linoleum, and even the light had a glinting-plastic quality. There were three floor-to-ceiling plastic bookshelves, swollen with books and papers. Massive kitsch family portraits hung on the walls, a dozen or so people in each, huddled together on some studio stage, all dressed up in what looked like church clothes—toddlers with sweater-vests and khakis, and some of the women in colorful African boubous and head wraps.

Max learned that Nadine's mother had gone back to Cameroon, where her two brothers lived also, to retire. She had grown up bilingual, French and English, and went to the American School of Paris for high school before coming back to the States to do pre-med. She was ahead a year and earned her MD at twenty-five, getting a residency at the hospital she worked at now. All the stuff in the apartment was furniture her family had left behind, the same furniture, plates, and trinkets she'd grown up with. She recognized the tawdriness but couldn't bring herself to replace any of it. "None of it's my style," she said, "but it comforts me somehow."

"Maybe that means it is your style."

She cocked her head and gave the wrinkled expression of someone receiving wisdom from an unlikely source. "Okay." She smiled. "That could be partially true."

She had such a different rhythm about her tonight. Her eyes shone but were smaller, lazier, ready to laugh over nothing. She danced between the table and stew and spice rack, steam waving out of the pot. Her thick thighs and hips and stomach contained a power that occasionally stole the air from Max.

She excused herself to go to the bathroom, and he took this opportunity to pour a glass of wine in his juice cup and chug it down. He felt like a champion. By the time he sat down, he realized he'd had too much.

Stirring the pot, her back to him now, she said, "You know, I met girls like Kelly in college, treating black people with some kind of romantic condolence or something. One of those girls who loves the idea of African Americans."

He stared at the padding of her butt. "The idea?"

"See, Kelly likes black people on a symbolic level. She's only interested in our oppression. She quickly got tired of hearing me say I'm doing fine. She'd say stuff like, 'But isn't it hard? I mean, living—'"

"'In the most racist country in the world!'" Max interjected.

"Yes!" She laughed, and he couldn't have felt any better about himself. "Unreal," she said, "I can't believe you've heard her say that same exact thing! I wrote it off as her just being young, but when I think about it, I was nothing like that when I was twenty-two. She only ever wanted to talk about the black high school dropouts, illiterates, junkies, prostitutes, and inmates. And Rodney played all that up big-time. Loved telling her stories about how some mean old white lady gave him the slant-eye at the supermarket like he was a thief or something." She took another sip of wine, still letting little puffs of laughter come through her nose. She swayed to the music. "Rodney. Rodney Rodney Rodney, what was I thinking?"

"Yeah," said Max.

"You know, this probably reflects more poorly on me than anyone, but I'll tell you anyway. I'd only been dating him for three months before he invited himself to move in with me. The man had just gotten kicked out of his other girlfriend's house." Her head rolled back and she gave a single "Ha!"

"Ha!" Max echoed.

She played with the silver stud in her ear, eyeing the corner of the ceiling. "You know, Rodney's kind of the same in a way." She finished up her glass and refilled it.

"The same how?"

"The same as Kelly. Only, he thinks of women as an idea."

"The idea of women," he said, feeling intimately involved, maybe even accused.

"It's all about how a woman can support the image he wants of himself. You know?"

God, Max wished he did.

"See, he wants to be with someone who helps him realize the portrait of his manhood he's been dreaming of since he was a boy. To have control of this portrait, he needs to have control of his woman. But it's no fun if she's too passive. He needs the challenge of taming a 'feisty,' independent woman." She let this thought sit for a while. "With me, he needed to feel like he was taking care of my needs, you know, like I was his little girl or something. Like he'd made me. I found it sweet for a surprisingly long time. Everyone likes being babied a little, right? Thing of it is"—she pointed at Max with her spoon—"if you accept being treated like a baby for too long, you end up becoming one."

"Yeah," he said. "That makes sense."

"I started getting tired of it when I understood he was trying to work the individuality out of me, you know what I'm saying? Like, he insisted on having the final say on what my opinions and needs were." What she spoke of resonated with something he'd seen before, if even a misshapen version of that something. But as usual, concepts that were close to being familiar and clear were the most confusing and difficult to comment on. "Back when I was excited about being with him, his need for control didn't threaten me that much. But when that excitement settled a little, and I could see clearly again, I caught on that he didn't like anything I liked. He didn't like any of the same people or music or books or politics, and it was on principle that he didn't like those things. It wasn't what I liked, in and of itself, that bothered him. No, it was the fact that I liked something that he didn't put in my head and, worse, couldn't take out of my head if he wanted to. He hated that he couldn't shape me. You know what I'm saying?" Max did know what she was saying, but not well enough to give any input or ask intelligent questions. It felt like it'd been a long time since he proved he was actively listening. "When I told him what I felt like doing, you know, to go to a museum, or for him to meet a friend of mine, or if I needed to have him listen to me babble a little, I could tell he was exercising all the patience he had in him. He didn't like me. Isn't that something? Entertaining the idea of a future with someone who doesn't even like you? Doesn't like to hear you speak unless it's praise for him. Doesn't like to know what makes you happy unless it was his idea first. Doesn't want to get to know any of your life outside of him. No, that's not the kind of man I want." She moved the wooden spoon around like an orchestra conductor, letting little droplets of red sauce fling all over the kitchen. Her bare arms under the plastic light looked immortal. "It really pisses me off that I shared some of my smartest and most intimate thoughts with that fool. He never was impressed by any of them either."

"Yeah," said Max, "you should like the person you live with. I think so too."

"And I'll tell you another thing. I'm not dumb. I knew he was having an affair. I didn't know it was with the inane bitch across the street. I confess, that was a huge surprise. I knew she wanted him, but she was always too ridiculous to be a threat. Rodney used to make fun of her behind her back all the time." She weaved her hips through the air, getting into the music. "Ooh, listen to that riff right there."

"But you knew he was sleeping with someone else and didn't do anything about it?"

"I needed to figure out how I wanted to play the situation. I've been having my fun on the side too."

"Wow."

She danced with a glazed grin. "That's right," she said, "I get mine. I'm not one of those victims." She dove her spoon into the stew, let it go, and clapped her hands as though her words were the lyrics to the song: "Lets herself get treated like an old useless cow / keeps it all hushed up / hoping for I don't know what / I am no damn cliché." This greatly excited Max. She transitioned to finger snaps while she grooved, bringing a gusto into that kitchen that tremored his abdomen. Nadine, the prettiest, smartest, best-smelling, loveliest being he'd ever known. His very idea of a woman.

"So what about you two?" she said, picking up the spoon again. "You all didn't know? Your dad had no idea?"

"I don't think he did. But I knew."

"What? You knew and didn't do anything about it? What's your excuse?"

"I just couldn't." He had a flash of his panting next to Kelly. His imagination had worsened the memory and added terrible details—her wearing significantly fewer clothes, her loose waist pressed hot against him, strands of her hair getting stuck to his lips, her hands making jerky circular motions in her underwear—and he felt a pang of self-disgust. He slumped deeper into his chair.

"Hmm." Still feeling the music, Nadine's hips flowed to the beat and she bit her bottom lip. "How's he doing these days?"

"He's fine. Working a lot, but fine."

"Isn't that everybody's truth. Everyone's working a lot, but fine. And how about you, are you working a lot, but fine?" She came over to the table, and when she sat down, her butt swelled out a little on both sides of her. She searched his face awhile, as if to say, *So, remind me what you're doing here again.*

"I'm pretty good," he said, though at this point it sounded out of left field. "Wait. I forgot to bring the sauce I made for the crab cakes. I'll be right back." He shot out of his seat and ran home. Still sitting on his kitchen table was the sauce: homemade mayonnaise mixed with Old Bay and lemon juice in a little bowl. He picked it up, set it down, filled and guzzled a half glass of vodka, grabbed the sauce, and darted back to Nadine's.

Imbalanced and out of breath, he put the bowl next to the crab cakes and sat.

"This looks delicious, Max, thank you."

He was hammered and had a strong urge to lie down. He looked away from her and at the framed portrait of a man he assumed was her father. The man's handsome, strong face steadied him. His head was tilted back as if he was looking down on the camera. He had uninterested eyes and graying hair.

She glanced over her shoulder at the portrait. "I hope your father isn't too mad at me. It wasn't right to come over and unload on you like that. You're such a good listener that I forgot who I was talking to. I've been holding it all in, and you were the unlucky one that saw it spill out first. I apologize."

His head spun fast. "That's okay. I liked it."

"You liked it?" She chuckled. "You looking to be a therapist someday?"

"No—it's just—it felt good for me too."

"Your dad thought it was pretty weird, and I don't blame him. A full-grown woman boohooing on my kid would make me think something was a little wonky. What are you smiling at?"

"I don't know. *Wonky* is a funny word, I guess."

"You guess a lot."

"I know."

She touched his arm and sent something through it that traveled down to his pelvis. It softened his posture. This was exactly why he'd come here tonight.

"You okay?" she asked. The burden in his jaw got too heavy, and he started mouth breathing.

"Fine."

She stood up to serve two plates of the main dish. Some rice with the stew. He thought of how the steaks had slowly come apart at the bottom of the pot. Steam rose up into his nostrils, but he couldn't actually smell anything. He took a big bite and didn't taste anything either. They should have started with the crab cakes, he thought. He tried for a second bite and threw up what looked like water and Play-Doh all over the table.

HE DIDN'T REMEMBER how he'd gotten onto the couch. Lying there with a sidelong view of Nadine, he watched her stumble a little as she filled up a glass with water, the kitchen table already cleared and the dishes done. He felt sedated and grateful and sorry. Keeping his eyes open was exceptionally difficult. She came back with the glass and a chastising smile. "You're a little young to be getting sloshed before dinner, don't you think? I smelled the booze on you, but you didn't look that bad when you first came in. Does this happen a lot?" She sat down in front of him, and the warmth of her backside touched his belly. She handed him the water, and he thanked her with an *anh* sound. Right before he let the glass crash to the floor, she grabbed it back out of his hands and put it on a little table behind his head, saying, "Why don't we save that one for later." He mumbled that he had something to tell her but couldn't remember what it was. She rubbed his arm and repeated, "That's all right, honey, that's all right, you can tell me all about it later," as he dropped off into sleep.

When he woke up, it took him a moment to understand he was basically spooning her on the couch. She faced out toward the kitchen and snored lightly. She must have gone from sitting, to leaning against the armrest, to sliding down into a lying position after he'd dozed off. He stared at the back of her neck, her thin dreadlocks grazing the tip of his nose like the soft side of Velcro. Her head smelled of crayons. Breathing her in, he fell asleep again.

He dreamed the two of them lay in a mattress-lined room, with wall-to-wall bedding. White sheets strewn about, they were on their sides, naked. He pumped in and out of her from behind, her ass shuddering every time she bumped him back. He couldn't see his own body clearly in the dream, but hers was a trembling masterpiece. White light somehow filled the windowless room, making the walls and sheets and ceilings feel limitless. The surge of his orgasm came so strongly that he might have been dying. He groaned loudly enough to wake himself up and realized that he had actually done it. He'd humped her from behind. He stiffened in horror. She woke up a beat after him, alarmed. "What are you doing?"

"I—" Blood rushed hotly to his face.

She sat up. "The hell?" She looked at Max, seeming to barely recognize him. Then she looked around her place as if she'd never been here before. "Okay. Wow. Little disoriented." She rubbed her eyes. "Sorry. I was having a weird dream." She gave his arm a friendly pat and got up. "You feeling any better? You're not so pale as you were."

She didn't know. Incredible.

Max studied himself in her bathroom mirror as the come hardened in his underwear. He was just a kid. He had an oily mess of thick, wavy black hair touching the tops of his oversize ears. His eyes stuck out like saucers on his slim and poreless face, his body short and weedy. He dressed like a juvenile, with his collar-stretched T-shirt, baggy pants, sneakers. If she had been awake while he humped her, she'd have doubtlessly thought he was having a nightmare and just squirming around, not believing he had a single sexual bone in his body. And even if she had recognized his squirming as adolescent lust, she'd have either been disgusted or, worse, instructed him (in some asexual way) on how to relieve himself, as Kelly had, as if helping him go to the bathroom. Glaring at his reflection now, he understood that he had no choice but to be a boy.

PART TWO: 1996-2000

TWELVE

MAX GREW ELEVEN inches in the following four years, topping out at six foot one, eight inches taller than his father. There had been nothing remotely uniform about the stages of his development. Sections enlarged one at a time. His shoulders rose up before anything else, too heavy for his back and rolling him forward into a hunch. Then his neck elongated and his ears flared out. His head looked like a dented pea, and his flop of black hair, cut into a bowl, resembled a toupée.

"Oh!" Mrs. Yang cried whenever she saw him. "You are changing again!" He'd become one of the Yangs' freakish plants.

His legs shot up next, pushing his hips up to where his chest had previously been, and only well after that did his torso lengthen in an effort to catch up. He had clumsy, gorilla-size hands flapping at the ends of his stemmy arms. His nose swelled wide and flat, the opposite of his father's hooked beak. Finally

Max's head filled out, making his eyes look only somewhat insectoid. There was an eight-month period with tremendous amounts of sprouting hair. So quickly and unruly did it grow that he had tender welts from ingrown hair infections in improbable places: behind an ear, on the back of his neck, on his ass, in his nostril, in an armpit. Strawberry fields of acne blazed across his face, along with blackheads, whiteheads, bumps, and divots. At fifteen he tried to grow a beard as cover, but the black stringy hair looked pubic and worsened his case. Wishing away his bad skin probably took up half of his waking mental energy.

He no longer existed in that comfortable middle distance at school. His theory about it had been all wrong. He'd gotten away with it before because he was beautiful. Of course, he hadn't appreciated how clean and pleasant-looking he was back then. Now he felt like a bother, a sore. He felt grotesque. Cynicism edged into his worldview, and he turned unsmiling.

Nadine's beauty became unbearable. Every time he saw her, he fell more deeply in love. He cherished that moment they had cried together, and the time they'd gotten drunk, and the physical contact that he was remorseful about but also regularly turned on by. The dream of them in that mattress-lined room was embellished upon and made more vivid by his memory. It was the guiltiest and most exciting material to masturbate to. She had very short-term boyfriends that he'd spot once or twice and then never again. After school, he visited her whenever he could. Sometimes she came back from work at ten in the morning after a night shift, other times at five or eight or ten in the evening.

At first he nearly begged her to give him yard work to do or to let him clean her house or wash her car. He accepted money for these little jobs when she threatened to refuse his continued help if he didn't. She watched him mow the lawn, following him, mildly suspicious of his motives, but maybe more tickled and curious than anything. He occasionally caught his father spying on them from the living room window, ducking out of sight when Max looked in his direction.

Things had been uncomfortable since his father had kicked Nadine out of the house that day. Rasheed's attempt at clearing the air came in the form of enthusiasm about banal things: "It's really a warm day today!" Or leaving uncharacteristic notes: *Max!!! Thank you for getting more OJ! I was so happy in finding the fresh carton this morning! What a way to start the day!!!* He even drew smiley faces on some of them. If Max didn't know any better, he'd have taken this as sarcasm or passive-aggressiveness, but really it was Rasheed's inability to acknowledge that something had been strangling their relationship from the moment he'd disrespected Nadine. It was then that Max had begun to question how he and his father operated. He realized that—aside from when he'd been told of his mother's death, under cover of the dark tree house—they had never spoken honestly and directly to each other. In consequence Max took a step back. With every subsequent step back, seeing Rasheed still not make any attempt at a personal conversation, Max further realized he'd actually never known his father well at all. He had just been accustomed to him. Knowing what his favorite dish was or how he liked his ear hairs cut didn't mean he really understood the man.

Max intrigued Nadine. She asked him a lot of questions about his interests, subjects he liked at school, books and art and music that appealed to him, sports and friends. He'd never enjoyed conversing with someone as much as he did with her. Her company energized him. At first he responded to her questions with an attractive version of himself in which he had a few close friends, loved literature (listing names of authors he'd heard of but whose first names he didn't know: Hemingway, Faulkner, Melville, Austen), and had a fascination with revolutionaries, left over from the days of Kelly's documentaries. At school, he followed the trend of embracing hip-hop, and liked the socially conscious stuff best, from Gil Scott-Heron to Arrested Development to Black Star. He listed off the social causes he was interested in, as rapped about by KRS-One, the Roots, and Common. She smirked in a way he dreamed was flirtation.

He'd always been captivated by stories of the brave and small up against the big and unfair, like Robin Hood or the Three Musketeers, and these rappers' objections to real-life inequalities were a continuation of this, an insight into the war of adulthood he feared he'd never be ready for. He'd gone from letting documentaries make him cringe at the world to bobbing his head along with those speaking out to change it. Even with their many words, hip-hop lyrics remained surprisingly generalist, like those of most songs, leaving room for anyone to latch their angst to them and momentarily transform it into an experience of heroism. Investing unanchored adolescent frustrations in these rappers' discontentment gave him a new confidence. Their anger was convincing, and he wondered for the first time if this anger could belong to him too.

He read the first and most of the last chapter of a book on Che Guevara, and developed a similar rapport with Malcolm X, Angela Davis, and Huey P. Newton. He loved the Zapatistas, because they were angry about some form of tyranny that pissed him off too. If it had to do with the underprivileged and combatting persecution, he privately threw his fist in the air in support. It was the fantasy of standing up against something much bigger than yourself that infatuated Max. Courage of this magnitude bewildered and enthralled him.

NADINE WAS ROUSED by questions of social justice too, though not with the same fervor she had for literary fiction and music. It was an addiction; she put on an album and dropped into her fictions right when she got home from work. She lent Max books and music and told him he didn't need to think up a job every time he wanted to come over. It took him a while to realize that she actually liked the insecure, confused Max, and he didn't need to pretend he had a rich life of friends and sports outside of her. He studied the books and music she gave him, and they talked at length about his findings and reactions. Over four years, she passed down a cultural education that his time in the public school system couldn't compete with.

She prepared unlikely combinations, books and music that had nothing in particular to do with one another, and told him to try them out. That was how she said it: "Here, try these out." Invariably one musician and one author at a time, she took creative license by marrying people like

RICHARD WRIGHT TO KEITH JARRETT, KEN KESEY TO AL GREEN, W. E. B DU BOIS TO LED ZEPPELIN, JIM HARRISON TO APHEX TWIN, BARRY HANNAH TO THE FUGEES, RAYMOND CARVER TO TALK TALK, KURT VONNEGUT JR. TO NINA SIMONE, SAUL BELLOW TO BAHAMADIA, OSCAR WILDE TO NICK DRAKE, DON DELILLO TO ANN PEEBLES, F. SCOTT FITZGERALD TO BOB MARLEY, FRANZ KAFKA TO DAVID BOWIE, TRUMAN CAPOTE TO CHUCK BERRY, ELIZABETH MCCRACKEN TO RADIOHEAD, BORIS VIAN TO THE TALKING HEADS, DONALD BARTHELME TO NIRVANA, MAYA ANGELOU TO BELLE AND SEBASTIAN, DENIS JOHNSON TO BILL WITHERS, VLADIMIR NABOKOV TO PINK FLOYD, ALBERT CAMUS TO THE GRATEFUL DEAD, JOAN DIDION TO SMOG, FLANNERY O'CONNOR TO STEVIE WONDER, JAMES BALDWIN TO DJ SHADOW, AMIRI BARAKA TO ANDREW BIRD, TOBIAS WOLFF TO PJ HARVEY, ALICE WALKER TO LOU REED, JENNIFER EGAN TO SHARON JONES, JEAN-PAUL SARTRE TO SEU JORGE, LANGSTON HUGHES TO PHILIP GLASS, JAMAICA KINCAID TO RAGE AGAINST THE MACHINE, SUSAN SONTAG TO MESHELL NDEGEOCELLO, JOHN CHEEVER TO CAT STEVENS, OCTAVIA BUTLER TO JONI MITCHELL, JIM CRACE TO CURTIS MAYFIELD, LYDIA DAVIS TO THE POLICE, CARSON MCCULLERS TO JAMES BROWN, HERMAN HESSE TO JEFF BUCKLEY, MILAN KUNDERA TO THE WU-TANG CLAN, WALKER PERCY TO PAUL SIMON, JAY MCINERNEY TO D'ANGELO, ALLAN GURGANUS TO MILES DAVIS, JONATHAN FRANZEN TO THE BUENA VISTA SOCIAL CLUB, J. D. SALINGER TO JUDY CLAY, MARK TWAIN TO THE CLASH, D. H. LAWRENCE

TO CREEDENCE CLEARWATER REVIVAL, ROMAIN GARY TO A TRIBE CALLED QUEST, IVAN TURGENEV TO YO-YO MA, MARGARET ATWOOD TO CAN, EUGÈNE IONESCO TO DEAD PREZ, DOSTOYEVSKY TO BALLAKÉ SISSOKO, GEORGE SAUNDERS TO BRIAN ENO, ARUNDHATI ROY TO JUANA MOLINA, HARUKI MURAKAMI TO SISTER NANCY, ETHAN CANIN TO ANI DIFRANCO, TONI MORRISON TO BOOMBAPTIST, BARBARA KINGSOLVER TO NEU!, SIMONE DE BEAUVOIR TO PATTI SMITH, ALEXANDRE DUMAS TO CHARLOTTE GAINSBOURG, WILLIAM GOLDING TO FIONA APPLE, GUSTAVE FLAUBERT TO IBRAHIM MAALOUF, HARPER LEE TO R.E.M., HOMER TO TUNNG, KATE ATKINSON TO TEARS FOR FEARS, NIKOLAI GOGOL TO CHILLY GONZALES, SINCLAIR LEWIS TO ERYKAH BADU, DEBORAH EISENBERG TO THE VIOLENT FEMMES, CLAUDIA RANKINE TO THE SILVER JEWS, RALPH ELLISON TO DUSTY SPRINGFIELD, KNUT HAMSUN TO RJD2, DONNA TARTT TO GODSPEED YOU! BLACK EMPEROR, RAINER MARIA RILKE TO OUTKAST, GUY DE MAUPASSANT TO SIMPLE MINDS, DEBORAH LEVY TO MAZZY STAR, ROBERT STONE TO WENDY RENE, EMMANUEL CARRÈRE TO GLADYS KNIGHT, STEPHANIE VAUGHN TO MAVIS STAPLES, SALMAN RUSHDIE TO AESOP ROCK, TENNESSEE WILLIAMS TO TINA TURNER . . .

Despite Nadine's demanding career and active dating life, she burned through books at an astonishing speed. Max read two to three novels a week from cover to cover now too, trying to keep up with her. He evolved into a new person with every set of artists she passed his way. His inner monologue mimicked narrators from novels, and his visceral responses to the music affected the way he held his body.

He developed an unsneering skepticism that gave him aplomb and a sense of purpose, as if he had a duty to investigate humanity, if only to report it to Nadine. He read the newspaper and was hypnotized by everything outside his small reality at home. How much bigger life was than he'd ever thought!

Oddly, the two areas to which his new interrogative drive did not apply were Rasheed and Lebanon. He avoided topics about Arabs in the news or in literature because it was excessively complicated and thus boring, but perhaps more than that, because it was in step with his vast distancing from his father. Max treated Rasheed as separate from this big new world he'd been learning about. He did his best to put aside the guilt and anger that budded inside him, and to fade his father out of his daily awareness.

Rasheed had gone into some sort of hiding, growing very old very quickly. His life of working and watching TV, and the way he had crawled back to Coach Tim because he needed someone to get drunk with, took on a piteousness that Max felt in his gut like a tangerine-size ball sitting on his stomach.

Max was happy to follow Nadine around as she tied up odds and ends, to go to the grocery store with her, or to listen to her talk about her day. They cooked and bounced ideas off each other—daily observations, pictures that popped into their heads, strong feelings at random moments, questions—in a way he'd never known to be appropriate or possible in human communication.

They talked about small things too, like how miso soup tasted like tears. They made up Italian words, saying they were *fatiguando* or that they were thinking about becoming *vegetariano* (which actually turned out to be the real Italian word for vegetarian). They questioned why people spoke of weak chins but never of weak noses or brows. They fantasized about giving anonymous letters to strangers, puzzling compliments or aphorisms that would make the day memorable for said stranger: "Your knees match your hands exquisitely"; "You were not put on this earth to explain yourself"; "You have the power of the Jupiter behind your skin"; "Patience isn't stealing all your time." They discussed why they didn't have the courage to actually give these notes. Did that mean they were more fearful than generous? Or were they just worried the receiver would suspect ridicule?

She exploded any expectations he could have had about a doctor's way of thinking. Not so calculated or scientifically minded at all, at least, not with him. She had a general confusion about being alive, about her unavoidable loop of happiness and self-destruction (which Max believed was what led her to someone like Rodney, and other men who were nowhere near good enough), and about how she rarely felt like one person, instead feeling like a massive crowd pulling omnidirectionally from the inside. It was Max's first real friendship.

DANNY DANESH'S STATUS had crumbled down to the ruins of an ancient empire. Having only one arm mattered in high school, because girls mattered a whole lot more. The number of kids had multiplied by five, and he was not the best basketball player by any stretch of the imagination, nor the most rebellious or daring or smart, or even the best wielder of gay jokes. His arrogance was considered unbefitting a one-armed boy, and his old entourage dissipated into the sea of other cliques. Max had seen girls exchange looks of laughing disgust behind Danny's back while pointing at the nubs of his missing arm, and their male counterparts tucked their arms inside their T-shirts to mock him too.

For a short while in their freshman year, Max had something that verged on companionship with Danesh. They found themselves eating lunch together most days. Since Max had no one else to talk to, he confided in Danesh about his feelings for his older neighbor, and tried out his analyses of the music and literature she assigned on him. Usually Danesh didn't have much to say in response. He waited for his turn to talk about the old days, back in middle school, reminiscing about all his fabulous pranks, and sometimes said nasty things about his old friends.

But one time, after Max had mentioned Nadine, Danny asked, "What does your mom think about this lady?"

"I don't have a mom."

"No shit. Really? Me neither." Danny seemed pleased by this point in common, and Max felt a deepened connection too.

How had he never known this about Danny? "Well," Danny went on, "I mean, I have a stepmom, but my real mom died when I was a baby. I guess she was nursing me when she croaked. My dad found me on her boob, and she was all cold. That's why he hates me so much. He thinks I like sucked the life out of her or something. And now that faggot can't get over the fact that I'm stronger than his ass. I have been for, like, five years now. Yeah. Last night he tried to twist my arm behind my back when I told him to stop talking to my stepmom like he does. She's cool as shit."

Max wasn't sure if Danny meant this literally. "Like, twisted your arm physically?"

Danesh blinked at him quickly. "Why are you so gay? Yeah, physically. He tried to pin my arm against me, and I swiveled right out of that shit and slammed my fist into his throat and told him I'd fuck him up for real next time." He took a heaping spoonful of Spanish rice and pork.

COACH TIM HAD told Max long ago that Danny's father was seriously bad news—had some kind of mental health issues and was abusive. Back then, Max admired even this information about Danny. Despite Max's avoidance of trouble and challenge, he believed that people with big problems had more meaningful lives.

But then he actually met Danny's father. He'd shown up to one of their basketball games. He had a sausage-shaped torso, a severe underbite, and a smashed pug nose. It was a wonder he'd helped create such a good-looking son. Danny played belligerently that game and fouled out. At this Mr. Danesh applauded slowly and sarcastically as he walked off the stands, circled the court, and approached the bench. Danny left the building, pretending not to see or hear his father clapping. Mr. Danesh took Danny's seat on the bench. Max was the only other player sitting; the others hopped up and down with the momentum of the game, neck and neck with St. James Catholic. Coach Tim gave Mr. Danesh a quick head nod and a glare that meant, *You'd better behave*. Mr. Danesh stared at the floor for a while. His hands pulled his face back and open into an eerie pumpkin-grin, his teeth the texture of dried corn husks.

He started speaking to the gymnasium's hardwood. It took a moment for Max to register that he was listing things that people with only one arm cannot do: "Can't button his jeans, can't cut steak on a plate, can't unscrew anything, can't wash under his arms, can't play guitar, can't clap, can't use scissors properly." When Mr. Danesh noticed Max listening, his face transformed, and he smiled those woody teeth at him like he was about to sell something. "Hey! Jeff, right?"

Max shook his head, "No."

"I ever tell *you* the time Danny got me to inject gasoline into myself?" he said with a touch of self-admiration.

He hadn't told Max this or any other story. It was the first time they'd met.

"Well," he carried on, "see, I'm a diabetic, and one day Danny gets the funny idea to fill up one of my syringes with gasoline." He gave Max a severe look that implied he was about to give him the unfortunate truth about Danny. "So, I slide the needle up a vein—Danny couldn't ever do that, see, you need both arms to inject yourself—and as I'm watching it disappear in me, I notice the color's a little off, you know. I look up and see him there, smiling wickedly at me. And Jeff, I cannot begin to describe the burning sensation I felt at that moment in time. Like my insides were corroding. The fluid takes over me, and I bolt out of the house. I hit the street and sprint like hell." He stood up and started miming his panicked running. "I could have won the goddamn Olympics with how fast

I was running. I ran down our street, through Copper Park, through downtown, through those farms before the airport, onto a runway, and just ran and ran and ran and ran and ran and ran until I thought I was going to take off like a plane, and then—I stopped." He sat down, beads of sweat ornamenting his upper lip. He slapped Max in the chest with the back of his hand and looked at him with screwed-up eyes. "You know why, Jeff?"

"No, why?"

"'Cause I ran out of gas." He maintained a grave expression for a few seconds before laughing madly. Coach Tim gave him a reprimanding look. When Mr. Danesh finished cackling, he said to Max, "All right, that's enough. See you next time, man. I'm going to find the champ." He got up and walked in the direction Danny had gone. It was the first time Max was consciously grateful to not be in Danny's shoes.

MAX NOW ROTATED his chicken sandwich 360 degrees in his hands. "And what did he say to that? When you told him you'd fuck him up for real next time."

"Nothing. He just looked at me like I stole his manhood or something. Or like he just woke up and didn't know where he was."

"What's your stepmom say?" Max asked.

"About what?"

"I don't know. Anything. Your dad or whatever."

He stared down the length of the cafeteria table. "I tell her not to talk back to him. She gets it worse if she does." After a while, he plopped his arm on the table in front of his tray, as if he suddenly needed to protect his food. "Sometimes I even tell her she should leave his ass and take me with her. But she says she loves him too much. Makes me want to kill him."

*

LATER ON, WHEN Max was no longer drawn to the derisive outlook he and Danesh had briefly shared, they stopped sitting together at lunch without any more of an official good-bye than they had a hello.

At the end of Max's sophomore year, when he'd all but forgotten about Danny Danesh, he learned that he'd gotten into drugs and overdosed on OxyContin. The story was all over campus. They said he'd flatlined and been revived by the paramedics twice. When he came back to school he temporarily resumed his role as the center of attention. His having died twice fascinated everyone, but the fascination lasted less than a week before he was discarded all over again.

Max was eager to talk to Danesh about his experience and sat with him at lunch one more time. He asked him what it was like to be dead, remembering how he'd almost died at the Yangs'. But Max hadn't quite crossed over to the other side like Danny had.

Danny looked embittered by Max's presence. To him, Max was like all the others, a deserter.

"I mean, I'm sorry to bug you, man," Max said. "I'm sure you're sick of telling people about it, but I just really want—"

"Yeah. I guess I am sick of telling it. You'll find out on your own anyway. You all will."

"But not live to talk about it."

"What the fuck does living to talk about it change?"

"Just tell me this, was it scary?"

"Do I look like a fag to you?"

"I—"

"All right." He sighed and leaned in a little closer. "If you want to know the truth, it was fucking awesome. You finally get to stop holding on, you know."

"Holding on." Yes, Max did recall a feeling of letting go at the Yangs'. His terror was climaxing into immense lightness before he was brought back down to life.

"Exactly. You don't realize how much effort it is to hold on to this garbage." He gestured to encompass their surroundings, and took a long drink of chocolate milk. "Even if you just sat here all day like a big piece of shit, without moving at all, you'd still get super tired. Ever think of that? You'd eventually fall asleep just from sitting here and doing nothing because it takes a fuck ton of centripetal force of physics or whatever the fuck just to keep your body alive. It's like, no matter what you do, you're using up your life to stay alive. To hold on. But fuck it."

What Danny said made sense. "Yeah. Fuck it." Death was probably the easiest thing on earth. Easier than just sitting here and doing nothing. You couldn't possibly screw it up. You were just cleared. Ready to go. Freed. Nevertheless, believing this didn't stop death from rumbling beneath all surfaces. Didn't stop it from itching all of the time.

AROUND THEN, ROCKET got lupus. Max and Rasheed took her to the vet when she started losing hair in patches. They gave her antibiotics and vitamin E pills, a topical ointment for her lesions, fatty acid supplements, and oral corticosteroids. They nailed her doggie door shut and let her out only after lathering waterproof SPF on her face and ears and bald spots.

Nadine and Max talked a lot about sad things without necessarily seeking answers. They knew there was no ultimate solution to being afraid of dying, for example, or the boundless source of what's-the-point questionings, or her regret at not giving more to her father before he'd killed himself. Her venting and confessions and self-deprecations were ways of rephrasing that Life Is Hard, not with the expectation of finding an actual solution but as a conversation piece to play with, to connect through, to see what else it inspired. Max and Nadine rephrased Life Is Hard to each other to feel understood, since feeling understood is the predecessor to feeling truly loved.

By the time he was seventeen, Max's skin had cleared up, his body had thickened, black hair whirled from his chest, and he shaved his face clean every day before school. He'd become a handsome man that women at the grocery store took notice of. He didn't respond to this new attention. He only wanted Nadine. She was the sole person in his life whose strength and poise and humor he admired, and who was also fundamentally kind.

After one of their dinners, she asked him if he'd ever had sex. This was the first topic he bald-facedly lied to her about. He told her he was sleeping with a girl from his English class, unconsciously describing the fictional girl as an older version of the little woman at the Yangs' from years before.

Nadine filled up her wineglass. "What's her name?"

"L—indy."

"Sorry?"

"Lindy."

"Lindy? Okay. What kinds of things do you and Lindy do together?"

"What do you mean, like what positions?"

"Yeah, sure."

"Oh, we do pretty much everything."

"Yeah? Are you any good at it?"

"At what? Sex?"

"Yeah." She gave a knowing smile that reminded him of their age difference. She knew he was full of shit.

"She seems to think so."

"Oh, yeah? Where do you guys do it?"

"All over. Her car, her house, my house, in fields."

She outwardly laughed at him now. "Really? Fields? And she's been over to your house? I've never seen her."

He smiled now too. "No, well, she comes in either really early in the morning or late at night. "

"That's smart, keeping it discreet like that. It's really nobody's business but yours. And so you go to her house too?"

"Sure, I'm there all the time. Usually after school. I go over there and, you know, we talk some, and then we get all—sweaty."

"You get all sweaty." She looked down and pretended she was trying to conceal her laughter.

"Yeah, definitely, we get all sweaty, and then I leave before her dad comes home, and everything's great. Okay, well what about you, when was the last time you got any?"

"I'm not nearly as active as you."

"Oh, come on! I see guys coming over, and what about that guy Graham you were seeing? That was like two weeks ago."

"Forget about Graham, that's boring. Tell me what kinds of things she does to you. I'm curious."

"Who?"

"Lindy."

And he did. Through Lindy, he spelled out the fantasies he'd been having about Nadine for years. His descriptions felt risqué, but she only laughed.

RASHEED WAS HOME for about an hour in the evenings. It'd been years since Max made a point of choosing to be there to share his company. Max was usually across the street during this hour, and Rasheed had yet to even knock on Nadine's door, let alone try to establish a respectful rapport. The Yangs hardly ever saw Rasheed either. He spent the little free time he had alone or at Coach Tim's.

Rasheed said to Max once, "It is strange that your only friend is an old single black lady."

With a cool rage Max didn't know existed in himself, he said, "She's not old, and I don't see what her being single or black has to do with anything."

Max felt he'd surpassed his father, knew more than him now. They were tense and self-conscious the rare times they were around each other, talking with a choppy and unfamiliar cadence. They seemed to be in each other's way, the hall and living room too small for both of them. In the kitchen, one always blocked the cupboard the other needed to get to. Max ate standing, hurriedly, and tried to get in and out of there as quickly as possible to avoid having to share the space with Rasheed. Speaking more than a few words would have given away what they kept from each other. At this point, the main thing they kept from each other was whether they noticed or cared about the degradation of their relationship. Max didn't know how they had remained stuck in this awkward formality for so long, and he couldn't remember what kinds of things they'd talked about before. All he knew was that his father's presence mined his energy, made him feel weak and tired.

Just as when Kelly was around, they maintained this amazing capacity to ignore the elephant in the room, to never address the strong, though annoyingly unspecific, feelings rocking their home from its very foundation. Rasheed probably thought Max would grow out of his need to distance himself, that things would go back to the way they were in time, that it would pass on its own, like bad weather.

Rasheed was getting two to three flus a month. Max brought food and water to his room, but nothing more. No stories, no good lies. The longer this standoff persisted, and Rasheed's bouts of depression sagged him, the colder Max became. But in a not-so-distant fold of Max's consciousness, he understood the truth. His father's increased depression was because he'd lost his son. Max wouldn't dignify this with much thought. Why should the onus be on him to give Rasheed back his position as the center of Max's universe? Even if Max wanted to, he couldn't give him that. Rasheed was not the center. So Max carried on silently, his father's despair hanging off him, pretending to be unfazed by the strain it caused. He told himself that allowing Rasheed to see how much he hated his depression would be precisely what encouraged it.

When Max felt guilty about ignoring Rasheed's sadness, he evoked the memory of his father's disrespect of Nadine and his continual rejection of her. This helped him get angry enough to shut him out again.

Max told Nadine about the adventures of Kip and his Man-Dog of a brother. "Every once in a while, when my dad couldn't come up with new episodes, Kip and his Man-Dog got into situations that were identical to scenes from *The Adventures of Tintin*, or *Indiana Jones, Jurassic Park*, and once, even *Dances with Wolves*." Nadine smiled. "The weird part is that not only did I not let on that I noticed he was copying those other stories, but I was actually able to forget that I'd heard them before. I could listen to them as if for the first time, as though everything he said was completely original."

"Now that's filial devotion," she said. "Don't make that face—I think it's sweet."

"No, it's messed up. It's like I brainwashed myself into thinking that everything he did or said was perfect."

"You just loved hearing him tell stories."

He shook his head. "I don't know. Don't most kids eventually call their parents out on their bullshit? It's like I wouldn't ever let myself be disappointed. That's got to be unhealthy."

"Well, you're expressing disappointment now, aren't you? Are you really going to sit here being disappointed that you weren't disappointed sooner?"

"Feels late."

"What will feel late is if you let this tension drag out any longer."

Nadine urged him to open his arms to Rasheed more, give him the affection he obviously thirsted for, even if he didn't know how to ask for it. She told Max to spend less time at her place and to be with Rasheed when he came home, that this disappointed phase would definitely pass. Max resolved not to talk to her about his father anymore. When she told him she felt like she'd come between them, he swore his problems with Rasheed had nothing to do with her.

"Whatever it is, don't waste your time being mad," she told him. "You're not teaching him any lessons this way, and you won't always have the chance to be with him whenever you feel like it."

THIRTEEN

MAX AND NADINE were peeling cucumbers at the sink, her bare shoulder grazing him from time to time. He stared out her kitchen window at the vein-blue sky, the rust of sunset slowly getting scrubbed away.

He'd thought about his stupid fantasy of Nadine and him as a couple. Seventeen-year-old boys and thirty-year-old women who got together were trashy people, the kind of people who yelled at the camera on early-evening local news stations, drank themselves dumb, smashed plates, and kicked dogs. They didn't know about Zora Neale Hurston and Oscar Peterson; they didn't talk about the Absurd or their fear of death or make fusions of French cream sauces with duchess potatoes and African fufu. They were not kind and soft with each other while also being sophisticated, confiding and articulating their deepest thoughts. High school kids and thirty-year-old women who got together were loud and lewd and stained.

She put a cucumbered hand on his cheek to turn his face toward her. He dropped his peeler in the sink. With the other hand she took his and placed it on her hip. She stepped into him, their waists connected. His heart drummed louder.

She said, "Max?" and then pulled his neck down to kiss him. A deep kiss that lasted a long time before their mouths opened and their tongues crossed over. She drew back to check what all this had done to him, and laughed a little out of her nose. She said, "Is this a really bad idea?"

"No," said Max. He brought his mouth down to hers again, but she pinched his jaw in her hand to stop him. She studied his face for a second before lowering him down, and slowly licked his closed mouth from left to right. She said, "We can enjoy each other like this. No big deal, right?"

He couldn't believe it. "Right. No big deal."

She took her shirt off, her breasts swelling out her bra, and told him to touch her, and to put his mouth on her nipples over the bra. To graze his teeth over them. Then to rub her up and down with his hand over her shorts. She ordered him to unzip and pull everything down to her ankles. She asked if he wanted her and how long had he wanted her. Speechless, as he stood back up from the floor, smelling the sweetness between her legs, he nodded yes.

She guided his hands to her ass and squeezed with him. Shook it a little. Laughed. Removing her hands, she told him to do it again, without her help. Her gorgeous ass in his hands. She jumped up on the edge of the sink, let her shorts and underwear drop off her ankles, and parted her legs to both sides of him. She said, "Take it out. I want to see it."

The heat from her vagina made his penis grow long, downward at first and then filling upward. His quick trembling breaths made it sound as if he were lifting something heavy. The moment his erection rose enough to scrape its head against her tight, shiny curls, it started losing all power, drooping. *Please, no.* It slunk inward until all that remained was the tip and an obscene rumple of foreskin. He'd dreamed of this moment for years, and now he shrank in terror.

"You okay?" she said. She reached between her legs and cupped his balls as if she were holding a baby chick. With her other hand, she tweezed the head between her fingertips and stretched it out of its hole. She brushed it up and down her pubic hair a couple times, trying to reawaken him.

He wanted to scream that this was not his penis. He had never seen this penis before in his life. His did not behave this way. He wanted to flick and squeeze and yank this dick until it became his again. But he didn't dare touch it. Masturbating the emasculated rubbery thing in front of her was more than he could handle.

"It feels so good," he said, his genitals cold and numb.

She looked over her shoulder and said, "The neighbors might see." She hopped down, and put on her shorts and found her shirt.

He pulled up his pants. "I'm so sorry," he said.

"I'm the sorry one. Look at me. I'm nearly old enough to be your mother. Have I lost my mind?"

"No."

She put a palm to her forehead. "I'm feeling a little pathetic here."

"Yeah, me too."

"Thanks."

"No, I mean because of me, not because of you. Really."

She pursed her lips. He felt he was supposed to leave now.

"Don't feel pathetic," he said. "Please don't say you feel pathetic."

She looked out the window for a long time. "When I love a friend, I want to get as close to him or her as I can. A minute

ago, touching you felt like an innocent way to do that. It seemed
light and easy, and now it feels so irresponsible and heavy." She
shook her head. "I cannot believe I did that." She wouldn't
look at him. "Max, if you stand there much longer, I'm going to
get truly embarrassed."

She walked him to the door, apologized again, and opened it
for him. He couldn't cross that threshold and go outside. If he
did, the dream he had gotten so close to would be forever gone.
There were a few seconds left before he would miss the opportunity to turn this around. He had never been proactive. Luck
had formed his life thus far and would keep forming it if he
didn't do something to change that fact.

"No," he said, staring out her front door, facing his house.
He shut the door and looked at her. He pushed her shoulders
against the wall and kissed her.

"Max. Please. I feel bad enough as it is."

He pulled away. "I want to feel closer too. You were right, it
doesn't have to be some big deal. I was just nervous." This time
she let him kiss her, and as soon as he felt her kiss back, fire
flowed through him. He was eager to prove his arousal and
pressed himself against her crotch. She pushed him back a little
at first, but he broke through her resistance. When he felt her
fully concede to his body, he huffed like a bull with excitement.
So much blood barreled up into his ears, it sounded like he was
on an airplane. They frantically ripped their pants back off in
the doorway, and he showed her his glorious erection.

She led him to her bedroom by his penis like a leash. Her ass
and hips swayed back and forth as if to say, *Okay, all right,
follow me; follow me.*

"Lie down," said Nadine when they got to the bed. "Take
everything off. And your socks."

She unclipped her bra and he watched them fall. She crawled
onto the bed slowly, her breasts swinging a little from side to

side. After taking him into her mouth for a second, she came up and straddled him, hovering over his penis. She had him suck on his fingers and put them inside her. She rocked back and forth on them, telling him what to do. Her wet walls ballooned in and out, and the very top had ripples like the roof of a mouth. Again, stunned by a surge of performance anxiety—*Oh my God, Oh my God, Am I doing this right? Does this feel good? Does she like this? Did she just groan? Shut up, just feel it, be in the moment, just relax and go with it, stop thinking about it*—he felt himself losing strength. *Oh my God.* The more he begged it to stay up, trying to flex it back into action, the limper it got. Feeling he didn't have much time before he'd lose it completely, he said, "I want to be inside you now."

She looked at him questioningly, and all he could think was, Please hurry.

She asked, "Are you a virgin, Max?"

"Yes."

"Are you sure you want to do this?"

"Yes. Yes."

The moment she lined it up with her vagina, his mouth slackened, the pressure to perform increased, and his dick curled into a shrimp. She managed to push it in anyway, and he could feel it getting even smaller in there. She tried to move on him but he slipped out. He actually wanted to cry. She glided her clitoris back and forth on it for a frustrated moment and then got off and lay next to him. He'd lost his chance for good now. The weight of the failure made him hold his breath.

She sat up, and Max presumed she was looking for her clothes, but she said, "You know, penetration isn't even the best part. Let's try this." She got on all fours and turned around. She said, "Smack my ass." He did it and laughed nervously. She said, "Again, but harder." He started getting into it. "Yeah, again. Good. Again. Now lick me, use your hands to open and lick me."

She wasn't giving up on him. He smothered his face in her, closing his eyes and breathing her in. She coached him on where to lap and flick his tongue and what to do with his hands, her wetness and his saliva all over his mouth and chin. She started sucking on him too.

By the time she turned back around and began sliding down on him, he had stopped thinking about his penis's functioning at all. He'd let it do its natural best. This time when he entered her, he felt every distinct and remarkable layer. He pushed through the rasp of her pubic hair, spread her lips, and sank into her hot inside. He moaned with liberating agony. It deepened until their pelvises blocked them from getting any closer, from becoming the other. She ground down on him and waved her hips side to side, back and forth. She looked at the ceiling with her hands on his chest. The perfumes of their sex, the pace that picked up speed, the panting, the thrusts, the clapping of their middles, their suctioning mouths, her gripping and pulling his torso red, was all part of the revolution that made his life mean something new.

THE SUCCESS LIFTED him so high he had the capacity and will to love all things more fully than ever before. Having been with Nadine even gave him the impetus to reach out to his father. Tell him that it was important they improve their relationship, and that there was no good reason things had soured like they had. He saw him the next morning, but Rasheed was on his way out the door, not leaving enough time to get down to it. Max smiled at him in a way that meant, *My arms are open to you now, Dad. We'll figure this thing out. We will. I love you.*

But his mood crashed as soon as he went over to Nadine's later that day. Things felt different, and not in the way he'd hoped: She didn't suddenly treat him like her boyfriend. In fact, nothing at all seemed to have changed. There was no kiss at the door; she simply let him in and walked back into the kitchen to tend to her stir-fry, singing harmonies to a Daft Punk album she had playing in the background, acting normally. And after the night before, normalcy felt like total rejection. He became fixated on the idea of being physical again, just a long embrace for starters, more for reassurance than anything. He didn't know what he'd expected exactly, but every second here was saturated with the possibility of It—the touching—happening again, without It happening again, and this made him feel tense and unwanted. She asked if he'd like to stay for dinner, and he accepted with a stilted "Yeah, gre— Awesome, I'd love that a lot, terrifically . . . um . . ." She gave him a funny look. Sitting at the table, he tried to think of something to say, but his throat filled with dry ice. This wasn't the charmed and butterflied awkwardness of shy love. What was wrong with him? He could tell by her body language that she felt it now too. Or was that in his head? He couldn't decide. Maybe she wasn't thinking about him at all right now, wasn't affected by what they'd done. Was there anything special for her about yesterday?

"So," she said, "I should probably warn you, I have to get out of here around nine."

"You covering somebody's nightshift?"

"Nope. Just going out for a bit."

"Oh." He swallowed. "Meeting up with a friend?"

"Yep."

After a minute, he asked, "Lucille?"

"No. Not Lucille."

A date. His body turned achingly fragile. Before, when Nadine had dates, he didn't have the illusion that she belonged to him. He was used to her being out of reach in that way, happy to spend any time with her at all. But tonight the vision of her getting intimate with someone else revolted him. And in no time at all, he was bursting with the brand of jealousy he'd read about in novels. The maddening kind that makes you behave ridiculously. The kind that makes you unwilling to accept anything less than an exclusive, possessive relationship as sworn eternal lovers. He knew he was thinking like an insane person, but he couldn't stop.

She sucked in her lips and gave him what looked like the face of apology. He felt pitied, and that hurt. "Max, we shouldn't let what happened change everything. We have a great thing here, you know?"

"No, yeah, I totally agree."

"You do?" She sighed in relief. "I'm really glad to hear you say that."

Then touch me, goddammit! he wanted to cry out.

She continued tending to her stir-fry. "So, what did you think of that Russell Banks book? Have you finished it?" She looked back at him. "Max?"

"Yeah. The book."

"Well, what did you think? Seemed right up your alley."

"Actually, Nadine—"

When he said nothing more, she turned. "Yeah?"

Her face was so perfect. "I can't stand it."

"What?"

"The book. I could hardly get through the first page." What was he talking about? "Totally insipid. Dead."

"Oh. That sucks, sorry." She shrugged and returned to her food.

"Yeah, no, the *book* kind of sucks."

She laughed a little and said, "You liked his other one," then went back to singing along with the music. He didn't respond, and she gave no sign of noticing. Her indifference was drowning him. Having never felt this crazy before, he worried he'd act like even more of an idiot if he didn't get out of there. "Yeah, anyway, I've got to get going. I'll see you around." He stood.

"Wait, you do? I thought we were eating together. I'm cooking for two now."

"I actually got to go. I got to go, actually."

"Got to go actually, do you?"

He didn't laugh. "I'm sorry." He started walking out.

"Max, where?"

"Hmm?"

"Where do you have to go?"

He stared back blankly. Of course there was nowhere else for him to be, nothing else to do. She knew by now he had no other friends, that his relationship with his father was shit, and that she was the only person he felt close to. He'd told her as much. Her asking where he was going felt a lot like cruelty.

"I'm going to help my dad with some house stuff."

"Okay. You suddenly remembered?"

"Yeah."

As he opened the front door to leave, she said, "Hey. If things got weird, we need to talk about it."

"Weird? Why? Are things weird for you? They're not weird for me at all. I just forgot I told my dad I'd help him move stuff around." He didn't stay long enough to get a sense of whether she believed him or not.

He WENT TO BED. She felt so far off. It was as if achieving his dream of having Nadine simultaneously took her away from him. Why couldn't he stop thinking so melodramatically? He obviously wasn't seeing the situation clearly. And what situation, anyway? Was there a situation, or was he just being a spastic? The best thing for him to do would be to take a little space from her to process it all, cool off, and then he might be able to go back to acting naturally. He gave himself three days.

At the end of the first day, he was morbidly offended that she didn't make any effort to see him. It shouldn't have surprised him, really. In all the years they'd been friends, she hadn't come over since his father kicked her out, and had never called. He'd always understood it to be out of avoidance of Rasheed, but now it felt like a larger sign. She couldn't have called one single time? He wasn't even sure she had his phone number. Who had he been kidding? They'd never been real friends. He was just the kid next door who had a flattering crush on her.

He determined a new approach. He would become a callous sex machine. That's what men were supposed to be anyway. He'd go over there and they'd have emotionless sex and he'd thank her and leave, saying he'd be back for more when his body thirsted for it. There. That's right. But on account of this plan being stupid, he made himself hold off on seeing her for a second, even more painful day.

And on that day, as if his nerves couldn't have been bundled any tighter, he received a letter from Kelly. He'd never gotten personal mail before. There was no return address. He ripped it open and unfolded the letter, and a check made out to him for five thousand dollars fluttered to the kitchen floor.

Dear Max,

I think about writing you this all the time. So why now, right? My newborn daughter, Angie, is sitting on my lap, and when I look into her eyes I see the answer. It's so clear to me just how overdue this explanation is. I'll spare you my details, but basically, when I barged into your life, I had nothing. I was such a wreck. Your dad said I could stay at his house for as long as it took me to get back on my feet. I couldn't believe it. We hardly knew each other. So what was the catch, right? Well, the deal was that you needed a mother. He gave me an allowance, and the more attention I gave you, the more money I got. Seemed simple enough at the time. I was young and dumb and was able to convince myself that I was doing good by you. He and I got really close really fast. I guess you end up trusting people you share lies with. The idea of having a friend he told everything to was a total novelty to him, and he ended up sharing the story about your mother getting killed. I got kind of obsessed with it, and when I asked about more details another time, certain things didn't match up to the first version. I kept pressing him and the story kept changing and eventually your mom was the bad guy and it was her fault that his family was slaughtered.

The final story, and the reason I'm writing you, is that your mom was not killed at all. She got away. Her name is Samira Jabbir, and she was eventually caught for her involvement in the Palestinian resistance, and put in prison for a number of years. She lives somewhere in Lebanon now. The truth really freaked me out, and I let it show. He realized he shouldn't have told me so much. He understood this weird illusion we were creating for you couldn't work anymore because he and I had different lying thresholds. He thought I would accept your mom's job even after learning she was still alive! He's so angry with her for what happened to his own family, he's killed her off in his mind, and I guess in yours too. I couldn't stomach this lie, and so he wanted me gone. He thought if there was no more money I would leave on my own. That supposed eviction notice was part of his strategy. When I demanded to see it, I found out there was nothing to see. You're still in the same house, aren't you? He ended up paying me off to leave. He has this trust fund in your name that your mother's parents put money into every

month. There's some good news—turns out you've got loaded grandparents. To find out whether this is all bullshit or not, show him this letter. He'll definitely lie, claim I'm a lunatic or something, but you'll know the truth the second you see his face while reading. Your dad confirmed he knew your mother was still living in Beirut four years ago. Who knows why or what lie someone's been feeding her all these years. But speaking as a mother myself, I can guarantee you she's been dreaming of her baby for the past seventeen years. I can't imagine the pain she has endured. Enclosed is a fourth of the money I owe you. I intend on paying it all back just as soon as I can afford it.
  Good luck,
  Kelly

P.S. Your real name is Hakeem. It means "wise" or "intelligent." And I think you live up to it completely. It was when "Reed" brought you over to the U.S. that he gave you the name Max, probably to make it all the more difficult for her to find you.

His mom had never been a real person to him. He'd never even asked for her name. She had only been "your mother" or "my mom," a character in one of Rasheed's stories, the story that was supposed to explain Rasheed's sadness.

His mind split into at least two. One read the letter again and became frantic. The other mind observed the first mind's shock, stunned but without thought or opinion or feeling. The stunned mind observed the frantic one in the same way it watched a movie or read an article about something outrageous happening far away.

The stunned mind slowly sympathized with the frantic one, but was still not upset exactly. This more detached mind knew that the word *mother* stood for an idea of great importance, but couldn't feel that importance right away, wasn't touched by it. It began to worry that this word, this Idea of Mother, wasn't rattling its world or creating any real urgency as it should. The word didn't cause Max to drop the letter and run to Lebanon.

Why should it?

Because you've been cheated. You deserve to know your own goddamn mother. That fucker lied to you about your own mother!

It's that word again, *mother*. Mother. Such a strong and sacred word, I know. Why should that word hold so much power?

Because it's not just a word anymore. It's her body that fed you. She is in your veins. She is in your face, she is the beginning of you, the roots you've been severed from. Your instincts are mashed together with hers. And she must love you. To her, *son* is the word that holds the most importance. You are the most important word that's ever been in her mouth.

Of course I deserve to know her. How could he have done this? Why? Why would anyone raise their child this way? Wait. This is coming from Kelly. We don't trust her.

Kelly was right about everything else. He is racist. We were not evicted. She's not lying. If you don't have the guts to go find your mother now, then at least confront him with this letter, see what he says. You have to. No matter how he handles it, she's right, you'll know by his reaction.

When Rasheed came home, he gave Max a flat smile. His back curved with fatigue, he trudged into the kitchen, opened the fridge, and took out the orange juice. His mustache was no longer the neat triangle it once had been but a bristly old broom, and his eyes drooped like a hound dog's. He gazed at the cabinets next to the fridge for a while, dreaming, longing for something—maybe rest.

"This isn't the life I wanted to give you, Max," he said, as though he knew what Max had in his hand. "I wanted more."

"Hakeem?" Max said, standing.

His father looked up. Max held the letter out, and Rasheed approached warily. He read through it standing, flipping it back to the front to stare at that again. He didn't raise his eyes from those pages for what felt like an hour.

Max wanted both to run away and bash him to pieces, to reclaim a sense of control or at least understanding by breaking it out of him. Anger glided up his throat, and it required all his strength not to scream and swing.

"Hakeem?" Max repeated.

"Trust me, it was right. It was the best I could do."

Trust me? What could he even mean by that? Max saw his father as absolute enemy now, the man who would destroy him if Max didn't destroy the man first. He uttered a single word that he would never have predicted saying to anyone, ever, let alone his father. A word that astounded Max the moment it existed outside him. A simple command: "Die."

For a moment the muscles in Rasheed's face failed, like when he came down with the flu. Then they reawakened, inflated. He lunged toward his son and, in one swift and precise motion, struck him for the first time in his life, backhanding him across the cheek. Max's head torqued hard to the left, and his neck's kickback realigned his face with his father's. He felt he was no longer in real life but caged inside his imagination. His cheek hummed, and his right eye gauzed over. It was like looking through a fly's wing. He turned and walked into the living room to lie on the couch. He squinted up at the white ceiling, too soft to stand up and go after Rasheed because it was all still unfathomable.

LATER HE GOT up and went to Nadine's. As soon as she opened the door, he hugged her for too long. The heat of her body felt like the origin of life. She asked what was the matter. He didn't want to talk. He stepped in, took her hand, and leaned down to kiss her.

She turned away. "Maybe we should just hold off on that. Let's concentrate on getting things to feel normal again. Are you okay? You look like a ghost. Come into the kitchen with me."

He walked right past her, through the living room, past the kitchen, into her bedroom, and stripped off his clothes. When she came in after him, she flicked on the light. "You're naked."

"I know. Tell me what to do."

"Put your clothes back on."

He shook his head no.

"Max. I just think it got complicated, you know?"

"It's not complicated. Please tell me what to do like the other day."

And he saw her, for the second time, pity him. This time it was so much worse. She bent down to pick up his underwear and handed it to him.

He took the underwear and then kissed her neck. She just stood there. He said, "Please." He yearned for her to draw him near so he could rest his head on her breasts a while. He hugged her again, but she didn't hug back this time. She only said his name. He closed his eyes, and an unwanted scene played in his mind. It was a closeup of his father eating. Rasheed would take too many big bites in a row without swallowing, and when he wanted to speak, he pushed as much food as would fit into one cheek and the rest into the other. His face bulging like a chipmunk's, he was fully capable of telling a long story, or speaking to someone on the phone. It made Max sick now. He opened his eyes, and Nadine asked him again to come into the kitchen to talk.

He said, "I'm fine. Just, maybe you could sit down here?"

She thought about it, and then sat on the bed. He dropped to his knees at her feet and told her to teach him how to use his tongue again. She tugged his hair playfully a little, generously trying to make light of the situation, saying "No way." Before she could stand, he placed his hands on her thighs to keep her down. He closed his eyes again and repeated, "Please."

Rasheed's stuffed mouth shoved its way back into his head. The image consumed him with irritation. He replaced it with that of pushing his tongue deep inside Nadine, then his lips, and then pictured putting his nose inside her, then his face. But his father's chewing intruded on his fantasy again, and an aggressive nervousness frenzied him, his eyes flared open, and he dove his mouth at her crotch, with the overwhelming urge to eat or be eaten, to break through her jeans and store himself inside her, to belong, to be kept. Owned.

"Stop!" she said. "Jesus, Max, what the fuck? Enough." She stood up and looked down at him. Naked and on the floor, he could see in her eyes how disgraceful he'd become. She said, "Get dressed and come into the kitchen. We need to talk." But he couldn't, he'd already begun crying. He put on his pants, gathered the rest of his things, and went home.

Nadine didn't go after him. He paced around his living room, looking out the window at her house every few seconds, saying to himself she'd better not follow but, of course, further injured that she didn't. After a half an hour of this, he went to the backyard, climbed up to his tree house for the first time in years, and lay on the floor. His breathing sounded like screaming. He could feel a broken piece inside him. It boated up and down his throat and stomach, searching for its origin, a justification for being. He didn't know how long that broken piece had been moving around in there. He'd noticed it before, in small flashes, but it had always dissolved when he telescoped all of his love into a single other person: first his father and then Nadine. It was during the gaps in his relentlessly focused love—which lasted long enough for him to hate himself—that he felt the piece grow big and sharp. And at this moment he did not feel love for anyone. He felt only fear. He saw how easily Nadine could take herself away, and how small and worthless it made him.

He finally fell asleep in there. Waking up in the middle of the night, he remembered the letter. His mother. Maybe he missed her. Maybe he'd missed her his whole life. The more he thought about it, the clearer it became that the letter was a blessing. He started to understand that he'd won something big. Magical. His mother was alive. What was he waiting for? She'd been looking for him. She would be as devoted to him as he could be to her, would put that broken piece back where it belonged and mend him. She would leave no room for his lying father. His father deserved forgetting. And he wouldn't need Nadine in this pitiable and enervating way anymore.

THAT MORNING, AFTER a fruitless Internet search, there being dozens of Samira Jabbirs in Lebanon, most of whom didn't have phone numbers or photos published online, he decided to launch himself into the quest in a real way; to leave this suffocating house, this suffocating street. He deposited the check from Kelly and went to the post office to order a passport. His plan was no more intricate than to fly to Beirut, locate a phone book, and solicit all the Samira Jabbirs of Lebanon. Time to be bold.

He filled out the forms, got his picture taken, paid for the passport to be expedited, and waited for it to arrive in the mail without telling anyone what he was up to. Enduring Nadine's inattention and noticing his father's absence more than usual felt like the experience of a brave soldier. It took a lot of self-restraint to resist telling Nadine he was leaving. The thought of excluding her empowered him, and though he wanted to revel in her reaction now, he knew the exclusion would be more complete, more effective, if he just left—that is, if she even noticed. Maybe he wouldn't ever come back. Maybe he'd move in with his mother and live happily in Lebanon. Forget all these other people.

There was another reason not to confide in Nadine about the trip: She'd talk him out of it, or offer a more logical way to go about getting in contact with his mother. He didn't want that. Didn't want to be logical. The only great part about his plan was that it was crazy. The old him would have tried to find his mother's phone number, but at this point it would require asking his father for help, giving him power, and that was out of the question.

Through his stinging confusion—fantasies of committing violence against his father and of telling Nadine off, explaining that he didn't need her and could disappear as easily as that—he had a growing determination to find his mom. He became increasingly convinced that this was not just about running from Nadine and Rasheed. His mortality had started haunting him the summer he'd choked on that taffy, when he'd nearly flung himself out the tree house window, when Kelly's documentaries had penetrated his censored world view, when he'd spent hundreds of practice hours in the awful tree house, preparing for the unbelievable certainty that we die, that we stop and others carry on. The woman with the pot on her head was the mascot for this certainty. She was the symbol of death, not an individual who had died. And now she had miraculously outdone death, crossed over to the side of living, become a real person who'd been looking for him. It was nothing short of an otherworldly phenomenon. She would help him transcend all his greatest fears. She was the answer to all the questions and cravings he'd never articulated or even been fully conscious of. If she had once inspired a prideful sadness in Max when dead, she now instilled a prideful hope.

Samira Jabbir became the point of everything. And it is when you think you've discovered the point of everything that you are truly blind.

PART THREE: SUMMER OF 2000

FOURTEEN

H E VOMITED WHILE landing in Beirut in the middle of the night. The inside of Rafic Hariri International Airport looked like a carless parking garage with a baggage claim, an immigration desk, and a few bored or sleepy soldiers pacing about with machine guns, smoking cigarettes. When he had boarded the plane in New Jersey, and as he stared out the window during takeoff, he felt exceedingly proud of this romantic jump toward the unknown. Now in this dingy airport, he experienced a distinct lack of reward. There was no one here to receive him and tell him what a brave thing he had done. He was very much on his own. He told the immigration officer chewing a cigar that he'd come to visit family. The man glared at him awhile before telling him to write down what address he'd be staying at on his customs form. Max wrote his mother's name and put down the Yangs' address, 2718 Marion Street. Without looking at it, the man threw it in a drawer, stamped his passport, and waved him on.

Max's lungs worked to filter the water and cigarette smoke from the air. His legs felt heavy and he had to push them hard to cut through the dense humidity. The one phone he found in the airport was out of service and didn't have a phone book. Shit, he thought. His simple and crazy plan was already coming apart. Outside, a taxi driver with one eye asked if he needed a ride. The man hobbled with a cane, his right foot landing crookedly and his knees collapsing inward with every step. It looked unnatural and agonizing. He had such dense stubble it looked as if charcoal had been smeared on his face, and it continued down his neck to connect with his chest hair. A hammer-and-sickle pendant hung from a gold chain between the lapels of his open white shirt. He opened the door for Max before limping over to the driver's side.

He asked Max, "You want downtown?"

"I'm looking for a phone."

The man took a cell phone out of his pocket. "Like this one?" He waved it around a little.

"Is there a way to call information here?"

"Call information?"

"Never mind. I think I need a pay phone."

"Where you go?"

Max said, "I guess I go to Beirut," not sure why he used broken English.

"To downtown Beirut?"

"Yes, I need to find a public phone."

"I am agree to take you, but there is very little phones in downtown."

The driver chain-smoked, the car jangled, and Max thought of loose screws. His nausea came back. The uncertainty of where this would all lead terrified him. All of his senses were telling him that he was far outside his element. Billboards proclaimed themselves every forty feet on both sides of the highway: ads for watches, cigarettes, cell phones, TVs, cars, whiskey, designer clothes, hair gel, nursing assistant positions, diamond-studded hijabs. Within a few minutes the driver declared, "You are American. I am not like a normal Lebanese. I hate Lebanon. I hate God. I hate every religious and political peoples." He checked to see what effect this had on Max and decided to go further. "I had grew up with cancers until I am age eighteen. Where was God? I am Communist people." He lifted his pendant off his chest as if he were showing off a sixth finger, as if to say, *I am a freak and proud.* "We are very little Communists in Lebanon."

He had a plastic cup of whiskey and Red Bull, the emptied can and bottle at Max's feet. He noticed Max eyeing the cup and shouted over the sound of the highway that he must drink in order to stay awake all night.

"This gives me the power," said the driver.

He asked Max for his religion, and when Max replied that he didn't have one, the driver patted him on the shoulder and awarded him his first name: Ahmed.

"You hate God too," Ahmed said.

Max didn't want to disappoint him, so he said, "I don't know, never even met the guy." Ahmed found this hilarious and repeated it a few times, maybe practicing to recite the line to others in the future. Spittle fired through his decayed teeth and hit the backs of his hands and the steering wheel.

THE SUN OPENED its eye and shot a beam across Beirut. The city was burrowed between the Mediterranean and mountains. Aside from the colorful laundry flagging out of windows and rooftops, the buildings were the colors of abandonment: weak grays and deadened beiges. Ahmed pulled over to idle on the side of a small one-way street that cars drove both ways on, and pointed out the phone booth before the Corniche, the seaside pedestrian walk that wrapped around Beirut. Max didn't really want to get out. He wished he could stay with Ahmed until he found his mother. He craved direction, orders, a promise of being cared for by someone who knew the ropes. But he could feel Ahmed waiting for him to exit and was too ashamed to ask for his help—not that he knew what he'd ask for, exactly. Max paid with American dollars. Before screeching off, Ahmed wrote his phone number down on the back of the receipt for the Red Bull and whiskey, telling Max to call anytime for a pickup.

The uneven and potholed sidewalk stirred up Max's nausea. Maybe if he didn't feel so ill, he'd be more mesmerized by his surroundings. The phone booth smelled of rotted clothes and piss, and he remembered his tree house. There was no phone book or receiver and he shouldered his way out, as if from a burning building.

He stood back onto the irregular ground, taking a lot of deep breaths, telling himself, *This is fine, no big deal, I'm not screwed, this is all part of the great adventure.* Worst-case scenario, he'd go back to the airport and buy a ticket home. He patted his wallet through his pants every twenty steps to make sure it was still there. He was broiling in the bath of humidity and pollution, his head wheeled round and round as the sun pounded on him. The gasoline and exhaust attacked as two separately stomach-turning odors. He hadn't eaten since the two bites he had on the plane, hadn't slept in two days, and was intensely conscious of his parched mouth. *Oh God, what am I doing here?*

He asked a young man with a soccer ball under his arm for another phone booth and was pointed in a vague direction down the Corniche. Feeling the sweat trickle down the back of his neck, he headed that way. The sun crushed his eyes even when he closed them, the orange bleeding past his lids like through brown glass. The top of his head started cooking. Whistling, honking, and shouting crackled through the air as the city woke up. People lived here like this? Every day? He saw another phone booth across the street, but the automobiles— nearly all of them old Mercedes or dusty motorcycles that carried four and sometimes five people, holding babies or baskets of figs—were an endless stream of droning hornets, flying by with hardly an inch between them. His vision pulsated with rainbow-colored spots. An old man with a plastic bag full of fish walked into the street, forcing the cars to skid to a stop. They didn't honk any more than they had before. The heat nearly flattened Max. He took a big lungful of the soaking air and stepped into oncoming traffic.

THERE WAS NO phone book or dial tone in this second booth, and besides, it looked like a phone-card-operated system. He picked up the receiver and smashed it against the phone twice. Through the glass of the booth he saw a few barefoot children laughing at his anger. He gently rested the receiver in its cradle, drew another deep breath, and gagged slightly. He meandered back into the denser part of the city to at least find shade while he reexamined his plan. Three fat men sat in front of a tall building on white lawn chairs that seemed on the verge of crumpling under their massive bodies. He slogged over to them and asked where he might buy water. The men conferenced in Arabic for a moment, and when they reached a consensus, the one in the middle grunted and motioned for Max to follow him inside the building. The fat around the man's eyes protruded so much it seemed like he had pits on either side of his nose with long, thick lashes growing out of them. It reminded Max of the time Danny Danesh had placed the back of a beetle against his eyelid and held it there with a squint, the legs kicking the air in search of ground. A young woman wearing a hijab stood erect behind the front desk. Her professional smile dissolved when she registered that Max was unwell. Whatever his face was doing made her very sad. The fat man went behind the desk and reached around her to open a mini fridge. His hand came up with a magnificent, glistening bottle of water. He gave it to Max without once changing the slack expression on his orangutan-padded face. Max said thank you and the man lumbered back outside to plop down on his tired chair. The young woman watched Max chug the water. With every glug of the bottle, her smile returned a bit more. She appeared sincerely impressed, as if he'd delivered fully on the spectacle she'd been dreaming of all week.

She offered, "Another one?"

He dipped his head gratefully before tipping back the second bottle. She watched in fascination again. He felt it important to keep her interest. She looked to be about twenty, with a uniform spread of light pimples across her cheeks that added to her prettiness somehow.

"Another one?" she said.

He chugged a third bottle for her.

"Another one?" repeated the girl, reaching for a fourth.

He forced it down and then his head spun further away. The air-conditioning in the building had felt wonderful at first, but now he experienced its shock to his body. His throat started its prevomiting convulsions and he was barely able to swallow it still. He said, "I'm looking for Samira Jabbir."

"I don't know. Does she stay in this hotel?"

"I don't think so. She's my mother."

"Oh. You cannot find your mother?"

"No." Darkness swirled in on him until he was peering at her through a closing tunnel. "I come from America. Please, help me." His eyes spooled back into his head, and he fell hard to the marble floor.

HE WOKE UP in a back staff room. An older woman stood by the young one. She looked serious, with the composure of a boss. She wore a cardinal-red business suit and had leathery skin, bristly brown hair, eyes set unequally, and the body of a forty-year-old rock climber: wiry and shriveled from too much sun. Max lay on a round table with his legs dangling off. When he got up and sat on a chair, the serious woman told the girl to bring the plate of pita bread and hummus they'd prepared.

He finished it all, and the serious-looking woman said, "I see you are terribly allergic to hummus." No one so much as smiled, not even her. "Jamila tells me you are looking for your mother. No one by the name Samira Jabbir is staying in this hotel."

Max said, "No, I'm pretty sure she's not here."

The younger girl, Jamila, enthusiastically restated, "Yes, we do not think she is here!"

"Right. I flew here to find her. We've never met. She doesn't know I've come."

Max felt them becoming ill at ease. He saw how idiotic it was to be in Beirut with no real information about his mom. In over his head, he was out of ideas and out of reasons to be in these nice women's hotel any longer.

"You are searching and have no address?" asked Jamila's boss. "Do you remember what neighborhood at least? If we have just one more clue, we may probably help you. It's not so hard to find people here if we have a little more data. It's not a big city. Does she have a job or something like this? Maybe a family name that is different than Jabbir we might know?"

He wished it appropriate to ask them to leave so he could lie back down on the table for a while before picking up his bag and getting a cab back to the airport. But then some inspiration emerged from his memory: Sunshine. Bathtub. Political science. AUB. All of which might be a lie, but he had nothing else to work with. "She may have gone to school at AUB."

The women looked at each other. The serious one said, "Ah, there. You see? Very easy. We must call AUB. They will have records."

Jamila was thrilled, lightly popping up on her toes. They brought him a phone and dialed the number for the American University. He was transferred to the registrar's office, where an older man with a high-pitched voice answered, *"Allô, marhaba."*

"Hello, my name is Max. Do you speak English?"

"Yes, of course. I am speaking English right now. We are the American University. We must speak English. What can I be of assistance about now?"

"I'm looking for someone who used to go there named Samira Jabbir."

"Yes?"

"Yes."

"It does sound familiar."

"Really?"

"Oh, yes, very much."

"Wow. Great."

"Okay, yes. But I don't think she is here now. Okay?"

Max sensed the old man was about to hang up. "No, no, wait. I don't think she works there or anything—she was a student at AUB a long time ago. She's my mother."

"Your mother? *Habibi,* you don't know where is your mother?"

"Yes. I mean, no—I don't know her at all."

"Repeat her name, please?"

"Her name is Samira Jabbir."

"Samira Jabbir. Ah, yes. It is really very familiar again." The line went silent for a good ten seconds. "Yes, I think I remember her more now. Jabbir, you say? Samira?"

"Yes."

"Ah, yes. I am remembering a little more still."

Another ten seconds elapsed. "Well, do you have any system of finding her?"

"Yes," the man said extremely slowly, clearly not responding to Max's question but to one of his own thoughts or recollections. "If it is who I think it is, she came here years before to find out more about another student. A very interesting woman."

"Okay." Max couldn't think of how to confirm whether they were talking about the same person. "Is there a way to look her up?"

"A man named Rasheed."

"Sorry?"

"That was the student she looked for. I believe."

"Oh my God. Yes, that's got to be her!"

"Good. Very good then."

Too much time passed. "Well, what next, sir? I mean, would you be able to find her file? I'm trying to get in contact with her."

"Yes"—again, suspiciously slowly—"are you far from the university? You come here. I will find her file, and you come here, okay?"

The serious woman said they were a five-minute walk from AUB's campus. "Yes," he said to the old man, "I can come right over." It truly frightened Max how uncomplicatedly this seemed to be working itself out. It felt like an omen that it would precisely not, in the end, work itself out.

The man said, "Very good. You will come to the second floor of the College Hall building and ask for Faraj in room two four five. This is me. Okay? Faraj."

"Okay, Faraj, room two four five, got it. See you in five minutes." But the man had hung up before Max finished his sentence.

The serious woman introduced herself as Rima and said she'd walk him to the university. As they left the hotel, he couldn't resist vocalizing his doubts. "I'm not sure about this. That guy seemed a little out of it."

"What is the risk of going to see if he can help? Getting your hopes up? You must already have hopes if you came all this way, no?"

"Probably."

"Probably? No, definitely. But I wouldn't worry too much. This is a very small country. Somebody always knows somebody who you are looking for. Every time. What would be strange to me is if you did not find your mother by the end of today. And if not today, then tomorrow or the day after or the day after that."

To himself, Max mumbled, "Or the day after that."

Rima moved quickly, her heels clapping different levels of sidewalk, unfazed by its patchiness, and fearlessly walking through traffic. Max's stomach had settled, but his body remained weak. He had trouble keeping his back straight and desperately wanted to lie down again. The prospect of gaining on his mother wouldn't allow for that. This abstract idea of Mother had been with him the whole trip over here, like a belt fastened around his chest, restricting his lungs. What would having a mother mean? Would she be the answer to everything that had been unclear or lacking? The idea of her became increasingly central; a promise of completeness. The counterweight to his father. Rasheed's lies had made Max's whole life feel untrue. Any sweet memories would be forever embittered by the dishonesty. She would fix that. Though he had to acknowledge the possibility of having false information about her. She might live somewhere else entirely now, she might even be dead. But he knew he'd find something here, something that would bring him closer to understanding whatever he needed to do next.

Max kept thinking he saw Rasheed out of the corner of his eye. They rambled past groups of men smoking and reading the paper, doctors walking hurriedly toward the hospital in lab coats, women in business suits and head scarves, others in full-on chadors. There was a mother begging on the sidewalk, pretending to nurse a boy who must have been eight years old, and a man yelling at himself as he turned in circles, who Max swore at first was his father. They walked by old bullet-and-shrapnel-riddled facades of buildings, one splayed open like an organ for dissection, exposing broken pipes and wires, with two adjacent walls intact. They passed by old homes with Ottoman arches and French windows next to abandoned buildings and a block away from brand-new high-rises spiraling into the sky and reflecting so much light they seared Max just for looking at them. More cars and motorcycles flew by, and the disproportionate wetness and fumes in the air bent the light into waves, like burning oil. They entered the AUB campus with a nod to the security guards, stepping into this oasis in the middle of the oppressive city. It had lush grass quads, adobe buildings, smooth walkways, tennis courts, ancient banyan trees; expensively coiffed students looking like TV personalities with backpacks; palm trees, benches, and cats. Emaciated cats everywhere, lounging about like entitled Sahara lions.

Rima led him into College Hall, arcades and palm trees at the entrance, and up to the second floor, into the open room 245. There was one man whose body hid behind towers of boxes and folders on his desk. He appeared to be only a head—a bald, hoary, white head shaped like an upturned Styrofoam cup—with gold glasses. Max presumed he was seated back there, but the man walked around the desk and showed his tininess. He couldn't have been more than four foot eight. He smiled graciously at Max and Rima as he closed the door behind them.

"Hello, sir," Max said. "Are you Faraj?"

"No, I am very sorry. I am not." Though he sounded exactly like him.

"Do you know where I may find him?"

"Faraj?" He shook his head. "I do not know him."

"No one named Faraj works here?" asked Max.

"No. I am very sorry. There is no Faraj here." He dug his hands into his pockets.

"You know everyone who works in this building?"

"Yes, of course. I have worked here since I was young like you."

Max turned to Rima and then back to the man. "This is College Hall, right? Room two forty-five?"

"Yes, yes, it is." The tiny man wrinkled his forehead, preparing with extreme keenness for whatever the next question might be.

"I swear I heard him say this building, College Hall. Room two forty-five." Max paced back and forth, not knowing what to do next.

Finally the man offered, "I am Faraz? My name is Faraz?"

Max stopped his pacing and stared down at this man's oddly shaped head. "Did you just talk to someone ten minutes ago who was looking for his mother?"

"I did, yes. Who, may I ask, is wanting to know?"

"That was me."

"Ah! Yes! Hello, welcome. I am Faraz, not Faraj." He took Max's hand as if he was forgiving him.

Rima showed little patience for this man. She spoke sternly at him in Arabic, surely reiterating the situation. Faraz's ghost-white face loosened and jumped and pinched as he listened, his

mouth opening and closing like a nutcracker soldier, as if afflic-
ted with absorbing a hundred times the stimulation of a normal
person, registering everything going on around him at once
with miserable attentiveness.

"Yes." He turned to Max. "And I have already looked her
up. When I saw her file, I remembered much more. I even found
some notes I wrote down on the file all those years ago, because
we kept a little bit of special track of her. She was involved in
many forms of activism on campus, very invested in politics,
and the arts too, but mostly politics. She was a very determined
and energetic young lady, even when pregnant. I recall it
now. The dean used to check her grades and so on to make
sure she was not a troublemaker, but her marks were perfect
across the board. Professors talked about her. Yes, yes, the
professors were afraid of her because she was capable to
point out their mistakes in the classroom!" He bent over to slap
at his thigh and give a hooting laugh. "But then of course she
was expelled."

Hard to decide how reliable this man was. "Why was she
expelled?"

"Op." Faraz glanced over at Rima. "For her involvement
with some of the outside groups. But I remember before this
that she carried her baby everywhere. She even brought the
baby to her classes sometimes, and people said this baby never
cried or made a noise during the lectures. We even wondered if
the baby was really alive at all! How old are you?"

"Seventeen."

"Unless you have a twin brother, it was you who was the
baby who did not cry!" He hooted again. "She was one of these
very nice girls who did not want people to know she was nice.
Very serious and in too much of a hurry to stop being young. I
was very sorry to learn all that she suffered through."

"Like what? What did she suffer through?"

"Op." He looked at Rima again for guidance. "She spent some time in a bad prison for her political involvement. A very strong woman. Yes."

Max braced himself with a held breath. "Do you know if she's alive now?"

"I have no way of knowing at this present moment, but I don't see why not."

"You said over the phone that she'd come looking for someone here a few years back."

"Yes, that's right. She came here some years ago, looking for a man." He moved some papers around on his desk arbitrarily. "No, I didn't write his surname down, but I remember his name was Rasheed. I don't know many Rasheeds, and I like this name. So I remembered it right here." He pointed at his own head. "But I remember also that I couldn't really help her. We didn't have any information about where Rasheed so-and-so lives now."

Rima cut in, "Faraz, can you help this boy find his mother or not?"

His face clenched in concentration and then broke free of itself. "Yes, yes, of course. I can help in many ways. I can tell you the year she graduated, her birth date, the address she had while she was studying here, and—Op!—maybe the phone numbers of some of her classmates who I believe still live in Beirut and who might know better where is she currently. How is that?"

Exhale. Faraz spent the next few minutes writing down information taken off his computer while humming the tune of "Lean on Me." Then he called two classmates he thought he remembered seeing Samira with, and who still lived in Beirut. He learned through the first phone call that one had died the year before of lung cancer. The second phone call was to a woman who explained that Samira's sister was back in Beirut and would probably be of most help. Her name was Anika. Faraz jotted down the number, called, and after an ecstatic minute-long conversation in Arabic he hung up and told Max he was to go to his aunt's house right away.

"My aunt's?"

"Op!" he laughed. "Another surprise for you!"

Rima said to Max, "This is Beirut. Every day another aunt you never knew appears in front of you." She handed him her card and said she had to get back to her hotel, but that he was welcome to stay there later. Also, she had plenty more hummus if he wanted. She had a dour but sincere kindness that Max hadn't ever encountered. He was sad to see her go.

FIFTEEN

THE HEAT AND pollution attacked again. Every other person they passed on the way to Anika's stopped to shake Faraz's hand and ask about his wife, and his children and grandchildren, and his brothers and sisters and aunts and uncles. It took about twenty minutes to walk the three hundred yards to Anika's. This place, Beirut, felt like an elaborate movie set. Just as soon as Max had that thought, he realized it was the exact opposite. No, Beirut made Clarence feel like a movie set. This, here, was real life. Every missing tooth, every red-haired Arab, every American-looking kid, each set of gorgeous eyes, each tennis bag, every beggar, every shiny necklace, every ficus or orange tree, was new and rousing and rich with meaning to him now. The meaning being no more specific than: The world is big, small, unfair, and sometimes beautiful.

Anika lived in the building noted as Samira's address in the AUB database, al-Nada building.

She buzzed Faraz and Max in and they rode the elevator to the eleventh floor: the penthouse apartment. The suspense of that ride bordered on intolerable. A black maid with a broad forehead and the compact physique of a jockey opened the door. She guided Faraz and Max across a spacious, marble-floored living room with Persian rugs. Glum black-and-gray paintings of ships in awesome storms hung on the walls next to dozens of photographs of men shaking hands like politicians. The antique furniture looked uninviting and bumpy, and if it hadn't been for all the sunlight flooding the apartment, thanks to the screen door leading to the terrace, the place would have felt haunted. As they reached the balcony's edge and admired the sea for a moment, Anika descended the stairs from the roof deck.

"Faraz, Hakeem, welcome," she said. Max almost corrected her when she called him Hakeem. She wore an all-white linen suit with a light blue headscarf resting on her head, her auburn-dyed hair exposed in the front. She looked about forty-five, had intelligent brown eyes, the pale, powdery olive complexion that rich Middle Easterners sometimes have, and walked with the slow privilege and elegance of a feline, every movement easy and deliberate. She gripped Max by the shoulders, her long, hard nails like little splinters. "The spitting image of your father," she said in an almost accusatory tone. She bent down to kiss Faraz on both cheeks and invited them to sit around the table under the patio umbrellas. Faraz and Anika caught up in a mixture of French, Arabic, and English. They talked for an excruciatingly long five minutes with no apparent reference as to why Max sat with them. Anxious as this made him, it gave him a chance to examine his aunt's face and way of speaking without the self-consciousness of being part of the conversation. Her hands moved delicately as spiders. He wondered if his mother looked and gestured similarly. There was something in her demeanor he didn't trust. Was it something vicious, or was she just guarded? Her eyes hardly ever changed; her mouth smiled and frowned, opened and closed, but the skin around her eyes never creased. They talked about where Anika had been all these years, how her husband and children were doing in Qatar, what had come of AUB, the shortcomings of bureaucracy, the wonderful professors and the doddering ones who'd been there since Anika's day. In English they spoke with the same accent as Rasheed, only Anika's grammar and vocabulary were better. The maid came to ask Max and Faraz what they'd like to drink.

Faraz laughed about how apologetically Max asked the maid for water and a vodka cranberry. Max knew he looked old enough to drink alcohol, especially after a few days of not shaving, but wasn't used to getting waited on like this. Seeing a black maid felt strange. How weird would this have been in New Jersey? At the Yangs', for instance.

Faraz excused himself; he had to get back to the office. Anika insisted he stay for tea and come up to the roof deck for a quick swim. She didn't seem eager to be alone with her nephew. But Faraz really did have to get going. He too gave Max his business card and told him that in absolutely no circumstances should he hesitate to call him for anything at all.

Once he'd gone, Anika turned and stared at Max a moment. Her mouth coiled into a tight ring. "You have come to learn about your mother."

"Yes."

"I'm sorry to disappoint you. I don't know much."

"Is she alive?" He held his breath.

"I'm pretty sure. Though I cannot promise that my mother would have told me if she had passed away."

"Do you know where she'd be living now?" he asked.

"No. The last time I saw her was many years ago. Nineteen eighty-five. But I believe my mother knows where she is."

"Your mother wouldn't have told you that, either?"

"No." She gave a bitter smile. "My mother would not have told me that either. Shall I call her and tell her you are here?"

"Is she in Beirut too?"

"She lives in Paris."

"France?"

"Yes."

Gratefulness and suspicion blossomed in him. He could have jumped off the terrace and soared over the city out of how possible everything felt, but also out of some instinctive need to escape this building and the mounting complexity of what he was after. Part of him wanted to go home and forget about the whole thing. How tempting it can be to quit right before getting what you want most.

He waited over a quarter of an hour before Anika came back. Still sipping on his vodka cranberry, he decided he must be careful here. He didn't yet know who had lied to his mother about him. Someone had probably told her he died, and Anika's not being in contact with her inspired distrust in him. After too big a drink, acid torched up his esophagus and back down. The acid came with a picture of Rasheed's face as he'd last seen it in the kitchen, right after hitting Max. A vengefulness heated his mind, a blistering fantasy to say hateful things to him. It was freeing to blame him so openly in his heart, so head-on, as though this was what he'd wanted to do his whole life. Hate his father.

The beeping and shouting and fumes down in the streets were subdued by the prayer call. An imam cried a long *Allaaaaaaaaahu akbar* through a megaphone from a nearby minaret. Other imams in close-by neighborhoods also sang the prayer. Three or four different voices and styles and volumes could be heard together, each a couple of beats ahead of or behind the others.

Anika told Max that his grandmother wanted to speak to him. Her face had changed. She had no more mascara on her eyes. That was it, that's what made her eyes smaller now. She had cried and wiped everything clean.

He went into a room with velvet curtains and vintage weapons mounted on the walls, like some sort of colonial smoking room, and took the phone to talk to one of his living grandparents. The parents of a living mother confirmed while at his living aunt's. A family of ghosts come back to life.

"Hello," he said.

"Hakeem." Her voice was grave but soft. "I cannot believe."

He laughed uneasily. "I'm good," he said, as though she'd asked.

"You are liking Beirut?"

"It's very nice."

"I miss it, you know. If I were your age in Beirut, I would be having too much fun. Are you having too much fun?"

"Yes."

"Good. You will call me Téta, and your grandfather Jiddo." She spoke to someone in the background for a minute before taking back up the phone. "Okay. You will now stay there with Anika until your flight to Paris. I have asked that they book you a nine P.M. direct on Air France. You will arrive very early in the morning. You are young and can handle this, no?"

"Yes, so my mother is there?"

"*Inshallah*, Hakeem, *inshallah*."

"Sorry?"

"Yes. She will come here to meet you. God willing."

Relief filled his lungs. His mother was alive. "Okay. Wow, unbelievable. So, she'll actually be there."

"I am sure."

"Where will she be flying in from?"

"She will be here tomorrow."

"Excellent. Yeah. But could you tell me where she lives now?"

"Yes, she is on her way. The way to meet her is to come here. To Paris. Okay?"

"But where is she now?"

She sighed and waited a while before admitting, "Not sure."

"You don't know?"

"No, we don't know. But she will fly here tomorrow."

MAX NOTICED A pain in his jaw. He'd been grinding his teeth since he hung up the phone. Again, things had only become more mysterious. Really? Fly over and meet your mom? She'll be here waiting, but we don't know where she lives? Don't know where she's been, or why we haven't seen her in fifteen years?

The maid brought him a towel and led him to the bathroom. He was to wash and change before their early dinner. Max asked if she could show him where they kept the vodka to top off his drink. She speed-walked away and returned a few minutes later with a martini and a sword of olives. He sipped on it while in the triple-headed shower, big enough for five people.

Refreshed, he meandered the apartment alone while Anika stayed on the phone in that colonial smoke room. He tried to listen in on her conversation by standing by the door, but it was all in Arabic. Ambling up to the roof deck, one of the highest outlooks in Ras Beirut, he discovered the swimming pool. The maid lay on her stomach at the pool's edge, reaching for a dead pigeon floating a few centimeters out of her reach. A Siamese cat perched on the balcony's handrail eyed the dead bird. Behind the cat stood Beirut on crutches—half-built gray and brown buildings, construction cranes, cinder-block homes studding the mountains like mushroom stalks, water tanks, holes—all set before a belt of smogged blue sky. The maid noticed him, and became self-conscious, as if she'd been caught breaking a rule. She said, "Sir?"

He looked around the roof deck: the table and umbrella, the pool, and the pool shed not much bigger than his tree house. In Rasheed's version, this space had been turned into a brothel. He pictured half-naked men and women pouring bottles of whiskey down their chins, and Kalashnikov rifles resting up against the wooden chaise longues.

DINNER WAS ALMOST ready, and Anika waited for him at the head of the table on the lower terrace. "If you knew how much you looked like your father." She said it less aggressively this time, but still, he was taken aback. If I knew, he thought, then what? What if I knew? And why does she assume I don't know in the first place? But in truth he didn't know he looked like his father because no one had said so before. There wasn't much physical resemblance between them other than the size of their noses, though the shapes weren't similar at all: Rasheed's like a butter knife, and Max's like a spoon.

"I was hoping you could tell me some things about my mother," he said.

She stood up. "Let me introduce you to Beirut before the food arrives." She led him to the balcony's railing and pointed out buildings and places in a bored tone, as though someone had told her this task was part of her burden as hostess. He listened attentively, awaiting the relevance of these sites to his mother, and despite himself, to his father too. She pointed out AUB, which looked like an airbrushed photo of an American university that had been cut and pasted into this beaten-down view. The flashy new buildings had this same out-of-place effect, making the older architecture look like beautiful tombstones from another era. The Holiday Inn was the tallest building around, and hideous. It looked like an enormous abandoned building firemen use for training, all scorched around the windows, and with huge chunks of cement that had long been rocketed out.

He didn't care about Beirut now. He asked her what his mother was doing in 1985. She acted as if she didn't hear him and continued describing sites in her jaded way—the Grand Serail, the Mohammad al-Amin mosque, an all-women's swimming resort. She did an expert job at pretending not to notice him staring at her profile. Max was sure she was running out of steam; that she couldn't maintain this description of everything her eyes landed on for much longer.

She surprised him when she said, earnestly, that she never stopped missing this city. Apparently she was only back here on business and lived in Qatar most of the year. Max didn't see what one could miss about Beirut. It was a striking place, sure, but it was also run-down and war-shadowed. Was its value thanks to its continually being on the brink of total destruction? Was that what made it so precious? Was that what made it feel more like real life than Clarence?

With her first semblance of a natural smile, she asked how many drinks he'd had. He told her two, and she found this funny. In this unguarded moment, showing teeth, she was pretty. She ordered herself a drink and kept describing the scenery. As she spoke, Max watched fisherman starting their workday at sunset, swaying on top of the sea. The water twinkled hysterically under a sinking orange sun. His mind wandered over to Nadine and the smell of her lips and sweat and head. He imagined her fear and regret at his having vanished, and how they'd left things. His heart warmed at the thought of her worrying about him.

Anika did tire out. She interrupted his thoughts by asking if Rasheed still went to mosque. He couldn't tell if she was making a dry joke. He said no, but then again he knew very little about the man. She gave the strenuous grin that only cynicism can pull across one's lips, then quickly finished her first drink and ordered the maid to bring them each a fresh one. A good sign. The alcohol loosened her up.

He tried again. "Why haven't you seen my mom since 1985?"

"For many reasons. We were never close. Also," she said into her new drink, "our father disowned her."

"Why?"

She looked surprised. "Because of what she brought on to Rasheed's family."

"Which was what?"

"Do you know any of this story, Hakeem?"

He told her he'd only learned his name was Hakeem a few days ago. Then he ran her through the version of his mother's story he'd lived with for the past five years.

She said, "It's very close to the truth," as if it should suffice. She scanned the cityscape from left to right, probably looking for something else to describe.

After she'd lit and nearly finished her cigarette, Max said, "He kept my mother from me."

She shrugged, seeming to say, *Sure, I can see why you'd be upset about something like that.*

"What did she bring on to Rasheed's family?" he asked.

"Your mother will tell you about all of these things. I know too little, Hakeem. I may mislead you if I tell you my version of things."

"I want to hear your version." He was resolved to keep pushing. His insistence would either break Anika open or cause an irretrievable rift that blocked further discussion. But she'd invited him here. Surely she knew he'd have questions. Did she really hope to avoid the topic altogether? Again: "What did she bring on to Rasheed's family?"

"She brought death to his family. "

Max kept his face still, wanting her to think him impervious, simply collecting facts. He asked, "How did Rasheed and Samira meet?"

"The Boulos family"—she cleared her throat and sighed—"lived always just below us. Samira and Rasheed played together as children. And then, of course, there was Ali, the third friend. Ali was a Palestinian boy from a refugee camp in Beirut called Shatila. The camp is famous because of the Sabra and Shatila massacre."

"I saw something about it in a documentary once." He couldn't have said more on the subject, having just a vague recollection of bodies and those names, Sabra and Shatila. He wanted to keep her going. "So they went to school with Ali?"

She encircled her mouth with her thumbnail, scraping clean any potential smudges of lipstick. She was one of those elegant people who are impossible to imagine naked. "No. Ali was the son of a very poor worker who fixed things in our home. The problem was, Ali grew up to be handsome, and he liked Samira too much. My father wanted Samira to marry Rasheed. Somehow he'd gotten it in his head that Rasheed would calm her down." She laughed at this. "Ali and Samira got into trouble, sneaking off to protests when they were ten or eleven years old only. Protesting things that had nothing to do with them even, like increases of tuition at the university." She shook her head and sucked on a new cigarette, caving in her cheeks. "They protested just to protest, because it excited them."

The maid came and quickly filled the long table with enough dishes for five people: char-grilled eggplant on triangular plates, cumin-powdered chickpeas in emerald and eucalyptus-green bowls, skewers of grilled meats and vegetables, a salad of toasted pita bread, cucumbers, tomatoes, chickweed, and mint in a wooden salad bowl, fried cauliflower, flat cakes of minced

meat and spices, stuffed zucchini, some kind of lentil concoc-
tion, cheese balls, falafel, and baba ghanoush. They sat down.
He didn't want to enjoy the food as much as he suspected he
would. Worried and stressed people were supposed to lose their
appetites. But feeling physically well again, he was ravenous.
He asked Anika if the maid ate with them. "No," she said, "she
eats her own food. Food from her country that she likes better."
Anika told him to stop thinking of the maid as a slave. Everyone
in Lebanon had at least one maid. Given all the different
kinds of people he'd seen on the streets today, Max had trouble
believing that. "This one here," Anika said, "Nadifa, sends a
lot of money back to her family in Eritrea. She is paying her
children's way through college. She is lucky to be here."

"So," Max said. "Ali and Samira's friendship."

She picked up a falafel ball with a pair of silver tongs and
dropped it on her plate. "Yes. Let me back up." She took in a
deep breath and exhaled the way people do when they are about
to explain something from the beginning. "My father loved
how Samira argued when she was a young girl, but later, when
she was still just as stubborn and the issues were very sensitive,
real tensions came between them."

"About what? What did they disagree about?"

"In short, they ended up on opposite sides of the war. My
father wanted the West's presence in the region because it was
an oil services company during the French mandate that gave us
this fortunate life. And Samira, following the Arab nationalist
movement, believed that the West's involvement was bad for
Arabs."

Max repeated *Arab nationalist, Arab nationalist, Arab
nationalist* in his head. He'd have to look up what that meant
later.

"Do you know about Arab nationalism?" she asked.

"Yeah, sure."

"It's people who believe the Arab world should be united as one, and that we are separate countries only because of borders drawn arbitrarily by colonial powers from the West." She stared at him long enough to make him swallow. He didn't know why she stared like that. When she said, "Like in Africa," he understood that she didn't trust him to follow what she was talking about.

"Yeah."

"Your mother's main obsession was the Palestinian cause. Our father believed it was unfair that what happened to the Palestinians should be our problem. He thought it was unfortunate the way Israel was created, but that we shouldn't be responsible for cleaning up a mess that is not ours. As things got more and more tenuous in this country, her Arab nationalism and sentiments about the Palestinians and Israelis strengthened, and so did his pro-West positions, which were of course indirectly in support of Israel. He was so serious about being pro-West that he even stopped—would you believe—speaking to us in Arabic." She had a perplexed smile, remembering her past with detached fascination. Again, Max noticed her prettiness.

"I was about seventeen, and Samira fifteen, when he came home one day to announce that from now on we would only speak French and English. Samira refused. For the rest of their relationship, he talked to her in English and French, and she responded in Arabic."

Anika looked amused by her own story, and he was entertained too, as though it had nothing to do with him. The alcohol sloshed around his head. He experienced a growing self-satisfaction for having come all this way on his own; as if he'd done enough, already succeeded, and could stop here with a pat on the back and plenty of rest. He swallowed his food, hardly chewing. "So, when did she marry Rasheed?"

She smoked awhile. "They married in Samira's third year at AUB. As a sort of joke."

"A joke?"

"They had an arrangement: They'd live together as best friends, make the families happy enough to leave them alone, and continue to indulge in their secret lives."

"What kinds of secret lives?"

She seemed to carefully organize her thoughts, nervous about saying the wrong things. "That's not an important part of the story."

She hadn't touched her falafel. Scooping up some baba ghanoush with a wedge of pita, she took a minuscule bite, chewing slowly. Max had almost finished his plate. "The story is the whole picture, right? What secret lives?"

"Samira and Ali were in love."

"My father knew this?"

"Rasheed? Yes, of course, Rasheed knew this. Rasheed had different, well, different preferences. His own private lifestyle, in certain—clubs." She narrowed her eyes at the lonely falafel ball, waiting to see if she'd said too much.

He kept cool as the wind took itself out of him. *She's telling me my dad is gay.* Whatever fluffiness he'd felt about the food and drinks and storytelling blew away. He had a flash of Rasheed standing in jean shorts and a white tank top at one of his basketball games, and zoomed in on the girlishly quick and small way he applauded when someone scored. Max had attributed all such details of his father's comportment to foreignness. But had it been obvious to everyone else in those basketball stands that Rasheed was a gay man? Then he thought of Coach Tim and how conflicts with him started the moment Kelly showed up. And how much time Rasheed spent over there before and after Kelly. Was Max the only one hidden away in the dark? Paranoia and betrayal and humiliation set in deeper.

But hadn't Kelly and his father shared a bed? Or was even that part of the illusion? Had they just been sleeping side by side as partners in this charade? Where could his father have gotten these twisted ideas of what defined a normal, healthy child-hood? On what standards did he base all his complicated lying? Why would he think Max too weak to handle the truth? Max had spent the better part of his life trusting and being close to only his father, giving him the entirety of his love and attention, and he'd never been trusted in return. He'd been deemed nothing more than a feeble little boy.

Anika explained that while her parents were still in Beirut, Samira and Rasheed lived in the small pool shed upstairs. Ali could come and go easily through a separate entrance without being seen. The parents avoided the shed, either out of respect for the newlyweds' privacy or out of fear of the truth.

"And they were all still in school?"

"Ali didn't go to school. He was a bricklayer on the black market."

"Why on the black market?"

"Refugees aren't allowed to work most jobs legally here."

"How are they supposed to survive?"

"They have to find ways. Anyway, Samira was in school, and Rasheed had finished with his schooling a year earlier. He helped his father with his dentistry in the apartment."

She took her time putting a spoonful of *tzatziki* next to the one falafel, letting her spoon clank loudly a few times against the white porcelain of her plate, and talked about how Samira spent her time in cafés where members of one of the PLO factions conferred. She also went to local civil groups led by academics from AUB, but was frustrated by the ineffectiveness of peaceful protest in a country that had no government what-soever and was at war with itself. She joined another leftist group that did not believe in strict nonviolence. Ali joined too.

Rasheed told Anika that Samira and Ali were getting mixed up with people who would endanger them. Anika said, "What can I do? If she won't listen to you, she of course will not care what I think." Also, at this time, Samira was pregnant.

Max asked what kinds of things his mother did with this new group.

Anika had only heard little pieces, rumors, about how Samira delivered packages for some militia or another, probably documents and maybe sometimes weapons and plans, who knew? Rasheed tried to cover for her absences but could only invent so many excuses. She became too extreme for her old friends from high school and at AUB. No one was involved enough in the resistance for her taste. After the doctors delivered Max in 1984, Samira took him everywhere with her: to school, to group meetings, and whatever else she did.

"She was even more insufferable," Anika remembered. "Politics and social justice was all she could talk about. She made everything you said sound silly in light of the suffering of others. There are few things that are more annoying than conversing with someone who is always putting things into perspective."

Anika continued to summarize liberally, and maybe therapeutically. He wondered if he'd ever actually meet this woman, his mother. The more he heard, the more unimaginable the idea of facing her seemed.

Samira had made the newspapers after getting expelled from AUB for being involved with an armed group in a campus protest. The group didn't use any violence, but the mere presence of armed men surrounding the campus and Samira standing with them was enough for her to get kicked out. She went from doing sit-ins to carrying a pistol and sleeping in abandoned buildings, shooting and maybe even bombing. It had long become too much to manage all of this with a baby in her arms, so she left Max with Rasheed. She was never around. Samira's father pretended not to notice for as long as possible, telling people she was just spending a lot of time at school and with friends, and that of course the rumors were not true.

The war got uglier, and people stopped believing it would ever end. Anika, her husband and children, and her parents left for France in 1985—much later than they should have, having waited that long because Samira refused to go—abandoning the apartment to hooligans and prostitutes and militiamen until 1990. The Bouloses were the last tenants crazy enough to keep living in the building.

Samira stayed behind under the pretense that she needed to be with her husband's family, but she only really holed up with the Bouloses after Ali was assassinated. She lay in their bathtub for days, refusing food or water. She believed they killed Ali because of a traitor in their group, a man named Fuad who she claimed was a spy for the Israelis. One day Fuad strolled in to get his teeth cleaned.

Max asked, "He didn't know she was staying there?"

"There was always a lot of bad information going around. People died all of the time because of misinformation. Yes, maybe he didn't know Samira was in the apartment. Or maybe he wasn't a traitor at all and had no reason to fear going there. But when Fuad laid his back in the dentist chair, Samira emerged from the bathroom and pressed her pistol to the crown of his head. Everyone screamed for her not to shoot, but she squeezed the trigger. She had to go into hiding after that. She didn't even stay to help clean up the mess, and it was very complicated for the others to know what to do with this body. As far as I know, that was the last time Samira saw Rasheed or you. Fuad's brothers came for revenge, and it fell on the Bouloses and their friends. Twelve people in all. You and Rasheed happened to have gone on a walk in the stairwell, and when the shooting began, he ran up with you in his arms and listened to everything from the corridor."

After Max's chills smoothed out, he asked if she thought any of the story about the two young rightist Christians holding them hostage, waiting for that militia leader's appointment for a root canal, was possibly true. She couldn't be sure, but had trouble imagining why Rasheed would have left that part out when he and Max arrived in Paris, as he seemed to fill the Jabbirs in on every other major event. And up until the massacre, the Bouloses had been in steady contact with the Jabbirs. They called as frequently as they could with updates, and despite hearing a lot of incredible anecdotes and horror stories, Anika didn't remember anything about two young rightist Christians. And no, she didn't hear anything about her sister wearing a pot on her head either. She found that detail harder to believe than any other. However, yes, the bit about a rocket going through the window and over the dentist chair was true.

Max almost had to admire Rasheed's ingenuity. Had he plotted all the fictionalized elements of the story before climbing into the tree house, or was it all off the cuff? It was the perfect amount of specificity; he'd given Max just enough for him to feel he was getting a complete story while also managing to keep the most important person, Max's mother, a purely symbolic character. If Rasheed had told of her being a fighter or getting depressed about Ali's death or any psychological complexities about her at all, he'd have risked spurring more of Max's curiosity, but as long as Samira stayed that generic, simple, loving mother with a pot on her head, she remained only a representation of Mother, a nonperson—a cartoon. And what additional information did Max ever demand of cartoons?

Anika moved the food on her plate around for a short while. "I am not shocked that Rasheed tries to forget about her." She snubbed out her cigarette and slowly pulled out another, taking her time to light it.

"Maybe, but he can't choose whether I forget her or not." He disliked the whininess he heard in his voice. He sounded like a child.

When Rasheed and Max flew to Anika and Samira's parents' home in Paris, their father had learned the story and said he never wanted to hear her name again. He didn't want to see Rasheed again either, but promised to help out financially until Max turned eighteen, as long as they went far away to start a new life.

Max remembered the accounts with deposits from Ziad Jabbir from all those years ago. "So your father is Ziad Jabbir."

"That's right. Your grandfather."

Gunshots popped off in the distance, and Max jumped. With a sardonic smirk that Max was getting used to, Anika said not to worry, people in the mountains shoot in the air to celebrate what some political or religious leader says on television.

Max asked, "How did you know your mom was still in contact with her?"

"My mother slips sometimes. She speaks, forgetting that someone is listening."

"So my mother was put in prison for what happened with Fuad?"

"No. This prison, which was run by the SLA, in the Israeli-occupied south of Lebanon, didn't care about such things. They were happy to see us killing each other."

"So what was she charged with?"

"Charged with? It didn't work like this. They removed you. Someone informed on you, or they suspected something and kept you for as long as they wanted, or until you betrayed enough of your friends, that is all."

"Torture?"

She nodded yes. "I also found a letter to my mother from Samira that dated from 1998."

"What did it say?"

"I don't know. I didn't read it."

"Why not? You weren't interested at all?"

"Not interested enough to risk having her anywhere near me or my family. If I read it, I'd know where she lived, and my curiosity might get the better of me. Listen, the truth is, over the years, I have come to share my sister's political views, but I want nothing to do with her lifestyle."

"What do you mean?"

"I mean, there are some people who don't read the newspapers because they feel helpless and it depresses them. Then there are other people, like me, who read the paper cover to cover every morning and complain for hours about the Israeli occupation and give a little money here and there to charities and NGOs. And then there are people like Samira who read the newspaper in the morning, pick up a gun in the afternoon, and by evening are fighting with all their life. I love this kind of character in books and so on, but don't want someone like that near my children."

Max imagined Anika's children for the first time, his cousins. He saw them as stuck-up, apathetic-looking boys with their hair parted hard to one side.

After another drink Max could tell Anika was getting as toasted as him. "My sister is a very strong woman," she said. "People either loved or hated her. That is a good sign, I believe. Means you have a strong character if at least half of the people hate you. You should never be impressed by someone who everyone loves. They are either weak or liars. Your mother was neither weak nor a liar." She frowned at the sky. "I was one of the people who hated her. I'm not surprised she hasn't contacted me since her release."

"Why did you hate each other?"

"I didn't say she hated me. She was quite unconcerned with me. I hated her because of how inconsequential she made me feel. My hate had no effect on her. I also envied her for other reasons."

Max consciously changed to a more delicate tone. "What did you envy?"

She daydreamed awhile. "How sure she was about everything. It seems wonderful to know so clearly what is right and what is wrong. Maybe that knowledge doesn't give her a happy life, but it gives her a purposeful one at least. This wasn't exactly the idea you had formed about her, is it?"

"I didn't have any idea formed."

"Strange. I'd have assumed a child who grows up without a mother would have all kinds of fantasies about what she was like. None of this surprises you?"

"No, it all does."

They didn't speak for a few minutes. She stared off at the mountains. Her face softened. "We were young. I chose the wrong side in the war."

"Because it was the opposite of hers?"

"No, I was on the side of my parents. Most are on the side of their parents. It was my father's wish, even though we were Muslim, for the rightists and the West to control the country. He, like most, worried about his own family's survival above any questions of ethics. He wanted us to stay wealthy. Samira was the odd one out in our family. She hated our money. Something in your mother's blood makes it impossible for her to just accept the great chance she was given."

"What chance?"

"The chance of being born rich. Of not needing to surrender her life to fight for what we should all have for free." She swallowed and rediscovered her tone of indifference. "Basic rights and so on."

Something bothered him. "Do you think she killed other people? Or just Fuad?"

"She fought with violence, sure. As to the specifics, I don't know. Unfortunately, the use of violence against the Israeli occupation continues to be inevitable."

"Why inevitable?" Mostly thanks to Nadine's influence, his admiration for armed revolutionaries had shifted to peaceful activists over the years. She had convinced him that civil disobedience and diplomacy were always superior options.

"Because Palestinians have absolutely no economic leverage with which to demand their human rights."

"I don't know much about this topic in particular, but fighting with violence gets more innocent people killed, right? Including more of your own."

"Sure, but you can't expect that all Palestinians will accept dehumanization to avoid more casualties. An occupied population has the right to defend itself. That said, perhaps you don't know, but most Palestinian resistance to the occupation has been through nonviolent demonstrations. But they are always crushed by the Israeli army, daily, and Israel continues to make more illegal settlements inside the Palestinian territories."

Maybe this was her way of feeling realigned with Samira. "Who decides if they're illegal?"

"This is not my defining, *habibi*. An overwhelming majority of the world's leaders"—she counted off on her fingers—"and the United Nations Security Council, and the General Assembly, the Red Cross, the International Court of Justice, the EU, and every single human rights organization across the board consider the occupation illegal, but not the United States. Your country doesn't see a problem with Israel controlling the roads, air space, borders, water, electricity, sewage systems, and access to oil in the Palestinian territories. And though Israel does not give these people they control the right to a vote, your country somehow reasons that they are the great democracy of the region. It would actually all be very funny if it weren't so sad. There is a moment when you must consider the consensus, no? When ninety-eight percent of scientists around the world tell me that global warming is real, I believe them and consider the deniers a little stupid. But in this situation, the most powerful country in the world, the United States, is the denier. What is this?"

He couldn't tell if it was a paranoid thought or not, but he had the strong feeling that condemning Israel equaled anti-Semitism. His impulse was to defend their state. He was conscious that this stance was an implicit critique of his mother. Even so, he felt more comfortable arguing for the Jewish people he'd heard had been persecuted for centuries. And maybe disagreeing with his mother was healthy. It didn't mean a rejection of her. No, he imagined she was the kind of person who would respect his willingness to disagree. He decided she was the synthesis of Nadine and his father. With his father he'd made the mistake of refusing to vocalize his differences of opinion, and though he would have surely felt at ease contradicting Nadine, he never did. He naturally agreed with everything she said, which was also suspicious. Finally, with his mother, he'd struck a balance. Respectfully opposing her, even if only through his aunt, was actually anticipative and exciting. "But don't Jews have the right to their holy land? I mean, after all they've been through? They needed a safe place to exist after the Nazis tried to exterminate them, right?" He wished Nadine and his mother had heard him say that. He sounded good just now—confident.

She looked at him as if he'd randomly taken his shirt off. "Palestinians had nothing to do with the Holocaust. You know that, right? Listen"—she put both her hands flat on the table— "the very idea of half a million traumatized people from Europe getting invited into the Middle East to make an exclusivist state, without the knowledge, let alone the permission, of the native population is absurd." She squinted at him. "You don't see that? And some of the natives who were violently forced out fought back, like the Native Americans in your country. Some of them tried to fight back as they were being forced out, no? Were they horrible terrorists for it?"

He resented this comparison, as if being on the side of the Jewish people was the same as being on the side of colonizers who killed Native Americans. "I'm not saying Israel is perfect or anything. I just think they use military force out of self-defense from terrorists. If terrorist attacks stopped, I'm sure they would let up."

"Ah yes, the losers will always be called terrorists. The crazy man who doesn't look anything like a Westerner, who straps a bomb to his chest and cries out 'Allah Akbar,' is of course a terrorist, but the handsome, light-skinned cadet dropping a bomb from an expensive plane onto a shantytown is not. He is a soldier following orders. He is well trained and well fed and speaks an impeccable English. But the fact that they kill at least ten Palestinians to every one Israeli doesn't seem to count when deciding who is terrorizing who." She was heating up. "And why does your principled antiviolence position only apply to Palestinians? Why should one side be allowed to use force but not the other? Because one side is better friends with America? And tell me, if Israel's main concern was really their people's safety, then why do they pay Jews from anywhere in the world, who have never even been to the Middle East, to move into these illegal settlements in the occupied territories, right on top of the Palestinians? This isn't about safety, Hakeem, this is clear-cut expansionism."

"No, yeah, okay." He nodded rapidly. He wanted out of this debate.

"It's always amazed me how afraid Americans are to criticize Israel's brutal occupation. I have no problem complaining about the racism in Lebanon and the backwardness and corruption here, and it doesn't mean I hate Lebanese. I went to graduate school in London and lived there for twenty years, but I will happily criticize Great Britain's foreign policy too. So why is it so hard for Americans or Israelis to admit that the way they treat Palestinians is disgusting? Disagreeing with Israel's repression of Palestinians doesn't mean that you don't like Jewish people. There is nothing Jewish about the apartheid enacted there. Don't be fooled, Hakeem, this is not a religious or racial conflict. It is a human rights issue. Period." She shook her head at her plate for a while.

As the maid came to clear the table, Max thought about meeting his mother, of their cheeks touching. What else was in her life than fighting for Palestinians? What did she eat for breakfast? Did she read any fiction? Did she spend a lot of time outside, or was she more of a hermit, like Nadine and Max? Did she listen to Pink Floyd? Which album was her favorite? Did she really exist at all?

He said, "I don't want to go to Paris if she's not there."

Anika clucked her tongue. "If my mother says she's coming, then she will come. Go to their home, Hakeem. It's the best way." She stood up. "Now, please, call Rasheed. Call him at once and tell him you are here and doing all right."

He didn't. A righteous anger streamed through him at the thought of Rasheed. The tangerine-size ball on his stomach that had maybe been a sorrowful love for his father before now shivered with sickening pity and hatred.

He called Nadine instead.

"YOU'RE IN LEBANON?" she shouted.

"Yeah." He could hear a trace of pride in his voice. "I just sort of flew here. And my mom's in Paris."

"What are you doing to us, Max?" she said.

"Us?"

"Your father's been over here three times. He's called the school and the police." It was hard to imagine Nadine and his father interacting at all, let alone collaborating on a manhunt. "Tim spent the last two nights with him because of how bad he's freaking out. He's been having a heart attack since you left. He looks horrible."

"I didn't know you two were such good friends."

"Don't be an ass," she said. "Why didn't you tell me you were leaving?"

"Because I acted like a psycho last time I saw you. And because you'd have talked me out of it."

"Yeah, I would have come up with some way to do it intelligently. Prepare a little. Did you even try to call her first?"

"I couldn't find her from there. I needed to do this, Nadine. I needed to do something for once. Anyway, it's more or less worked out thus far. I'm going to meet her in Paris tomorrow."

"So she lives in Paris?"

"I don't think she actually lives there. No one seems to know," he said, starting to whisper now, "or they're not telling me."

"That's weird. Why wouldn't they tell you?"

"Not sure yet. We're all meeting at my grandparents'."

"Well, at least give me their phone number."

"No, I don't know it. Nadine, please don't worry about my dad anymore. You shouldn't be paying attention to him. And do not tell him where I'm going, okay? I can try to call you from there, but promise you won't tell him."

"Don't ask me to keep a secret like that. He's hurting badly. I mean, he looks sick."

"I don't give a shit."

"Yes, you do. Saying you don't give a shit invariably means you do give a shit. Come home. Your dad's in really rough shape."

"You're joking, right? I'm a day away from meeting my mother."

"Are you nervous?"

"I don't know what I am."

SIXTEEN

H E ARRIVED IN Paris at six thirty in the morning. His grandparents' apartment was the whole top floor of a Haussmannian building next to the Arc de Triomphe. Even with the tall ceilings and large windows, the inside had the same great but somehow airless feel as their Beirut apartment.

His grandmother, Téta, opened the door. Not saying a word, she studied his breaths as though each one revealed a profound truth about universal life. Based on their brief phone conversation, he would have guessed her to be high-energy and assertive. But it's easy to be that way over the phone. She looked frail in her blueberry-and-cream polka-dotted summer dress. Her skin, wrinkly and soft, would probably rip under a light scratch. Wrapping her arms around him, she smelled tart, like face creams that have gone sour. Over her shoulder he could see Jiddo. Max followed Téta through the living room. Her steps were light and surprisingly even and self-possessed. Like Anika, she had controlled and deliberate gestures, except for the constant side-to-side motion of her head that seemed to be saying, *I don't know, I don't know, oh God, I really don't know.*

Jiddo's appearance was familiar. Max must have caught a younger version of him in one of those photographs in the Beirut apartment. He didn't rise from the sofa placed in the center of this grand, wood-floored apartment. His legs stayed crossed as he caressed a *masbaha*, a string of prayer beads, with his thumb.

Jiddo scrunched up his eyes as Max approached. The couch and table, with little else around it, were a good thirty feet away from the door. The liver spots on his peanut-brown skin looked strangely handsome, medallions of experience. His lips were slim and the color of ground beef, and above them hung a thick gray mustache. He had broad shoulders and spoke loudly. "Ah, yes, Ali! Come here, my boy! Please, sit, sit."

Shit, Max thought, now I have a third name?

Téta said to Jiddo, "This is not Ali, Ziad, this is Hakeem, Samira's son." She spoke kindly but with that directness and authority effective schoolteachers use. "He has come to meet us for the first time."

Jiddo gave no sign of registering what she'd said. Max sat on an antique wicker chair across from him. The black marble coffee table—littered with silver antiques, a dozen more *masbaha*s, and two curved daggers in ruby-studded sheaths—separated them. Jiddo wore a corduroy vest and a green-and-red Christmas sweater underneath, though it must have been eighty degrees. Téta went to the kitchen to tell the maid to prepare some tea, leaving Max and Jiddo alone.

"You see," he said, "Ali, I have been meaning to inform you of some things. When you order food in a proper restaurant, you should not look at the menu, you should look at the waiter directly in the eye." He interlaced his fingers. "Because you know what it is you want." He moved his head forward and backward knowingly. "I ask you to try this when the waitress comes back. Also, always dry your hands well enough to shake with another person immediately after you come out of the bathroom. You never know when you will run into an important acquaintance, and a wet handshake puts a very disagreeable pall over a conversation."

"Yeah, all right."

"Good boy. Another thing. Stop stacking the plates at the end of the meal. We have people to do that. You and Samira try to help the waitress. You believe it is a considerate and helpful thing to do, but in fact you are degrading the waitress's duties. You must allow people of all standings to do their work honorably. Understand?"

"Yes."

"Good. *Shh*. Here she comes." Téta walked through the living room and sat with them. Jiddo winked at Max and said, "So, Ali, tell me how is school? Are you going every day like we spoke about?"

Max had no idea how to play this. Before he could think to answer, Jiddo cut in. "Where is Samira?"

"What?"

The pleasantness drained from Jiddo's face, and he looked at Max as if he'd caught him stealing. His brow lowered and his eyes darkened. "Are you having trouble with your ears today, Ali? I asked you a simple question. Where is my daughter? Look at me. Where is she?" He tried to stand up a couple of times but couldn't. "You dirty peasant swine." He wept. "They put her in prison because of you. Are you proud, you pig? Nine years. Are you proud now? They hurt my baby. Ways that never leave the body. Ways that stay on the inside. They don't ever leave the inside. They won't leave the inside. They won't leave." He shook his head as if he were wicking water off his hair, softly repeating, "I'll kill you, I'll kill you, I'll kill you," through his sobs.

Téta took a lollipop out of her pocket. "Don't worry, Hakeem. He is only very confused." She unwrapped it, leaned over, and planted it in Jiddo's mouth. This distracted him enough to stop his crying. His expression changed into an easy, pleased smile. He gazed at the table like a glassy-eyed kid watching cartoons. Téta said, "Come with me into the kitchen, Hakeem, to help with the tea."

As they walked to the kitchen, Jiddo talked around the lollipop at Max's back. "Where is she? Where is she?"

In the kitchen, Téta introduced him to the maid. She was Sudanese and at least six foot three, with a sweet round face and shaved head. She bowed a hello, and Max bowed back. The kitchen was as large as one of Max's classrooms back in Clarence, with a big island in the middle, brass pots and pans hanging above. The clock on the oven read 6:45, and the amber daylight climbed the walls like a rising water line. They could hear Jiddo barking it now, like a protest chant: *Where! Is! She! Where! Is! She!*

"What year are you at school, Hakeem?" Téta asked Max. She seemed to want to pretend, at least for a short while, that there was something casual in this visit.

"I'm going to be a senior in high school."

Jiddo was going hoarse in the living room, screaming that they had hurt his baby in ways that never leave the body.

Téta said, "Good, good. Good. You look so much older than that."

They should have had a million things to say to each other, but nothing came. Samira's absence hung too heavily between them.

"How is your father?" she asked.

"He's fine." Jiddo sounded like a mourner out there. No words, only wailing.

"Is he doing all right financially?" He saw she regretted saying it as soon as it came out of her mouth, and ignored the question.

Jiddo's lamentations simmered down to a drowsy blubbering. Max heard the ticking of a grandfather clock coming from some other room for the first time since he'd arrived.

Waiting like this made for a terrible restlessness. Waiting to address the reason he stood here in this oversize kitchen. Waiting for Jiddo to tire out. Waiting for the kettle to whistle and the long-limbed maid to stop moving around aimlessly, cleaning what was already perfectly clean. Waiting to meet his mother. Sleep hadn't come to him on the plane to Beirut or the one here; the waiting had kept him up the whole way. An obsessive concern for the future: the very definition of anxiety.

The kettle whistled, and the maid prepared the silver tea tray, everything appearing miniature in her large hands. Téta looked at Max with rose-rimmed eyes of alarm and pain, and maybe wisdom. He couldn't decide if she saw him as an angel or as a curse that had landed in their house.

He volunteered to bring the tea to Jiddo, and on the way he determined that the nervousness in the air wasn't only his own. Téta was afraid of Max too. Of course she was. Max represented a memory they'd tried to erase. She had probably never expected this day to come. Had she been the one to tell his mother he didn't make it? That he'd died? Was that the arrangement? You, Rasheed, tell her son that she is dead, and I'll tell my daughter her husband and son are no longer of this earth?

But as with Anika, why had Téta invited him at all? Did she have a change of heart and realize the wrongness in all the lies spun over the years? He walked toward Jiddo, angry but emboldened by this idea of forcing confessions from everyone.

Yes, emboldened by the idea that he wouldn't stop until he found his mother and all the light they would bring each other.

Jiddo sat folded over himself, hanging his head all the way down to his lap. Max thought he'd dozed off at first, but he was holding a wristwatch in his hands, staring intently at it, his nose almost touching its gold face. The lollipop had fallen to the Persian rug.

Max sat a few minutes, observing Jiddo's steadfast obsession with his watch's second hand. Téta should be here to take her share of the awkwardness. He marched back through the swinging door and into the kitchen, where the enlivening smells of pressed pomegranate, coffee, and the olive oil and *labne* being spread down a long plate coursed up his nose.

Max asked, "Will I meet her soon, Téta?"

She washed her bent and knotted hands in the air. "She should have arrived hours ago. This means she had some delays in coming."

His instinct was to conceal his edginess. "But coming from where?"

"Amman, Jordan," she whispered as though it could get her into trouble.

"Jordan?" He didn't know exactly where to situate Jordan, but he was pretty sure it was closer to Lebanon than to France.

So what the hell was he doing here? Did no one understand that he was looking for his mother? He'd come all this way for his mother. Not for tea and pistachios with grandparents. Not to learn about his Lebanese origins. Not to debate the Israeli-Palestinian conflict. Not to hear stories about Samira Jabbir, or see pictures of her, but for her to be sitting and breathing and talking right there in front of him. Why hadn't Téta told him where his mother lived before? Why didn't they give him her fucking phone number when he was with Anika? What was going on? So far, of all the people, only Kelly had been straight with him.

If Téta knew or could have found out where Max lived all these years, since they were depositing money in Rasheed's account, and she had his mother's phone number, of course she could have connected mother and son. Ask her why she never did, he told himself. What are you afraid of? Ask her. Ask her that one question, you coward.

Téta washed her hands more rapidly. "She works at a refugee camp there."

"Could I call her, please?" he said.

Her head shook a little faster, and her eyes glazed thickly, as if they sat in egg whites. She'd looked on the verge of tears since his arrival, but had yet to shed one. She didn't answer for a long time. "Yes. You are right. I will call her in the study room. Wait here."

She exited.

She'd already left by the time he'd formulated what he should have said: *No, I'll call while you wait here.*

He stayed in the kitchen, doing slow laps around the island, avoiding Jiddo.

He didn't want these grandparents. Not until he found the woman that connected them to him. He wanted his mother to teach him how to read and appreciate Téta and Jiddo.

He dragged his feet to one of the large windows, pressed his forehead against the glass, and stared down into the street. He heard Téta's voice rising from behind a closed door somewhere. The apartment was easily six times the size of his home, but elevated, like a giant tree house: a fort, a prison, a casket in the air.

There was a white delivery van in the street with an extraordinary amount of pigeon shit concentrated dead in the center of its roof like a giant spinach omelet, green and white and yellow. The cars parked in front of and behind it were spotless. He wondered what it was about this van that attracted pigeons to take aim at it so incessantly. To remove all those layers of shit would require a metal scraping tool, a strong spatula of some kind, and boiling water and soap too. A minor surgery of sorts. He understood why the owner of the van didn't clean the roof. He might avoid such a job himself, considering so few people look closely at roofs anyway.

This is crazy, he thought. What am I waiting here for? He lifted his head and nearly ran toward the sound of Téta's voice until he came to the study. He entered as she hung up.

Without turning toward Max, she said, "Hakeem, your mother is not well."

"What do you mean?"

"I mean to say she is not like before. She is not stable as she once was. Like Jiddo."

"Like Jiddo?"

"No, not like Jiddo, really." She faced him.

"Téta, why didn't you tell me she was in Jordan while I was in Beirut?"

She looked at the ground like a culpable kid. "It is better to have everyone meet here, I think. It is better like this. Here, with us all together. This way we can all meet." She put her hand on Max's shoulder. "Okay. There was a simple complication. No problem. She will come, you will see. I promise. She will come tonight, I am sure. We will see her tonight."

"What complication?"

"A traveling complication. But she is on her way now."

"Really?"

"*Inshallah*, Hakeem. *Inshallah*."

"Right. What time is she coming then?"

"Tonight. This evening."

"I would like to talk to her myself on the phone."

"Hakeem, she has made bad decisions."

"Yeah?"

"Yes."

"Well I'll learn all about them when I meet her. For now I'd just like to speak to her on the phone and make sure she exists."

"Exists?" She took a big, brave breath. "Okay. Yes. Fine." She picked up the phone and held it awhile, staring at him, like she was calling his bluff. When he didn't react, she dialed a long number and handed him the receiver. There was that waterfalling sound between rings that comes with international calls, and it felt like once the ringing stopped, his judgment would be decided. It rang and rang. He understood his mother had been talking to Téta a moment ago, and now she wasn't answering. Every ring was a spasming fish trapped behind his breastbone. A nervousness that caused a physical ache. Air bubbles in his heart. It rang nine times before the machine picked up. A woman spoke briefly in a watery Arabic, and then, *beep*.

He said, "Hello? Hi, this is—" and then blanked. He hung up a few seconds later, not sure who would get the message, or what he could possibly say even if he did know his mother would hear it.

"She is on her way," Téta said.

WHEN THEY SAT around that low coffee table in the living room, Jiddo addressed him again as though for the first time. "Ah, Ali! I am glad to see you. I want you to invite your father for dinner. I find it is not correct that we never see each other except when I need his services. You will tell him we insist that he come this evening."

Max looked at Téta. She said to Jiddo, "Of course, Ziad, we will have a nice dinner tonight. Now let us enjoy this breakfast."

"Very well." He turned to Téta. "Miss? Do I have dinner plans for this evening?"

"No, we do not."

"Well, tell Ali to stay with us and invite his father and the other children. Doesn't that suit you, Ali?"

The maid brought everything: the *sobeir* cactus fruit, *labne*, hummus, *halawi, man'oushe*, fresh pomegranate juice, white tea, and coffee. After she'd laid everything out, Jiddo asked where Samira was today. Max took his first bite of cactus fruit, trying to relax under his grandfather's murderous gaze.

Max didn't answer, so Jiddo pointed the question to Téta. "Still at school?"

"Hakeem," Téta said, "why don't we go look at some family photos after we finish eating? I have decided to tell you a few things you don't yet know."

"Okay."

IN HER BEDROOM, Téta opened a green marble box, saying these were the things she'd managed to save. Inside were a few pictures of Samira, Ali, Rasheed, and Anika as children. Ali jumped out at Max first. He looked like him, same nose and eyes and bone structure. Max was more built than him, but otherwise they were twins. It was unsettling to resemble a dead man this much, the same dead man Jiddo kept mistaking him for. There was a delay between that thought and his recalling what Anika had said about how much he looked like his father. He understood who she meant now. Of course. Ali, the man his mother had loved and avenged. That's who they were saying was Max's father.

HE LOST THE ability to swallow. His midsection turned into a cloud; his torso floated a few inches above his waist. He had no urge to address or confirm the surreality of this new under-standing. It was too big. Along with Rasheed's sexuality, his mind's defense was to shelve it for another time.

RASHEED WAS THE only one smiling in the photos, laughing even, with one arm around Ali and the other around Samira, and Anika standing a few feet apart from them with her arms crossed. They were on a seafront. Téta said they were at one of Rasheed's aunt's homes in Byblos. Rasheed's carefreeness in the pictures annoyed Max to no end.

Samira wore faded jeans and a dusty white T-shirt, her big maple-brown curls cut short and parted in the middle. Her features were both wide and angular, strong and intelligent. She had the broad jaw of Indian chiefs on old television shows, and large, impenetrable eyes. In another picture, years older than the first, she had the physique of a swimmer, full shoulders and bad posture, holding Max in her arms. The people in the background were out of focus, but you could make out the outline of someone reclining in a burnt-orange dentist chair behind her. And behind the chair, lining the walls, were a bunch of even blurrier people, sitting or squatting.

Téta showed him a more recent picture of Samira. After nine years of prison, losing her family, and the unforgiving nature of time, his mother's eyes brimmed over with disquiet and fatigue. They were big, pink eyes mapped with veins, but they had a keen and begging quality to them, not so different from Téta's. Strands that had gotten loose from her ponytail created a sort of angelic orb of fuzz around her head, like a little girl. She was surrounded by dozens of children, and wore a poncho-like gray thing that Téta called an abaya. It covered her from the neck down, cloaking the form of her body. Téta said this was her at the refugee camp with the students.

He spotted a letter in Téta's box and unfolded it without asking permission. The blue Arabic characters that looked like billowing sails had been bombed and blotted with teardrops.

"This letter is to me," she said, and took it from him.

"I don't get it," said Max. "She writes you, but you haven't seen her in fifteen years?"

"She wrote me only this one time."

"Does she know about me?"

"Of course. She's coming here only for you tonight, Hakeem."

"And that's why you wanted us to meet here. So you can see her too."

To deflect his accusation, she gave more information. She said that Samira had come to Téta and Jiddo's Beirut apartment in the summer of 1996. No one but Jiddo and their maid, Nadifa, were home. Jiddo opened the door and was face-to-face with his daughter for the first time in over ten years. Nadifa stood back at an angle, able to see everything. She would later describe Samira as no longer womanlike. No longer beautiful. As having a crazy person's blank stare, and a few big scars on her face. It looked as if her nose had been broken and her hair cut with a knife. She'd very recently been released from al-Khiam prison.

Jiddo couldn't look at her for long. Samira said, "Baba, it's me." He told her to go away, that Samira had died years ago. Samira stared on. They stood like this for minutes. Finally Samira said something that Nadifa couldn't hear. And Jiddo responded with something along the lines of *Everyone is dead now. Please leave.* He closed the door on her and turned around to find Nadifa, telling her that if she said anything about this, he'd throw her to the street without her passport—Jiddo confiscated all of his maids' papers when he hired them. She listened through the front door to Samira's heavy breathing.

For three years Nadifa kept this secret, too afraid to say anything. Finally unable to hold it in any longer, she told Téta what she remembered. Téta didn't let Jiddo kick her out, promising to leave him if he tried such a thing, and returned Nadifa's papers to her in case she wanted to leave on her own accord.

Téta started speaking to Jiddo again when he finished losing his mind two years before. Now Jiddo talked about Samira all of the time. He continued to speak English, and Téta took up Samira's old habit of answering him in Arabic, save for when they had non-Arabic-speaking guests. Their relationship was the best it had ever been now that he was like a baby, and she was like a mother again.

There was something unnatural about this most recent photo of Samira, in that she looked both there and not there, paler than everyone else; she alone focused her eyes into the camera's lens, mistrustfully, a warning to the viewer to step no closer. The children laughed and daydreamed.

"When Samira was five years old," Téta said, "I knew she would never be a happy person."

"What do you mean?"

"It is a curse to be so concerned with unfairness, and even at that age she was cursed. She fasted for Ramadan that year. It's too young. We are not even religious people. We tried to force her to eat, but she refused. And she got worse with age. She wanted to feel what it was like to live a hard life. She saw beggars and wanted to live on the street like them. We compromised by letting her bring them things like blankets and food and so on. Most people forget the outside world—you must in order to carry on with your life—but she could not. She hated her good fortune. This is her curse. She cannot believe she deserves her good luck. Doesn't deserve money, education, not even family. The life she chooses is an unhappy one."

His mother's rejection of a life of grandeur with a maid and too much food was to Max a sign not of unhappiness, but of strength and uncommon virtue. Téta, Jiddo, and Anika were the unhappy ones. No one should be as rich as Téta and Jiddo. And now his mother had decided to revisit this castle in the middle of Paris because Téta had lured her here with Max, who she'd been hiding from Samira for years. Punishing his mother in the same sick way Rasheed had.

"Now Samira has started an NGO in the camp for preschoolers before they start at the UNRWA schools," Téta said. "Do you know UNRWA?"

"It's a UN thing."

"Yes."

"Have you been?" he said.

"No. Never."

"Does she want to see me? Did she know about me?"

"Yes, of course."

"Which? She wants to see me, or she knew about me?"

"Yes, of course." She hastily put the pictures back in the box on top of the letter, as if somebody would burst in any second and catch them snooping around someone else's things.

It made sense that he avoided pressing Téta for the obvious information: Why didn't his mother ever find him? What had Téta told her? Had Téta, like Jiddo, kept Max away from his mother?

You don't ask such important questions of people you don't trust; people who have been complicit in the greatest lie of your life. He'd find out the truth about all these things tonight, assuming Téta wasn't lying about his mother's arrival. A few more hours shouldn't make a difference. Max had to be patient a short while longer. For now, he needed to get away. He excused himself to go for a walk and said he'd be back for dinner. Téta gave him a key and a map of the city, and studied his face and body as though he might not return, telling herself to never forget what he looked like.

SEVENTEEN

MAX SAT UNDER a big manila sun and a fleece of clouds. He'd left his grandparents' street of buildings that looked like giant yellow wedding cakes, then passed the Arc de Triomphe, walked the Champs-Elysées, the Place de la Concorde, through the Jardins to the Louvre and then back to the Tuileries, an area that looked exactly how he'd imagined Paris: an aristocratic landscape of ancient statues, enormous arches, designer shops, cobbled streets, skinny men and women, and fancy shrubbery.

He'd parked himself on the lip of a marble fountain with smoothly sculpted fish-children spitting water into arches. Square-trimmed walls of tree surrounded the park, patrolled by mothers pushing strollers. Gangs of French toddlers, in bright red and yellow and white polos, parted from their parents to experiment with what could and could not float in the fish-children's fountain.

The toddlers learned that a dead sparrow floated in the pool. So did a clump of dirt, for a short while. A dry, bowed leaf floated if placed delicately enough. A toy boat did, but inelegantly after being dunked under a few times. They waited for it to resurface, making a gulping sound they enjoyed. But they respected it less now that its canvas sails were heavier, less graceful. A goose feather floated until it had its hairs taken under in bunches. Sometimes a rainbow of heavy water shot it under, cracking its spine, and other times it glided behind the cascades untouched. The toddlers watched, loving the lack of pattern; loving the idea of surprise. Some rooted for objects to stay afloat, but most expressed the greatest satisfaction when things sank. So far, no rules were apparent, only happenstance.

Max considered himself more authentic than the tourists around him, with their oversize backpacks and trail shoes, or the older ones with cameras and children and awestruck smiles at every monument or gargoyle. He felt sophisticated in how lightly he traveled and the mere fact that he had not, and explicitly would not, visit the Eiffel Tower.

He wanted to discover the Paris Nadine had talked about, with its Africans and Arabs and open-air markets. He looked at the map and found the names she'd mentioned, all in the northern part of the city: Château Rouge, Château d'Eau, Gare du Nord, and Barbès. He set out to Gare du Nord and then Pigalle by Métro. He surfaced so he could walk Boulevard de Rochechouart into Barbès, a lively place, grittier and more energetic than where his grandparents lived.

He moseyed down the center of the boulevard—with a pedestrian walk wide enough to have its own bike lanes, trees, benches, bathrooms, and loads of strolling people—toward Barbès.

He saw a large German couple wearing massive packs and cargo shorts, looking flustered as they spoke to a blind Indian man. The German man shouted to the blind man as though he were hard of hearing, "I think I know exactly where is it, but we are going the opposite direction!"

The German woman chimed in, "Ya! We are late to get our things and meet our plane! We are not from here, you know?"

Panicked and flushed, the German man saw Max looking at them and called out, "Excuse! Excuse! Are you speaking English?"

"Yes."

"Help us, please. Can you show this man to Barbès? We must catch the plane and we have not the time."

"Yeah," he said, "actually, that's where I'm going anyway."

They thanked Max a few times and left. The blind man looked about thirty. He turned to face Max, clouds of gray sitting in the middle of his white eyes. One of his cheeks was flattened and aslant, and he had scrapes and bruises on his chin and forehead, like he'd taken a bad fall recently. There were also anthills of razor burn on his jaw and neck, giving his face a granular quality.

"You ready?" Max said to him. "It's not far at all, I don't think."

"It is a fine day," the man said, hooking arms with Max and starting them off walking.

"It's really nice."

"Who are these people around us?" he asked.

Max looked around the pedestrian walk. "Who are these people?"

"Yes, the people walking around us now."

"Oh, lots of different people just strolling. I'm Max, by the way."

"And my name is Hanuman. What do the people look like, Max?"

"Which people?"

"Any of them."

"Let's see. Well, I guess there's a bit of everything."

"Men and women, I suppose?"

"There are both men and women, yes."

"Young women?"

"Some," Max said, noticing that the city had gotten very loud.

"How about over there?" He pointed at what happened to be a charming young woman sitting on a bench.

"Wow. Yeah, actually, there is one right there."

"Does she have big tits?"

Uncomfortable, Max mumbled, "Pretty big."

"Could you repeat?"

"I said, 'Yeah, pretty big.'"

He glanced back at the woman, and she gave him a disgusted look, as if she knew what they were talking about.

"What's she wearing? Something kind of—"

"Just a shirt and a skirt and boots, okay?"

"The skirt is quite short?"

Max said, "Normal, average length. Do you mind if I ask how you hurt yourself? Your face?"

"No. I do not mind if you ask. What was the color of her hair?"

"Brown. Straight. Pretty."

"Pretty, huh? Soft skin?"

"I don't remember. We've passed her now. So, how did you hurt yourself?"

"I was beaten up by *racailles* on the Métro."

"Racailles?"

"Yes, this is the pejorative word that means 'scum.' They are most often the children of immigrant families from Africa or the Middle East that live in the peripheral ghettos of the city called the banlieue. They have baby faces and military haircuts.

They are poor and uneducated, and they are profiled and bullied by police. They are treated neither as French nor as members of their parents' home countries. They are the result of social exclusion. Monsters. When my eyes face them, even though I cannot see, they ask if I want to take their fucking photograph."

Max took a minute to absorb this thorough description. "And so they attacked you?"

"Correct. They were going behind people on the Métro, slapping the backs of their heads and laughing like some drunken wolves. I could feel them behind the young woman next to me, who smelled of flour and jasmine. One of them came around to face her, and with a voice like an electric blender asked the girl if she thought he was a handsome man. The girl did not answer, and I felt the heat of her fear expanding. Then he yelled at her, saying, 'Oh, you don't like Arabs, huh? Your daddy will not let you be with a dirty Arab?' Etcetera, etcetera. He stopped yelling, and everything became very still. The boy cleared his throat and spit in her face. His friends howled with terrible laughter. She spat heavily, and the boy who spat on her said, 'It is okay, baby, do not cry, honey, I'm sorry,' in this very cruel and horny-like voice. 'I'll take care of you, come with me, baby, come with me, and I'll take good care of you.' All of the other passengers sat inside themselves like helpless prisoners, watching this girl be tormented. I was pumped with outrage. I stood up and said, 'Stop.'"

Max waited. "So then what happened?"

"Then I heard the loudest sound. Like someone taking a big bite out of a very crisp apple, only one hundred times louder than that even. This sound was the breaking of my cheekbone. They kicked me while I was on the ground, curled like a snail. At the next stop they exited the car, very happy about their victory."

"Jesus. What happened next? Where did the girl go?"

"Oh, I do not know. She cried for some time and then got off at the following stop. Only when the *racailles* were far away, and I still lay on the ground of the car, did the other passengers come to life. They fought over who got to take me to the hospital."

Max told him how brave it was to stand up to those guys, and Hanuman said it wasn't courage but an impulse. He explained he didn't think about what could come next. Didn't think about how those boys would love the chance to break his face. He reacted in the moment. Had he thought about these things, he would have stayed seated.

"You regret standing up to them?"

"No, I don't regret it. Today, I get to hear you call me a brave man." He laughed, and they had to slow down a little. "What I am saying is that a natural reaction should not be called bravery. You cannot mistake temerity for courage. Real courage requires conscious sacrifice: to realize what the stakes are and then to go forward with the action anyway. There was no thought in my decision to stand up. It was rashness. And like I said, had I thought more about it, I certainly would not have done it." They picked up the pace. "How about now, Max, any enchanting women around us now?"

Max stared at his profile, the white eyes looking as much like injuries as the bruises and cuts. He looked up at the sky and invented this next woman for Hanuman. "Let's see, she's tall, has black curly hair, a mole on her cheek, red lipstick, curvy but with slender legs—"

"Not too slender, though. Right?"

"Excuse me?"

"I do not prefer stick legs. Are they thicker? Thicker is nicer."

"Yeah, believe me, I'm with you on that. They are kind of thick."

"What about her mouth? Tell me what you know about her mouth."

"Soft."

"Yes, and kind of pulpy?"

"That's it exactly," Max said.

"Is she alone, or with another man?"

"She's all alone. Just by herself and looking real lonely."

A corn-yellow smile stretched across Hanuman's face. Then he tightened his hold on Max's arm with concern. "You do not mean desperate, though, right?"

Max got defensive. "No. Not desperate. Of course not."

"Good. A little bored, maybe. It is natural, no one is even talking to her."

"Not desperate, but there is a general loneliness about her."

"How do you know that?"

"I think it's in her eyebrows."

"Furrowed?"

"Yeah."

"Plucked?"

"Nothing overdone. But there's a slight tension there that makes it seem like she's thinking about something deep. Like her head is somewhere else, or something, you know?"

"So, in fact, her being elsewhere is what you are calling the loneliness?"

"I guess so, yeah."

"Hm. Anyway," Hanuman said, "she is tremendously bewitching, yes?"

A dreaminess took over. The shimmering canopy of leaves overhead and the sounds of the city lightened Max. "Yeah. She really is."

"Does she have the nicest ass?" Hanuman wanted to know.

"Oh yeah. Really, really sweet ass."

"Sweet? Sweet like what? Like an onion?"

"That's interesting," Max said. "I don't actually think of onions as being especially sweet."

"The onion ass, though. I know you know that is the sweet one!"

"Yeah, yeah, I guess that is pretty sweet."

"I imagine where the small of her back meets the beginning of her oniony ass is something much like heaven."

"Yeah, and her breath too."

"Like your mother's?" Hanuman suggested.

"Like my mother's? What do you mean, 'like my mother's'?"

"Hm. Like what, then? Smelly like something pretty good, though, right?"

"Oh man. Something so good."

"And her voice is pure as mountain water."

"Pure, yeah, but not overly innocent or anything. Kinda sexy too."

"Yes, that's right! Like the late-night hostesses on Radio Nova."

"Sexy and a little bored."

Hanuman squeezed Max's arm on emphasized syllables. "Very *sen*suous. *Slin*ky."

"Yeah."

"I would love to feel her trumpet on my cock."

Max winced. "Her trumpet? I don't think she's really like that."

"Of course she is. I mean, not in public. She is a lady in public. But in the bedroom she must become the complete freak."

"She's got pretty feet."

"Naturally. You could lick marmalade off the feet, they are so clean and pretty. Very nice high arches too. Tender arches. She really is something. I want one like her."

"Me too," said Max.

The city went mad around them.

"They only cost forty euros at Barbès," Hanuman said.

"What?"

"The whores. They cost fifty at Pigalle and only forty at Barbès. But I do not think the quality will be quite as good. We'll see."

"Oh." He hadn't thought to ask where he was taking Hanuman.

"Well, we must have almost arrived, I can hear the Métro on the bridge. You were right, that was very quick."

"Um, yeah." He looked around and sort of lost track of why he'd come here himself.

"Great. Listen, it has been very enjoyable speaking with you. You can leave me right under the bridge, and I will manage finding her from here."

"She's going to meet you here?"

"No, it's across the street and in this alley right near here."

"Well, what about getting across the street and finding— everything."

"No need to worry, my friend. I will find her."

"Alone?"

"I will ask someone to get me across the street. And then the alley is right there. She will be waiting for me."

"You're going to ask some stranger to get you there?"

"Yes."

Max looked above, frowning at the bottom of the bridge, the Métro clacking over the tracks. "Yeah, yeah, I mean we're here and everything, but—"

"Great. Well, thank you so much, Max. It has been a major pleasure."

"Yeah. Okay then. Listen, good luck with everything."

When they unhooked arms, it took a little wind out of Max. Hanuman brought out a folded cane from his pocket and poked the ground with it. The stick eventually hit a bridge support, and Hanuman turned in a circle.

Max watched until Hanuman started talking to another man. Max couldn't stand it any longer. He got between the man and Hanuman and hooked arms again.

"I'm just going to take you all the way," he said.

"Max?"

"I was going this way anyway, and it's so close. Let me take you there myself. I'd feel a lot better about it."

"All right. It is only that—"

"What?"

"I do not want you to get attached."

"Oh, come on. She's yours—I get that."

"No, not to her."

"Then to who?"

No answer. Hanuman shrugged, shifting from foot to foot.

"Come on. Let's go," Max said. They crossed the street together. "You pretty excited to meet her?"

"Sure. I suppose. I do this most days of the week, you know?"

"You're a lucky man, Hanuman. It must really be something."

They rounded a corner and came upon a row of prostitutes. Max only really saw one. The one. A much older version of the exact woman they'd described earlier: mole on her cheek, curly black hair, red lipstick. He couldn't believe his eyes. He smiled bashfully at her, crinkled his nose, and made little near-curtsies.

"Max?" Hanuman said.

"Yes. Sorry. Well, here she is," he said, walking him up to her. "Hello."

"*Salut. C'est quarante pour une demi heure.*"

"*Très bien,*" Hanuman answered, unhooking his arm. "Well, thank you again, Max. Have a good one."

"Oh, yeah, I definitely will. Hey, I never actually told you what I was even doing in Paris. It's a pretty crazy story. I'd be happy to just wait for you until you come back down, and then I'll tell you all about why I'm here. It's kind of a big deal."

"No, no, I would not feel comfortable with you waiting around for me."

"It's really no trouble at all, it'd be my pleasure, honestly. It's a lovely day, and I could just sit and think. And then I'd walk you home, and we could discuss how everything went and, you know, I could tell you about how I'm looking for my mother and everything."

"Your mother?"

"Yeah!" Max said, feeling he'd piqued Hanuman's interest.

Hanuman put a hand on Max's shoulder. "Hey. Look at me. No, look at me. You'll be all right."

"I don't like the idea of just leaving you like this."

"I found her, right? We made it. I will be fine, you will be fine, everything is fine. Now you go on and continue enjoying this marvelous day. Go on. You can do that, I know you can."

"How will you get back?"

"I've been getting around cities for a long time."

"So, good-bye?"

"Until chance reunites us. How about that?"

Hanuman winked his beautiful discolored eye at him and walked off with the woman Max thought they had invented together.

EIGHTEEN

MAX TREKKED MOST all of Paris after leaving Hanuman, simultaneously coming to terms with the fact that he'd meet his mother soon and trying his best to forget about it, pretending he was just a normal guy walking around a pretty city. At about eight in the evening, when he got back to the apartment, there was a lot of commotion. It sounded like a party of people in there, but it was only Jiddo shouting at the wicker chair about how hedge funds own shares of stock that pay dividends, and Téta in the study, yelling in a tired, rasping Arabic. Presumably into the phone. Jiddo didn't lose any momentum on his financial sermon when Max strode by him and to the door of the study.

Téta was not on the phone. She was on her knees. Her back facing Max, she rocked back and forth at another woman's feet. Her shouting had transitioned to moaning and begging something of this woman. Max could see the crown of the woman's head as she bent over Téta, trying to gently pull her up. She wore a navy-blue abaya, and her maple-brown hair was in a loose ponytail. He knew who she was but didn't.

The woman lifted her head and said, "Hakeem," her voice smoky and low. Now Hakeem felt like it might be his real name.

He let out the breath he'd been holding, a puff of something between laughter and getting socked in the stomach, *Haah*.

"*Ya Allah shu hilweh*," she said. Her face was that of an alcoholic who spends her days in the sun, squinting, grimacing, laughing, weeping. She was striking in a worn-out, hard sort of way, with lines and scars scored across her cheeks like the palm of a hand.

"Hello," said Max.

Téta let herself be helped up, her face red and puffy. She said something accusatory to her daughter while pointing at Max.

He and his mother stood ten feet apart. "You don't speak Arabic," she said.

"No, I don't."

"You came alone?"

Max glanced over his shoulder and then back at her.

"Rasheed is coming?" she said.

"No."

Téta attacked her with a few more Arabic words. His mother kept her eyes on him, looking defensive, suspicious of some kind of setup or trick. She said, "When did you arrive?"

His heart slammed into his ribs, trying to break free. "Yeah—I got here this morning."

"Yes. You are happy to be here then?"

"I'm so happy." The tears had already begun welling over.

"Good. So you are enjoying the city."

"It's a really nice city."

"Very good."

He could only look at her for so long. His eyes dashed around the walls of the room, at the portraits of a young Jiddo welcoming or being welcomed by different men from all over the world: in suits, in kaffiyehs, gandouras, and dashikis; handshakes and smiles at dinner parties, and one on a landing strip in front of a fighter jet.

He looked back at her, propelled to break the distance between them that was harder and harder to sustain. He took a step closer. Her shoulders tensed. He stopped. He could see she wanted him to stop. She wasn't ready.

"It's really so nice here," he said again.

"How are you at school? Are you a good student at school?"

"I am."

She looked at the floor. "I will not stay for long, Hakeem."

"Oh. No. Yeah, okay."

"You must stay for your son!" Téta said, and then came to his side and put her hand on his shoulder. It felt like a warm iron, heating his skin up to an itch. She said something biting to Samira again in Arabic, and wiped at her nose with a ball of Kleenex.

His mother said to him, "I have too many obligations there. You understand, Hakeem?"

"Of course."

"I don't travel like this usually. This is exceptional. Your Téta told me you were ill. I came because over the phone she said you were very ill. Now she has confessed this is not true." Though her expression didn't change, he could see her chest lifting and dropping underneath the abaya, her toughness failing her. "I am happy to find you are healthy."

"Yeah, I'm healthy."

When she spoke, it sounded like she was giving herself orders. "Now that I am here, it is my duty to tell you these things face-to-face."

"What things?"

She answered with a question. "What is it you wanted? To see me? To talk like this? Something else?"

"What I wanted?" He hadn't thought of it in concrete terms. It hadn't occurred to him that anyone, let alone her, would ask why he wanted to know his mother.

"I mean to say, what did you hope for when you decided to look for me? What was your intention?"

He suddenly felt ashamed of his tears. "I don't know. Since they lied to you the way Rasheed lied to me, I thought maybe you'd want to know me." As he said it out loud, it sunk in that he'd gotten it all wrong. She wouldn't answer, and her gaze turned unfocused, as if daydreaming. Her stare stopped just short of him, and he felt a minuscule bottle pop inside his heart, followed by an immediate and profound need to sleep.

Still in her daze, she said, "Of course it is a great chance to be able to see you. But it will cause more suffering, you understand? I sacrificed my right to be your mother many years ago. I have no right."

He felt his eyes grow heavy, like he really was falling asleep. "You knew I was alive. All this time."

Her nostrils flared.

"You never once looked for me?" he asked, resting his eyes for a few seconds.

"I had you, and then I left you, Hakeem, for too long. I have no delusions about that. I could not have done it differently. I was a bad mother even before we separated. I had no right to come back into your life."

In an oddly detached way, he said, "I would have given you the right."

She snapped out of her daydream and took in a big breath. It sounded like a sob perched at the edge of her throat, a little bird that she managed to vacuum back down just before it flew out of her mouth. This woke him up some. She said, "It would be wrong. Irresponsible. I chose another life." She peeked around him and out the open door of the study. "You are sure Rasheed is not coming?"

A neediness crept through him, a hunger to break their distance, to get another glimpse of her emotions. "I'm sure."

"I did not plan to see you again. I have long grieved you as my child."

Max's body craved her more than ever.

"But you are welcome to visit the school at the camp if you like, in Beirut."

His voice warbled. "You're not in Jordan?"

"No. I'm in Shatila, in Lebanon. You were told this so we would all meet here." She glanced at Téta. "She wanted to unite us all here. She lies to get what she wants."

A prickle of heat started in Max's lower back, and then another, and then a whole desert of them crawled up to his neck, crossing paths with cold droplets of sweat. His voice got shakier. "I thought you were—I mean—you knew I thought you were dead?"

"Yes."

He looked at Téta again. Because it was easier to talk at her than to his mom. "And you all just decided that was best. Let me believe I had no mother." Téta stared back at him with the alarm of a deer feeling an arrow stick in its side.

His mother said, "You would have come looking for me, and then I would be getting in the way of you and Rasheed. He holds me responsible for the murder of his family. I could never force myself back into his life."

"What he told you is better than this truth," insisted Téta to Max.

"Which is what?" he said, even though it had been made perfectly clear.

They didn't speak for nearly a full minute. He focused on the grandfather clock to his mother's left.

At 8:09 she said, "The truth is, we are strangers to each other."

At 8:09 and ten seconds he responded, "Did you want me in the first place?"

"I was happy when I found out I was pregnant. At that time I had the vision of both fighting and being a fully committed mother. But because I knew Rasheed would take care of you, I allowed myself to be away for long periods. He loved you better than anyone, much better than I did, or your real father. I took advantage of this and was gone often. I promised myself I'd make it up to you, that I'd be a good mother later." She smoothed back some loose strands in her ponytail. "But I was failing you, and it extinguished something inside of me. Then Rasheed's family was killed, and I had to hide. The SLA caught and imprisoned me. I learned that I am not so strong. They broke me. I told them everything I knew. Nine years of hell, only to give it all up. I could not go back to fighting with my brothers and sisters in the resistance because I had betrayed them, and also because I didn't want to fight in that way anymore. My father would not have me in his family, and I could not come to you and Rasheed. His hate for me was too strong, and this hate would take you away from him. I found his address a few years ago and wrote him the letter that explained I was out but would not come bothering you two. I had already taken too much. We couldn't share you. And by then I understood that one either is or is not a mother. There is no telling yourself, I will be a mother later."

"And now you work with children," he said.

"Yes. I did live in Jordan for a while, but years ago I received the message that it would be safe for me to come back to Beirut. I met philanthropists in Amman, and we raised some funds.

The people I had betrayed were not so angry with me anymore, and they agreed to let me move into the refugee camp and build the school—"

"*Khalas*," Téta interrupted. "We need a break from this kind of depressing talk. I will make some tea now, and we can sit in the living room with Jiddo and tell some of the nice stories to Hakeem for a while. Samira, tell him about your kitten when you were a little girl." She put on a grandmotherly smile and turned to Max. "It only had three legs! Very cute. Very cute story. Samira loved this kitten too much. Tell him, Samira. Tell him."

Before Téta could go to make tea, the front door of the apartment rang loudly, startling as an end-of-the-game buzzer. Someone from the street was asking to be let up.

"Who is that?" Samira said.

Téta stared her down for a beat and then went to answer. Max and his mother stayed glued to their respective stances in the study and listened to Téta open the door. They heard the surprise in her voice at who had come.

MAX COULDN'T LOOK at his mother straight on. She was too beautiful, and too horrible. Rasheed's voice traveled through the apartment, and then Nadine's followed. It was them. They were here. Nadine had told Rasheed, and now they had come to find him.

His mother said, "You told me Rasheed was not coming."

"I didn't know," he said, on the verge of dropping to his knees and begging for her forgiveness, as if everything would have gone well had Rasheed not shown up.

She came toward Max, and now he tensed up, as if she was about to strike him. But she hugged him. With all the might he felt in her arms, he could have let his legs go and she would have continued to hold him up without difficulty. Her hair smelled like warm bread, and her abaya like a new cardboard box. It was a wonderful blindness to be so close to her that he couldn't see, only feel her. Their breaths harmonized, he relaxed, and her warmth crossed over into his body. It was exactly what he'd come for, and with Rasheed and Nadine's footsteps approaching, he understood it would now be taken away.

He hugged his mother tighter. She abruptly pushed him off and held him by the shoulders. "I promised myself I would not touch you," she said, "and now look at me."

He heard Nadine, from the living room, ask, "Where's Max?"

"Who?" Téta said. "The boy?" It echoed like in a cathedral.

His mother looked over his shoulder, and her eyes shot wide open at whoever lurked in the doorway. That was when she said, "Good-bye, Hakeem. Visit Shatila if you want. Anytime."

He turned and saw Rasheed creeping into the room. This man who had pretended to be his father and scared away his mother. Samira took one large side step away from Max, the three of them in a triangle now. She kept her head down, transforming into an icon, a statue—no longer alive. Rasheed didn't need to so much as glance at her to sap her life. His eyes never averted from Max's face. He looked sick, yellowish, sweaty, and determined. He lugged himself closer. Samira spoke another soft good-bye as she walked out of the room.

"Wait," Max said, watching his mother's back as Rasheed reached him.

And then Nadine appeared in the doorway. Out of context, these people were appallingly dreamlike. Nadine got out of his mother's way to let her pass.

Rasheed was hugging him. His heart beat up against Max's chest, banging on a wall. Behind Nadine, and into the living room, Max's mother got a little bit smaller. Jiddo was still on the couch, scowling at his wristwatch. Téta stood behind him, washing her hands in the air while her daughter crossed the wood floor to leave.

Max heard the locks unclick, the shrill of the hinges yawning open and then closing, but before it did, Jiddo blurted, "Samira!"

She must have turned around. There was complete silence.

Jiddo said, "Do not waste any more time with Ali. He is beneath you. Obey me and go to your room now."

Then came the clap of the door.

Rasheed pushed down on the tops of Max's shoulders and got so close it made for a fish-eye view of his great sad face. Max hadn't gotten fifteen minutes with his mother before Rasheed scared her off all over again. He'd waited seventeen years for those fifteen minutes. Max imagined her riding the elevator to the ground floor. He pictured her stepping out onto the sidewalk, then walking toward the Métro. She was already on that plane. She'd landed in Beirut. She was in a cab toward the refugee camp. She was holding an orphan. Giving a class. Eating with people she cared about. She was in her own bed. And Max was standing here doing nothing, staring into this sick man's face.

Hanging off him, and out of breath, Rasheed said, "You should not leave home this way."

Max wanted to throw him. He had an overwhelming urge to throw him.

"Max," Nadine said, "be fair."

The ludicrousness of the situation tightened its grip on him. While taking Rasheed's hands off him, he asked Nadine, "What did you two talk about on the plane?"

"What?"

"You've lived across the street from each other for years, and suddenly you're traveling to Paris together. That's funny to me. I'd just love to know what you all chatted about." His heartbeat throbbed up into his cheeks. "You two have become a little

team, huh? Rasheed, good for you for tolerating 'those people,'"
he said, pointing at Nadine. "And Nadine, thanks for telling
him where I was. It was the one thing I asked you not to do. It
may even be the one thing I've ever asked you not to do."

"We came together for you, Max," Rasheed said in an
unbearably suppliant way, bending to the side a little as though
he had a stomach cramp. "You killed us by disappearing like
that."

"Us?" Max said. His anger swelled into a power he would
soon have to release. "Let me guess," he said to Rasheed, "you
two have fallen in love and now you're getting married. Oh, no,
I'm being silly. You don't like women in that way, Rasheed.
You're more of a man's man, aren't you?"

Rasheed looked away from Max.

"Max," Nadine said.

"Hakeem," said Max. "Funniest thing. My name, as it turns
out, is Hakeem."

Rasheed put his hands back on Max's shoulders. "I need to
explain many things."

"Get your hands off me."

Rasheed clenched his teeth and twisted up his face as he took
one hand off Max's shoulder to clutch at his chest like he was
having heart pains. "Max," he said, "calm it down. Please,
calm it down and listen."

"Calm it down? No."

Rasheed stared at the ground like he was about to vomit.
Nadine came to Rasheed's side and put her hand on his back,
saying, "He's not well, Max."

"I can see that, Doctor, thank you."

Rasheed defended her with a grumble. "You do not need to
speak to her like this, Max."

What the fuck was this allegiance between them? He grabbed
the top of his head and felt his mind slipping.

"Calm it down," Rasheed whispered to the floor. "Please, calm it down." Nadine told Rasheed he needed to be sitting.

Max said, "It'd kill me if I calmed it down any more than I have. You are a liar."

Nadine said, "Stop it. Do not do this right now."

When he looked down at Rasheed, it maddened him. All he saw was a pitiful sagging man. A man who appeared to be saying, *She is gone for good, and you are my son again. You are my son, and you will come home with me and live like me and become me.* Max's tears narrowed Rasheed's body, turning him into a pin-man. He said, "You're weak. You disgust me, do you know that?"

"Hakeem," Téta said.

And at the same time Nadine shouted, "Max!"

"I have grown out of you, do you understand? I don't want to know you." Then he whispered, so as not to let the lump in his throat win his voice, "I hate you so much."

Rasheed straightened his back. Panic scribbled his lips as he reached out to put his hands on Max's shoulders again. Max shoved him as hard as he could. Rasheed caught his fall ten feet away. He took yet a few more steps back until he bumped into a small table. A phone on top of it plunged to the ground and made a lasting ding sound followed by the dial tone. He slowly sat down on the carpet and leaned against the leg of the table.

"What are you doing?" Max said.

Rasheed slumped to his side. Invisible hands throttled him, and his head trembled. His mouth tipped open into a muted lion's roar. It looked like theater, like bad acting. But he wasn't acting. His face purpled. The tendons in his neck became pronounced tree roots. A blood vessel popped in one eye and bled across the white.

"Dad." Max's tears cleared, his eyes becoming brand new, and Rasheed was human-size again. Nadine dropped down and put her hand under his head as she shouted for Téta to call an ambulance. As if high voltages ran through him, Rasheed lay both stiff and vibrating at once.

"Dad, what are you doing? Stop it. What are you doing? Get up."

The fright on Rasheed's face—that absolute shivering fear— was the sole thing Max hated so much now.

Nadine put her ear up to Rasheed's chest. He stopped moving shortly after that.

"Dad, get up. Stop it, Dad. Get up."

NINTEEN

IN THE HOSPITAL, at around ten that evening, a doctor came out to tell Nadine what was going on. She translated for Max, explaining that Rasheed had suffered some kind of attack that led to a devastating stroke.

"A heart attack?" Max said. He had felt he was dreaming when he shoved Rasheed across the room and watched him sit down. The dream had since crumbled only to reveal another, even more impossible reality.

Nadine said, "It mimics a heart attack. It's called transient apical ballooning syndrome." She tried to embrace him, but he put his hand up to stop her.

"No," he said. "No, no. This is wrong. This is a mistake."

A clot had formed in the left ventricle, the main pumping chamber, where the clot embolized to the brain, causing the major stroke.

They said to expect significant change in Rasheed's behavior when he woke up. He might not remember people. There'd been brain damage, but they didn't know how limited his motor skills would be quite yet. He'd probably need intense physical and occupational therapy. Other than that, there were only blood thinners to take, to prevent another clot, and lots of vitamins.

Rasheed was not connected to any machines. The doctors had even removed the IV drip. It created swelling in his brain because his water retention was too high.

When Rasheed came to, muscle seemed to be clinging to his right cheekbone with a last bit of strength, moments away from dripping off his face. His eye on that same side was slanted, the heaviness of his brow too much to support. Half of his mouth dragged to a frown, like a dead fish being held up in the middle. They warned Max that Rasheed might have lost a fair amount of lucidity.

"Hi, Dad, it's me." Max sat at his side. Everyone else left the room.

Rasheed's voice crackled. "Who else would you be?"

Max scanned his face a long time, still unsure if Rasheed recognized him. He saw his nose hair poking out like little witch brooms. His nails were curled and yellowish. "Do you remember my name?"

"Why? Have you forgotten it?"

"It's Max."

"I know that. I named you myself. Squeeze my hand, Maxie."

"Okay, Dad."

"Squeeze it harder. As hard as you can. I don't feel anything. Harder. Don't look like that. It's nice not to feel anything." He gave a crooked smile. "Tell me a story." After a moment, he said, "No? Okay. You are tired of stories. Did you know that some of the stories about Kip and his Man-Dog brother— What was his name again?"

Max felt as if the ball in his throat was about to pull off him, like a rock breaking free from a cliff. "I'm. I'm so sorry."

"Stop that. Tell me, what was his name? The Man-Dog."

He took a big breath. "Paul."

"Ah, yes. I remember now. His name was Brandon. You always think it is Paul. I don't know why. Anyway. Please, stop crying. Do you want me to say what I was going to say? Or not?"

"You need lots of rest, Dad, okay? You need lots of rest to get better. That's how you're going to get better."

"I have too much time for rest. Now I want to confess to you something about Kip and his Man-Dog brother. Okay?"

"Okay."

"Some of the time, when I couldn't think of a new adventure for them, I borrowed adventures from other stories. Adventures from Tintin and Peter Pan, and so on and so on."

"I know, Dad."

"You know? You know and you didn't say anything? You're a good son. Don't shake your head. You'll upset me. I'm feeling under the weather. Tell me—they gave me so many drugs I can't see perfectly—how do I look? Really."

"Handsome. Handsome as ever."

"It bothers me when you cry like this. I'll tell you about all of my other tales. Do you want me to tell you all of the truth so help me God?" He gave another faint smile.

"That's all right, Dad, not now."

"Squeeze my hand." Max studied this new face for a few minutes before Rasheed spoke again, his eyes shut: "Let me ask you something."

"Anything."

"Do you love Nadine?"

"What?"

"The black woman neighbor. Do you love her? If I knew I was going to be dying in a hospital one of these days, I would have asked you many more things. And maybe told you some more things too."

"You are not dying."

"Do you love her?"

"Yeah."

"Does she love you?"

"Maybe not the same way, but yeah. I think so."

"Do you two make love?"

"What?"

"What, what? I am a curious man."

"Sort of."

"Sort of you have made love to her?"

"Yeah."

"Wow."

"Yeah. I know, wow."

"And she is a good friend to you also?"

"Definitely."

"She is a good woman. Much too old maybe, but you have chosen a good woman."

"I've always liked Coach Tim too."

Rasheed let out an amused puff from his nose, and then said, "Don't let this go on too long, okay?"

"What do you mean?"

"This. Me like this. I don't care for this to go on too long."

"What?"

"I know you hear what I'm saying. Remember what I'm telling you. I do not want this for too long. Squeeze my hand. Harder. Harder, please. Max?"

He spoke so softly now that Max had to put his ear right up to his mouth. Rasheed said, "You were too happy for a long while with me, I think."

"Yeah, I was." Max watched him sleep.

When Max reported this coherent conversation to the doctors, they looked at him as though he'd imagined the whole thing. The horrifying part was that the next time Rasheed woke up, fifteen hours later, he didn't speak to anyone. He had the expression of a mystified baby. Innocent again, he absorbed the visual overstimulation of the people around him, maybe recognizing some of them but not knowing from where. He moved incredibly slowly. He looked down at where Max touched his arm, confused by the contact. His jaw wobbled left to right, in what looked like unceasing worry.

He cried for a woman named Noor. Whoever came, he called out that name, Noor! Noor! When Téta arrived, she said that Noor had been Rasheed's nanny when he was a young child. Max asked the doctors why they were giving him so many drugs, and they said they weren't. He wasn't on any drugs at all.

Rasheed couldn't form comprehensible sentences anymore. He gave up trying to communicate. Nadine believed he still understood what they said to him. No one knew how long he'd be stuck like this, but for the moment, his brain functions were breaking down one section at a time.

He could move his arms and hands, but had little coordination. He had trouble keeping his back straight in the wheelchair on the way to labs and to get CAT scans and MRIs, so Max or Nadine had to pin his chest to the back of the chair with a hand. The nurses spoon-fed him soft foods. He could have anything that slipped down his throat without any chewing required. Max developed a weak stomach and vomited a few times a day at random, and had clanging headaches that made it hard to see or hear properly.

NADINE WENT BACK to work in Clarence. The world had to carry on. Max stayed at the hospital for a week, and Rasheed's condition stabilized, not improving but not getting any worse either. He looked frozen in a state of astonishment. When the occupational therapists came in, his incessant look of alarm intensified, as if they were there to torture him.

The doctors said that 50 percent of subarachnoid hemorrhage stroke victims, the kind Rasheed suffered from, do survive. Fifty percent, Max thought, like flipping a coin. They told him that 10 percent of the ones who do not survive die within a week, 20 percent within a month, and 30 percent within a year. Nadine called Max and the doctors every day. Not being a citizen, Rasheed couldn't benefit from the French health care system for any sensible price. Eventually everyone agreed Rasheed could be flown home and cared for in his own house.

Téta bought them the plane tickets and told Max, "You will take the credit card, okay? Now you are in charge of the money." She looked at Rasheed again. "Until he is feeling better." It was the card linked to the Banque du Liban account that held the Ziad Jabbir deposits.

They checked out of the hospital and flew to Clarence. Nadine was there to pick them up once they landed.

When they got back to Marion Street late in the night, the house felt foreign. Max went to turn on the lights, but Rasheed grunted. It sounded more like a no than a yes, so he kept them off. Nadine rolled Rasheed to his room. Walking in darkness did one or the other to Max: compressed space so that walls and corners seemed inches away from smashing his face, or made him feel he was about to walk off a precipice to his death. Now he experienced both of these sensations intermittently, the claustrophobic tightness with each inhalation and an unendurable openness with every exhalation. He was apprehensive about where his feet landed, as if he were at the edge of a hole that could bring him under and into a space like his tree house.

When his eyes adjusted, the silhouettes of the couch and TV and table looked like they'd been cut out of the blue darkness.

With her hands on her hips, Nadine looked at the one tiny window high above Rasheed's bed. "No lights going to come in here, is it?" She said this would not do at all. He'd be spending a lot of time in one place and needed a room with more natural light; she wasn't open to letting him sit in the dark all day as he would have preferred. They wheeled him to Max's bedroom, where the three big windows kept it lit most all of the day.

Rocket smelled cleaner than usual, and Max picked up on Mrs. Yang's perfume. Nadine grabbed Rocket's face, kissed her between the eyes, and whispered severely, "I love you so much." Rocket sneezed as soon as Nadine let her go.

She had to show Max how to transfer Rasheed from the chair to the bed, how to undress him, how to clean the catheter condom and put it back on him, and how to roll him over to avoid bed sores. She'd already called Complete Home Health Care and arranged for a telephone meeting for Max in the morning so he could introduce himself as Rasheed's official guardian and care-taker. The nurses would watch Rasheed at the house during the day, continuing his occupational therapy while Max went to school and Nadine was at work. He said he'd call, but though tomorrow was his first day of his senior year, he wasn't going back to school yet. He'd tell the nurses they could stop in to do the therapy sessions but that he didn't want them staying all day.

Max and Nadine tucked Rasheed in like a little boy and sat on the bed until they heard him snoring. Then they gushed silently.

Nadine got her pajamas from her place and came to bed with him. She didn't want to leave him alone and admitted to needing the company too.

The next day, Nadine brought pills that Max was to give to Rasheed if he couldn't sleep. But since the attack, Rasheed had been sleeping sixteen or more hours a day. Max took the pills himself to get rest he wouldn't have otherwise, and Nadine did the same.

She pretty much moved in. In the mornings, he made her breakfast while she got ready for work. At first they put Rasheed in the wheelchair and sat him at the kitchen table, but later they decided it easier to eat in his room by his bed. Nadine returned home from the hospital with more blood thinners and supplies, like new pillows for his wheelchair, a hot water bottle, vitamins, sponges, and lubricating ointment for cracked lips.

When Mr. Yang showed up, he said, "Hello, Mr. Boulos!" with his usual enthusiasm. "Ah, Mr. Boulos"—he shook his head, looking around the room as though it were terribly messy—"we must change the environmental feeling in here. Then you will feel much better. You will see."

With his garden wagon, he carted over all the plants and flowers from his greenhouse that he thought could survive in the bedroom: around sixty or seventy of them in all. The room overflowed with greenery, the floor and windowsills covered with ceramic pots, stems holding up leaves and bulbs at various heights, corn silk orchids and black orchids, cacti, ferns, and small trees. Mr. Yang dropped by every day to teach Max how to tend to them. Watering the soil, spraying the leaves, pruning, and positioning them in the light at certain times of day was both a distraction from and an extension of taking care of Rasheed.

Mrs. Yang spent a couple of hours a day in the room with Rasheed and Robby, knitting and humming, feeding Rasheed mashed-up grapes, telling stories loosely based on Chinese folklore and about a brother of hers who'd had an attack like Rasheed's and recovered fully within a couple of months. She claimed her brother was now even sharper than he was before the attack. People said he was much nicer now too!

When Mrs. Yang laughed, Rasheed's eyes brightened, became a little less fearful.

Nadine told Max she'd managed to get his mother's phone number from Téta before leaving, so whenever he was ready to give her a call, he could. He said he'd get it from her some other time. He had all but forgotten his mother and would now give anything to have another conversation with Rasheed. Most of all, he dreamed of Rasheed nodding his head and acknowledging how much Max loved him. Because when Max said "I love you," Rasheed only looked back at him with that stupefied expression and trembling jaw.

It'd been ten days since the end of Max's summer break, and his school had been calling to check in on him, asking when he thought he'd be coming back. He said he didn't know yet. Physiotherapists arrived in the afternoons to bend and twist Rasheed around. Max could tell he hated it. In the evenings that Nadine didn't work, she and Max had drinks and ate dinner at Rasheed's bedside, feeding him and talking about their days. Rasheed watched them like a startled cat.

Nadine brought a shower chair from work. They sat Rasheed on it in the tub and washed him with a sponge glove. They had tacitly decided to act as casually and unsentimentally around Rasheed as possible, as though they weren't overcome by his new condition. At times Max caught himself succeeding at this so well that he stopped thinking of Rasheed as a person. Max cleaned him like a car, naked and slumped in the chair, the water combing his body hair into groves. Only after a good five minutes into the scrubbing—leaning him to one side to get under a butt cheek and then the other, rinsing him down, caring for and forgetting him at the same time while listening to Nadine talk about work as she put almond oil in her hair or brushed her teeth or plucked her eyebrows—did he remember the picture they inhabited: Rasheed a prisoner in his own body, the dependency that humiliated him, how his son had done this to him, and his moans that unquestionably begged for mercy.

But the hurt caught up to Max most of all when he left Rasheed alone. When he'd gone to do the dishes or take Rocket for a walk, or when he lay in bed with Nadine, waiting for the sleeping pills to take effect. That's when the injustice and guilt and grief pounded down on him hardest, and he went faint with an impotent rage.

THE MOON WAS full. Its copper light poured through the tiny window and splashed across Nadine's cheek. She was awake. Max could actually hear her blinking, like hands clapping in on themselves.

She worried they were getting hooked on the sleeping pills so decided to stop using them for a while. "You want to know how to fall asleep?" she said. "It's like in that movie." Her eyes reflected apostrophes of the orange light.

Max drummed a little beat on his belly. "What movie?"

"I don't remember what it's called, but it's a war film," she said, as though there were only a few. "They said the trick is to try as hard as possible to stay awake. And when you convince yourself you absolutely have to stay up, sleep takes you."

"But now I know it's a trick."

"It doesn't matter."

"Why not?" His right eye closed more than the left, the outside corners of his eyelashes crosshatched with sleep.

"Because I've done it before. It's one of those things that works even when you know you're lying."

The bizarre moonlight made his skin look like an apricot soaked in a jar of water. The glow individualized every distinct hair and crease and birthmark, as if they were separate creatures that just happened to gather on his body for tonight.

"Then why don't you do it?" he said. "Why don't you convince yourself and sleep?"

"Camaraderie, sweet boy. I'm waiting for you. Once we agree to go through with the plan, we'll execute it together."

"Right." He clapped his hand on his stomach.

"Do you want to close the curtain on our prison window up there?" she asked.

"No, I want to see you," he said, staring up at the ceiling fan.

"Oh, so you're fully awake now?"

"I'm applying your method."

"It doesn't work if you talk."

She rolled into him and let her nose mash up against his shoulder. He turned and yawned into her forehead, letting his teeth bump her skin. She sniffled like she did right before temporarily drifting off.

They found themselves in improbable positions. Her limbs unhurriedly splayed outward, like a firework exploding in slow motion. She smelled of something that didn't resemble anything he knew outside of her. She pushed him to an extremity of the bed, Rasheed's old bed, her feverishly hot knuckle sticking him in the side. When he thought of Rasheed lying in the other room, he was capable of sweating out all his liquids in a matter of seconds. It turned the mattress into a damp sponge.

An hour or so later, Nadine said, "You still awake?"

"Yep."

"Want to know what I was thinking?"

"You know I do."

"I was thinking, why is reincarnation always about becoming animals or plants?"

"What do you mean?"

"What if we turned into other stuff? Like a shock of electricity or a gust of wind or something."

He looked at her profile. She beamed with discovery and said, "I could be reincarnated as a thought. Or a note in a laugh. A single strand of sunshine. The very end of a taste!"

Max loved her more viscerally in this moment than the one before. As he pressed his wet cheek against her shoulder, he observed an entire lifetime. His hand gravitated to her chin, cupping it from below. His fingers grew up her face, caging her lips. She kissed and then nibbled the meat of his palm and scooted it up with her nose to her brow. His fingers lay on her hair like a lazy benediction.

"Okay, I'm ready," he said. "I'll never fall asleep again."

The night carried on like a lost boat on placid water.

TWENTY

COACH TIM BROUGHT birds. Two mosaic canaries. He said Rasheed loved birds. Max had no idea but embraced such new bits of information. Tim looked bad: chalky skin, black circles around red eyes, an overall droopiness.

Max pointed him to where Rasheed slept. He heard Tim set the cage down among the plants, and soon after, listened to him wail like a trumpeting elephant. When it had quieted down in there, Max peeked in. Tim looked weirdly effeminate nestling his nose into Rasheed's neck, lying on his side with his legs drawn up to his chest, whimpering and smiling and half sleeping all at once. The same man who shouted drill sequences on the court, who had talked to Max and his teammates before a game with the vehemence of sending kids off to war—telling them to go out there and play for their school, their loved ones, and sometimes even their country. He drank American beer, used sports analogies, tucked his bright polos into light blue jeans, and shielded his bald head with that Spurs cap. Coach Tim, melting desperate against Rasheed's diminished body. Rocket mewled from her plant-encircled bed, and the canaries chirped like a pedestrian walk sign.

Images of Tim and Rasheed kissing, cuddling, and having sex changed the meaning of all those nights Rasheed came home doe-eyed and drunk, not knowing how to look at Max, and ready for sleep. Max had once interpreted these looks on Rasheed's face as his needing a woman. Seeing Tim transformed the way he thought about Rasheed's body. He'd never considered it a sexual entity, and this added an extra dimension to the tragedy, to what Max had taken away.

Rasheed's eyes were closed, but Max could tell he wasn't sleeping. The deadened half of him faced the wall, so he looked a lot like his old self from Max's angle. He thought he saw him smile—as Tim dragged his sad head up and down like a child sucking his thumb, driving into sleep—but he couldn't be sure.

Tim stayed for dinner and wordlessly observed Max prepare *banh chiao* and some other Cambodian dishes for them, along with soup, mashed potatoes, and homemade applesauce and chocolate pudding.

Nadine walked in the front door, and the sight of her enfeebled Max, the way beauty sometimes can. Her mortality, her impermanence, her life, occasionally saddened him so much he wanted to lie down. What's the point if even she doesn't last forever?

Seeing Nadine and Tim in the same room reminded him of the car incident. How Tim stood in the background and watched his then ex-lover get batted around by Rodney.

They sat among the plants and flowers around Rasheed's bed. Max said to Tim, "You shouldn't have let me get so much playing time," as he passed Nadine the plate of spring rolls.

"What are you talking about?" said Tim.

"I probably cost us half of our games when I played for you. I mean, the others were so much better, Danny Danesh and company."

He didn't mean it as a real reproach against Tim. He actually felt it a good conversation starter, maybe even a little funny. Shouldn't they still aim to be a little funny? It made Nadine smile at least. But Tim stayed quiet, his forehead wrinkled. Then he mumbled that Danny Danesh was an idiot.

Something about the way he said it made Max crack up. A drained, senseless laughter took hold of him for so long that his stomach muscles felt like they were ripping. Eventually it infected Nadine and Tim too, but not in the same way. Max was hysterical, repeating Danny Danesh's name in a high-pitched pleading voice. He felt high for the first time in weeks. He stopped when he worried he'd choke.

"No," Tim said, "you're right. You shouldn't have been playing much at all, really."

Nadine said, "Seriously?"

"Yeah, sometimes I told myself he'd surprise everyone this time, but mostly it was because I liked him. Or maybe I thought I was expressing my feelings for Rasheed publicly by having him play."

Rasheed hadn't eaten. He'd been refusing food all day. Max suddenly felt provocative. "Tim. Why didn't you do anything when Rodney was hitting him that day? Remember?"

"Of course I remember. After Kelly moved in with you guys, we had a number of fights. In the end he told me not to, under any circumstances, come near you or him again. I guess I was teaching him a lesson by following his rules to a tee. The hardest thing was watching you go to pieces. You weren't a boy who expressed himself much, hardly at all, really, and watching your face was the heart-wrenching part. As for Reed, I knew a couple of slaps wouldn't be the end of the world for him. I needed something even more dramatic before I could come fighting for him, after all the cruel things we said to each other."

There were no other clues of Tim and Rasheed being lovers that Max could think of, other than Tim's absence during the Kelly months. He was dumbstruck by how little he knew about the world he'd grown up in.

"But you made up." Max felt a pang of jealousy.

"Yes, he came back to me. But sometimes I think he did so he could have someone to talk about you with. How much he loved you. Wouldn't shut up about how proud he was and how you'd grown beyond him."

Tim's effort to quell Max's regret didn't help. In fact, it was aggravating. Max wanted to ask if he knew that Rasheed lay here paralyzed because of his own son. Did Tim know that? Did he know what it was like to disable the man who raised you? Did he know what it was like to have ignored that man for the past four years? Not caring for him like he should have? Like he obviously should have. Did Tim have any idea? Did he know that Max would never sleep soundly again? And now this pain, this pain that Tim endeavored to relieve, was the strongest thread of attachment Max had to Rasheed. He hated when anyone tried to take that away from him. To sever them again. Nadine had told him he wasn't responsible for what was happening, but he made it clear to her that he didn't want to hear it. His culpability was necessary to him. It allowed him to be emotionally obsessed.

Tim addressed Nadine. "You're over here often."

She stared him down a beat. "I am I guess, yeah."

"Do you love him?" he asked.

Max felt a fight instinct surge through his stomach, ready to defend his relationship with Nadine.

But Tim wasn't asking about Max and Nadine. "Do you love Reed?" he said.

"I'm a doctor and a friend"—she put her hand on Max's arm—"but I've never hoped for anything romantic with Reed, rest assured. Besides, I don't think I'd have much of a chance even if those were my intentions." Max hadn't thought about how people on the outside interpreted Nadine's living with them. Of course they thought she was in some deeper relationship with Rasheed. Not Max. Changing the subject, Nadine asked Tim, "Did Rasheed ever make up good stories for you like he did with Max?"

"Constantly."

"About what?" she asked.

"Everything from inventing fictions a hundred times more entertaining than they should be to sleeping around on me."

"No kidding," Max said, again baffled by how much of Rasheed's life eluded him.

"But let me tell you one of my stories. A true story."

Nadine and Max followed Tim to the kitchen, and he started doing the dishes. "Five years ago, right after my dad died, I went and stayed with my mom in La Paz, Mexico, where they'd retired. She was in a bad way. I don't know if you know, but people can actually die of loneliness. She didn't want life without Dad. For her, being alive was a deal to be taken up as a couple. Long story short, her body quickly caught up with her mental state, and she started fading. In the middle of the night, about a half an hour before she gave out, I woke up with this funny feeling and rushed over to her room. I took her hand and saw she was dying. Like, right then. I was about to say good-bye, positive that she was ready. That this was all okay.

"But then I hesitated, you know? What if now—in this moment when she couldn't speak—she actually wanted to live? Wanted to be rescued and given another five, maybe ten happy years. Why couldn't she learn to live happily alone? She could see what it was to exist without serving my father, like she had for the past fifty-some odd years. To live now could be her greatest chapter yet. I needed to call the ambulance to try and save her, but I didn't know the number for emergency medical services in La Paz. The times we visited, it never came up.

"I asked my mom but couldn't make out what she was saying. I went looking for the phone book but couldn't find it. I went to the used computer I'd brought them a few months earlier, in the study. I switched the thing on, and five whole minutes passed while I watched the thing light up and squawk to life. Then of course I had to connect to the Internet, which took forever in those days, making all sorts of strangled-cat sounds. Finally I was connected and found the number. I picked up the phone, put it to my ear, and then hung up. I realized that I might have just spent the last ten minutes of my mother's life waiting for a computer to boot up in the room right next to hers. When I got to her, she was already dead."

Unmoved, Max said, "Why didn't you just go to the neighbors?"

"Yeah. Good question. Why didn't I do a lot of things? But you know what? I don't think her final fifteen minutes are more important than the rest of her life. We put so much emphasis on finales. It's not only about a good ending; remember that. The good stuff can be behind us, and that's got to be as good as if it were all saved up for the end."

"What's your point?" Max said, again resenting that Tim was trying to make him feel better. He felt Nadine's eyes on him.

"What do you mean?"

"I mean, why did you tell us that story? What was the point?"

Looking hurt, Tim said, "I'm on your side, Max."

Max somewhat aggressively took over the dishes, boxing Tim out with his body. "Fine. That's fine. But why did you tell the story?"

"Just to say that it's okay. That this is going to be okay. You know?"

"Yeah, I do know. And I know exactly what 'It's okay' means. It means that nothing can be done. I don't need anyone to ever tell me 'It's okay' again."

SITTING WITH RASHEED on his bed the next evening, Nadine decided he was dehydrated and needed to get on an IV. She'd go to the hospital after dinner to get one. Max saw that she could feel it now too, in the quiet of Rasheed's heartbeat, in his loss of appetite, in the arid wrinkles on his knuckles that looked like tiny screaming mouths. Something happens to a space when a person is falling apart in it; something obvious as the gray orb of seeds on a withered dandelion. A strong breeze away from blowing off.

In the middle of the night, Max unfolded Nadine's arms from him and crawled into his old bed with Rasheed. Nadine came to say good-bye to them in the morning, checking on the IV bag. Max didn't get up to make her breakfast, telling her he needed to rest. She kissed the top of their heads and left for work.

Max lay with Rasheed all day. Nadine brought home takeout that no one ate. It was a hunger strike against God or whoever made life this hard. Max had whispered to him, "If you don't eat, I won't either." But Rasheed never opened his mouth. When Nadine insisted, he'd screw his eyes up tight. Finally, she threatened to drive him to the hospital. He made a pleading wheeze from his nose. Max sided with Rasheed, saying to leave him be. Nadine said that if by tomorrow he didn't eat anything, she was taking him in. Max said he'd get him to eat. Alone with Rasheed, he tried again. It's horrible to force food on someone. He could only be so insistent. He needed to either physically pry his father's mouth open or give up. He quit when he heard the metal spoon clink against Rasheed's front teeth a second time. Worst of all was the questioning cast on Rasheed's face: *Why are you doing this? Don't you remember what I told you? Not to let this go on too long. You know what I want now.*

Max let the canaries out of their cages and flung food all over the floor for them to pick up as they pleased. The fight that burned inside him now was against the unimaginable confusion and suffering Rasheed endured. If he was to die soon—tomorrow or in fifty years—let it at least be fearless and painless. And give him back his faculties and senses. Let him say good night one last time, with a clear head and all his memories. Let him acknowledge how much he is loved and how much he has loved.

At night Rasheed's eyes snapped wide open. Two stunned bulbs gazing at the ceiling, waiting. He mustered up the strength to turn and look at Max, staring as alert and uncomprehending as a dying horse; a hyperawareness of every movement and color. Max wanted to inflict pain on himself.

Max had gone two nights without the sleeping pills and two nights without any sleep. He tiptoed to the bathroom and brought the pills and a glass of water to the bedside table. He decided to take half of one in an hour, if he still hadn't managed to fall asleep. After saying this to himself, he swallowed two pills.

He dreamed of lying on his side in a black field, spooning Rasheed tightly, holding him together, keeping the life in a little longer. But the life poured out slowly and uniformly, as if from a watering can, until the final drop. A globe of blood appeared at the corner of Rasheed's mouth. The blood grew black legs and spots, transforming itself into a ladybug. It crawled across his cheek and ear, and onto Max's nose. The ocean seeped up from the black field and lifted the two bodies. They floated easily together, swaying back and forth on gentle waves like fragments of a boat. The ladybug had nowhere to fly and clung tightly to Max's nose.

Awake, he saw the first light on Rasheed's face. It was blue and gray and cold and dead, his skin a hardened paste. The glass of water lay between them, soaking the bed. Next to the glass was the emptied bottle of sleeping pills. Rasheed had taken them all. Max began rocking him in his arms. *No, no, no.* Nadine knocked on the door. His reflex was to get up and lock it. He wouldn't let her in, telling her they needed to be alone and that he promised to get Rasheed to eat today. He felt her standing out there a few minutes before leaving. After he heard her drive away, he opened the window and popped off the screens so the birds could leave. He didn't have a thought in his head or a feeling in his body. All movement was senseless and mechanical. He disconnected the IV from Rasheed and carried him to the bath. He undressed and washed his slight body. After drying him off, he brought him back into the bedroom, laid him on the floor, with a pillow under his head, between small trees and flowers and fat leaves. He threw away the sheets and clothes that had been messed, and then went to the bathroom to get the razor and scissors. Propping Rasheed's back up against the wall, Max cut his ear and nose hairs, then brought in a bowl of hot water to shave him. He trimmed his mustache into a trapezoid, clipped his nails, and brushed his hair. He dressed his father in his nicest shirt, his yellow one, and his khaki slacks and brown shoes. The canaries flew out the window.

Locking the doors, even the chain lock, he turned off all the lights and shut the windows and blinds before lying down too. Rocket whined and scratched at the bedroom door. Dragging himself across the floor, pushing plants aside, he let her in. Some of the Yangs' flowers and plants had already begun to sag. They'd been neglected for a couple of days. Rocket licked Rasheed's face and then began to yowl. Max could hear Rasheed's voice, saying what a pretty girl she was.

Not much time passed before Rasheed had an odor. Max went to the cologne collection in the other room and sprinkled a generous amount on him. Within a couple hours Rasheed's smell beat the perfume, even after Max had dumped all he had left on him. Soaked his neck and shirt. It was the stench of a dirty city river. Max retched on the floor sometime after that, his stomach already empty, so it was mostly dry heaves. There was a knocking at the front door. At first, a questioning knock, and a few hours later came the louder knocks. He'd locked them all out. They would separate him from Rasheed, and it wasn't time for that yet.

After the knocking stopped, he picked Rasheed up and brought him into the other bedroom. He sought more darkness. He closed the curtain on the tiny window and lay on the bed next to him. Once in this darker space, his senses awakened and panicked, dilating and receiving so much stimulation that they exhausted themselves into complete numbness. Then a new spike of overwhelming stimulation shredded through the numbness. He squeezed his head between his hands in an attempt to freeze time. A stomach-aching cry came and then left him gulping for oxygen. A rush of air finally cleared him for a few minutes, nestling him back into a daze. His senses stabbed and overloaded again, his entire nervous system inflamed, and then broke back down into the heavy numbness, enveloping him in deafening sorrow. This was the cycle: everything at once and then great nothingness. All of life, and then all of death. Back and forth. Max interlaced their fingers. In his mind they weren't lying in Rasheed's dark bedroom but inside the tree house, safely holding hands inside that cool box.

Sometime later Nadine shouted into the house, through the opening of the front door made by the chain lock, "Max? What's going on? Max, if you don't answer, I'm going to break this door down. You know I will. Max, let me in."

He lay there, dying of thirst, his head a growing wildfire, his hand as cold as Rasheed's, as he fell in and out of the numbness. He passed out and dreamed about Kip and his Man-Dog brother. They walked around some suburban streets. Mailmen and Girl Scouts and people watering their lawns waved, delighted to see them.

He woke to the sound of banging on the door. He heard the chain lock getting clipped. When the firemen came in, they lit Max and Rasheed with their flashlights and brought their hands up to their noses. Max was more dead than alive, sitting inside himself, watching everyone panic around him through the holes he peered out of as they carried him from the house on a gurney.

Later that night, in the hospital, he was excruciatingly alive again.

PART FOUR: TEN YEARS LATER

TWENTY-ONE

Max is twenty-six years old. He stands in line at the grocery store, overhearing a little girl in front of him tell her parents that she has a bad headache. Her mother moans in sympathy and then asks, "Why?" as if the girl might know. The father, emptying the cart, volunteers a reason—"It's because you didn't get enough sleep last night, honey." The checkout clerk chimes in. "It might be this sudden change in weather, sometimes the different air pressure messes with people's inner balance." A woman behind Max suggests that it could be that bug that's been going around.

Then they all settle on hunger. It was the mother's idea. The girl simply needs a snack. The mother, father, checkout clerk, and woman in line nod in satisfaction at the final diagnosis. They've gained command of the headache by identifying its origin. Sense has been made out of what—deep down—they know they cannot make sense of. And why question their conclusion? Why challenge the victory of having resolved the girl's pain? There's hardly a fiction in the world that's more comforting than having a clear explanation for pain. The truth is not always what's most important.

For years there was a single explanation for Max's depression: the death of Rasheed. Anytime he felt like hiding for a couple of days, not wanting to interact directly with the world outside, not answering his phone, he could later see his teachers or the Yangs or Tim thinking, Of course you need to crawl inside sometimes. We understand. He knew they thought this by the way they touched his shoulder and bowed their heads in a moment of silence, as if they were all still at the funeral, even months and then years later.

This explanation made a lot of sense because it was true. He was absolutely submerged in the wreckage of his grief. But despite his best efforts to cling to the hurt, the numbness thinned, and holes stretched in the gloom that had once blanketed everything. And then one day, after waking up with a familiar depression, he sat on the toilet and had the world's most alleviating bowel movement. The sensation thrilled him to tears. It was an important moment because he allowed himself to see his self-loathing as unconnected to Rasheed. This relief had nothing to do with Rasheed. It had to do with the green pepper and onion pizza he'd eaten at three in the morning before bed. His body was sick with junk food, full of literal waste he needed to expel. Until then, Rasheed had been the sole mascot of hard times, the center of his son's world. Max had reflexively associated all pain with missing him. But on this special morning, he could attribute his crawling in his own skin to something else. Green pepper and onion pizza.

He let himself believe his depression on subsequent mornings was triggered by things other than Rasheed too. Maybe the BBC news radio he woke up to contributed to his feeling low:

fourteen dead in a car bombing today in a market in Islamabad. Or maybe it was that he didn't have any friends his age. Maybe it was because he didn't exercise. Maybe he was sad about something he was only subliminally in touch with, some subconscious taste of his insignificance in the universe. Or maybe his body was fighting off a seasonal flu.

With this new flood of possibilities, he rediscovered that ancient practice of human beings everywhere: making up reasons for why we feel the way we do. It emancipated him from having one origin for his misery. Always Rasheed. I killed my dad. He is still dead. I miss him. I miss him so much I hate the sound of my own breathing. But now, he had reclaimed the wonderful ridiculousness of all free, confused people, and joyously swam in the infinite mess of reasons to be unhappy. Reasons that could be followed by reactions: go to the bathroom, turn off the radio, meet people, jog, draw a picture, write a poem.

MAX REMEMBERS HOW Nadine and Robby stayed clasped to each other for the entirety of Rasheed's burial ceremony. Tim and Téta stood on either side of a wheelchaired Jiddo, and Max's old art teacher, Mr. Virgine, had come with a couple other colleagues. Some of the more religious neighbors who they'd never really interacted with stood with them too. A few Arabs materialized, people Max had never met. When they saw he didn't speak Arabic, they gave their condolences in English, saying what a wonderful man Rasheed was. Other things were said over the coffin, but it all sounded like it came out of a kazoo. Dull vibrations jammed together.

But when his mother's voice came through the telephone later that day, it was clear and distinct enough to nearly knock him to the floor. He'd felt so deadened only seconds earlier. "Hakeem.

Rasheed was a truly good man. Like you cannot find elsewhere. You are fortunate to have had him for as long as you did."

He used all his strength to not come apart. "I know," he said.

She told him about how kind and funny Rasheed had been, and what a phenomenal liar too. He'd spent a lot of his life hiding things from people. He lied about finishing his degree in economics at AUB—his grades were abysmal, and he never actually received a diploma; he lied about his sexuality—it was his idea to stage a fake marriage with Samira; and he was so good at shaping his political views around whatever his current company wanted to hear. It was always convincing.

Max said, "Did you ever wear a pot on your head?"

"What?"

"When I was a baby, during the war, did you stay with me in the bathtub with a pot on your head?"

"This is something Rasheed told you?"

"Yes."

"No, this never happened. I do remember, however, that Rasheed had a nanny named Noor who used to play with him for hours, and they would wear pots on their heads. It was Rasheed's favorite game. I also remember that he would often go to lie in the bathtub when there was a lot of mortar fire during the war. He held you in there for days, unwilling to come out. Hakeem, you know, if you are interested in visiting Beirut for a while, you are welcome here. Is that something that interests you?"

"No—it's not—not right now. Thank you."

They didn't stay on the phone much longer, and his mother more or less said to contact her when he felt like it. He didn't count on ever seeing her again.

But he did. A month before, he'd flown back to Beirut for the first time, taking a cab directly to her place. She was staying inside the refugee camp, under a corrugated tin roof, on a cot over a dirt floor.

She's someone who is certain of how she wants to live. She doesn't doubt or dream, isn't searching for anything at all. Her drive to give everything away—food, money, medical supplies, clothes, books; English, Arabic, math, and history lessons—keeps her alive. Her compulsive generosity and obsession with moral responsibility is her way of self-preservation. She cares for the kids with such a lack of sentimentality that it borders on coldness. They are sometimes intimidated but will feel admiration for her in retrospect. She is a mother with a hundred children swinging on her neck and remains stoic as an oak tree. What once felt like a devastating underreaction to Max that first time he'd met her, he now realizes was a great expression of emotion.

The camp community has a high regard for Samira's commitment to the school, her past as a fighter, and her insistence on living in the camp. And at around the age of twelve, when Palestinian kids begin to understand that life isn't the same for everyone in Lebanon, they find a solace in people like Samira, who wouldn't know how to abandon them if she had to. Her sense of duty is contagious. The community protects her when she needs no protection, brings her food even after she's already eaten, and insists on friendship, though she is someone who could live with or without it. She is still, in so many ways, a fictional character.

There's no telling how Max's budding relationship with his mother is affected by what happened to Rasheed. There will never be the sense of an even trade-off, or anything resembling fairness. No, the part about losing Rasheed continues to feel like an amputation. But now, at least, the amputation has stopped blackening other gains. It can be lived with.

Max has already died once, his grief having been potent enough to bring him part way to the other side with Rasheed.

In a way, this straddling of life and death, at the height of his grief, was the most alive he's ever been.

IN MAX'S LAST year of high school, he and Nadine continued to talk about novels and music when she wasn't at work, and he got a job at a gourmet market. They also went to movies, parks, museums, and made sobbing love to each other, like a real couple. It wasn't until Rocket passed away that they started talking about Rasheed with nostalgia and not just anguish. How Rasheed used to carry Rocket like a baby when she lost interest in their walks. Or how she used to curl her body around his feet while he brushed his teeth, trapping him at the bathroom sink. How Rasheed always said, "Bless you, my lady," when she sneezed or farted. And how he asked her what she thought they should watch on TV tonight.

People whispered about Max—about Rasheed and Coach Tim, about his relationship with a woman fourteen years his senior. And black. He didn't listen much to what they said. The less he listened, the closer they approached, observing him like some fascinating but potentially dangerous animal, daring themselves to get as near as they could.

NADINE BROKE MAX'S heart in his first year of college. She told him she would always be in his life, that her home was his home, but that the physical aspect had to end. Her resolve to keep their relationship platonic has endured seven years, during which time she had a bright-eyed daughter named Elise with a good man she didn't stay with. There was nothing particularly sad about Nadine and Elise's father not staying together. Nadine was sure she wanted a child, but less concerned with whether she and the child's father would have a lifelong romantic partnership. They live happily apart now, and he takes Elise on alternating weekends.

Max has tried to not let their separation be a source of hope. But he can't help it. As of late, he is convinced that Nadine's resistance to his romantic bids have lightened. She recently accepted his invitation to a formal dinner that she laughingly refuses to call a date. He knows it is flirtation when they argue over this point on the phone. He knows it, and remains openly and insistently in love with her.

NOW MAX IS home from the grocery store, where the little girl's headache was explained. He bends down at his doorstep and picks up a package from Nadine. The package contains two videos. They document the opening of Mr. Yang's camukra flowers: one fourteen years ago, the day Max choked on that taffy, and the second of Mr. Yang's latest *camukra*, blossoming successfully, an event Max attended yesterday.

The first video is from the perspective of the tripoded camera from that summer of 1996. The camera stays on the flower until it falls. Then the shot is of a window that faces Max and Rasheed's house. Though it's out of focus, you can make out where the Yangs' property meets the Boulos's yard, and a slice of their brick chimney.

You can hear the cries get more dramatic, and hear Rasheed shouting for Max to calm it down, please, calm it down. Finally there are the aftereffects of Coach Tim slugging Max in the solar plexus. The guests applaud as Rasheed bawls and Max sucks for air.

For the past fourteen years Mr. Yang's been cultivating another *camukra* flower. This second recording is from the perspective of Nadine. She stands a couple steps up on the staircase that leads down into the Yangs' kitchen and scans the heads of all the neighbors and friends. Leslie and other members of the church are there. Tim, who's gotten into photography, is firing away with a sleek-looking camera that looks a lot like a rifle. Robby, now in his early thirties, wears a suit that is too small. An old Asian man is talking to him, using a lot more hand gestures than is probably natural. Robby is bored. His mouth dangles open as if he's snoring.

Nadine focuses in on Max, and he smiles at her before returning his attention to the flower. The Yangs look exactly as they do in the first video, except that all of their hair is paper-white. The whiteness makes their faces appear smoother and more radiant. The guests are hypnotized by the small potted flower, moments away from opening. Nadine zeros in on the closed petals, then back out again. She finds Robby, who is now standing next to Max. When Robby sees he's being filmed, he tries to hide the pleasure it obviously brings him. Both excited and embarrassed by the idea, he fixates on the camera with timid liking.

Nadine says, "Say hi, Robby!"

Robby says, "Hi, Robby!" Nadine laughs, and he opens his mouth to say something more, but changes his mind. He giggles at Max before turning to face the flower with him. Nadine keeps filming the back of his head, saying, "Too good for the camera, huh?"

Someone in the crowd cries out, "Wasai!" And it has begun.

Nadine zooms in through Robby and Max's shoulders and gets a good shot of the flower. It unsticks its petals in little jolts of separation before growing on smoothly. It yawns so widely that it looks like it's about to turn inside out, but then stops and begins closing, curling inward, dying. The people watch like mesmerized infants, witnessing what could only be magic. The glistening red and purple and white and brown drain from the petals. Its center dehydrates and grays with extraordinary speed.

It bends down as if politely running out of breath, and finally drops limply. Hanging by its tired stem, it reaches for the ground. The weight tugs the roots and pulls up on the soil. Everyone claps and cheers. They exclaim how gorgeous it was, how unforgettable. Wow, just wow.

Max rewinds and replays the life dozens of times, forward then backward. The flower wakes with a jerk of animation. The stem unrolls, thickening with fluid, hardening, digging roots back down into the soil and raising its heavy head. The flower fills with color, the neck arching back, its nose in the air. It rounds its posture into a crescent and thrusts out its jaw. Crouching and blanching into a pale green, it closes into pre-nascent sleep. Playing it over and over, he watches it open and die, close and live, bowing up and down like a gracious opera singer. He can't help but marvel at the love and time and admiration that went into one short life. He feels it. He feels it skipping across his skin. It chills, pierces, aches, lifts—and then begins to let him go.

ACKNOWLEDGMENTS

I HAVE LOOKED forward to writing this part well before finalizing the novel. I'm grateful to have so many people to thank. Firstly, I am indebted to the time and support of the Michener Center for Writers. Without which this book wouldn't have been remotely possible, and without which I wouldn't have had generosity and encouragement—lifelines to this young writer—redefined for me by treasured mentors, particularly Elizabeth McCracken, Jim Magnuson, Michael Adams, visiting writer Naomi Shihab Nye and alumnus Philipp Meyer, who never once spoke of *if* this book would be published but always *when*.

I'm obliged to both my agent, the faithful Ryan D. Harbage, and to my scrupulous and kind editor, Lea Beresford, for heroically standing by my work. There's nothing quite like strangers who fight for one of your inventions.

The following people actually volunteered (!) to read sections—if not all—of early, and very shaky, drafts and returned to me with invaluable feedback and wisdom: Abe Koogler, Karan Mahajan, Corey Miller, Taylor Huchison, Eamon Aloyo, Greg Koehler, Thomas Kim, and my inspiriting sister, Kenza.

I'm also deeply beholden to the following for their insightful conversations that directly informed the world of this novel (most of whom couldn't have known it at the time): Catherine Geyre Dimechkie, Mrs. Nada Maaluf of al-Nada building, Hussein Balshi, Nadya Kaddoura, Talal Dimechkie, Riad Dimechkie, Rana Jabbour, Anthony Browne, Cory Gustason, Tiffani Allen, and Sahand Arshadmansab.

Most of all, I thank the woman and brilliance who lets me keep my orbit around her every day, Nana Afua Mensah.

A NOTE ON THE AUTHOR

Karim Dimechkie was a Michener Fellow. Before that, he taught English in Paris. This is his first novel. He lives in New York City.